EXPERT WITNESS

NICOLE LUCKOURT

Expert Witness

A Romantic Suspense Novel

Published by Nicole Luckourt

Copyright © 2016 by Nicole Luckourt.

All rights reserved.

Cover image by: Wicked By Design

ISBN: 978-0-9972149-1-8

For more information: www.nicoleluckourt.com

DEDICATION

This book is dedicated to my children. For, in encouraging them to ceaselessly pursue their dreams, I somehow found the courage to realize my own. You are and will always be my greatest inspiration.

CONTENTS

EXPERT WITNESS

A ROMANTIC SUSPENSE NOVEL

CHAPTER ONE

"Mr. Lancaster," Jordan said, extending a hand to the older gentlemen. "I'm Dr. Clayton."

He grasped her hand, his long bony fingers wrapping loosely around hers. "I'm sorry. I don't recall meeting you," he said, articulating each word deliberately while searching her face. "I'm not even sure why I'm here."

"We haven't had the opportunity to meet until now." Her tone was warm and reassuring. Having already reviewed his file, she was aware of Bradley Lancaster's potential memory lapses and confusion. "Let me tell you more about why we're meeting today. I've been hired by the court to conduct a psychological evaluation to help determine if you may be in need of a guardian." She passed him a consent form and went on to explain what having a guardian to oversee his care and financial affairs would mean and the limits of confidentiality, given the purpose of her evaluation.

"I'll be glad to do this...though I'm not sure it's necessary." His speech was slow and hesitant. He pushed his pen painstakingly across the signature line on the form and returned it to her. "I know my son is worried about me but I'm fine." His voice faltered on the last word.

1

"Why do you think your son is worried?" she asked, careful to keep her voice neutral and her posture open.

Mr. Lancaster didn't return eye contact. Instead, he gazed around the room and, finally, down at his hands. The buttons on his shirt were misaligned, and he was wearing two different-colored socks. Looking more closely, she saw that his hair had been left uncombed and he had several days' worth of growth around this chin. She jotted down notes on his appearance in the legal pad on her lap.

"I don't know. I've been forgetting some things." He paused to inspect a loose thread on his shirt cuff.

She waited until it was clear he wasn't going to say more. "You were saying?" she prompted.

"I'm sorry. What was the question?" He turned a tired gaze back to her. His fingers lingered on the unraveling cuff as he sat in silence.

"What types of things have you been forgetting?"

"Oh, just some appointments, things like that. I was a little late on a couple of bills these past few months. It's not like I don't have the money. Hell, part of the problem is I have too much damn money!"

He was less soft-spoken and more on edge now, but she didn't stop him. Whatever he was about to say obviously meant something to him.

"Takes more than one accountant to keep it all straight—can't be surprised some things fell through the cracks. I don't know why everyone has gotten so up in arms about it. My hard work has kept my son pretty comfortable all his life," he said gruffly while jabbing a finger in the air. "If I want to slow down a bit now, I think I'm entitled. I'm eighty-one years old, you know. Not many people are doing what I am at this age. I should have cut loose years ago, when my wife was still here. There's so much we could have done, but I was always too busy."

She nodded as she listened. Everything he'd said so far was consistent with the records she'd reviewed when she'd been assigned the case earlier in the week. His son, Keith Lancaster, had reported his father's current difficulties emerged following a knee replacement surgery about six months ago. Keith had assumed his father's role as head of his multimillion-dollar corporation so that his father could focus on his recovery. However, despite the respite, the elder Mr. Lancaster had continued to suffer from colds and other viruses, eventually being hospitalized with pneumonia.

The mental problems had been reported to begin shortly thereafter. While he'd returned to work, Mr. Lancaster would misplace things, forget appointments and leave bills unpaid. His appearance had also changed. A once fastidious dresser, he began wearing clothing that was wrinkled and disheveled. The most significant event in his recent past was the death of his wife. Keith conveyed that his father had been rock-steady during that time, managing her funeral and their financial affairs and being a constant state of support for him.

But that was no longer the case and his son reported that nothing he'd tried had helped. He'd stated that he felt like his father's condition was getting worse, and it would be only a matter of time before he left a burner on or fell victim to some scam artist trying to take advantage of his vast financial resources.

"When did your wife pass away?" she asked gently.

"Fourteen months ago. Four days before Keith's birthday. He took it hard." His eyes became watery as he spoke, but his memory regarding the timing of her death was accurate.

"What about you?"

"What do you mean?" he asked, a puzzled expression on his face. "I already told you I'm fine. I'm here, aren't I?"

Jordan observed the unspoken message. He was here. His wife, however, was not. She didn't delve into the statement though. She was performing an evaluation, not therapy—though a recommendation for grief counseling was certainly a consideration at this point. "I'm sorry, Mr. Lancaster. Let me clarify. How did you manage after her death?"

The older man took a deep breath and exhaled slowly before responding. "Oh, I don't know. I didn't stop, really. After she was gone, what would have been the point?" He raised his hands, palms up in front of him, rocking his head back and forth in answer to his question. "I should have stopped before it was too late, and now, I can't go back and do it any differently. The best thing I could do for her was take care of Keith. We were her world, you know. Anybody who knew her told us that at the funeral. She was a good woman, a family woman. I was damn lucky she put up with me for all those years."

"How long were you married?"

"Fifty-eight years. We were high school sweethearts, though I knew her when we were just kids. Used to spend every moment together swimming around an old dock by the bay where we grew up." A faraway look took residence in his eyes as he continued. "I decided one of those summers I was going to marry her someday. Even told her so when we were about nine years old." He chuckled at the memory. "She wasn't so keen on the idea back then, but I pestered her for enough years that she eventually came around. Started dating our tenth-grade year and were never apart after that…" His voice drifted off, and he appeared to reluctantly return from the memory.

"Sounds like you were very fortunate to have had each other," she said, her tone sincere.

In some ways, doing custody work had exposed her to the worst parts of relationships and the incredible hurt that occurred when they fell apart. Hearing Bradley Lancaster's story was a beacon of hope for her. Despite the hardships he'd mentioned, he'd clearly been as much in love with his wife on the day she'd died as on the day they'd been married.

She spent a couple of hours with him completing the interview and administering several neuropsychological tests to assess his overall cognitive functioning and capacity to manage his affairs and property in various domains. By the time they were through, it was late in the afternoon.

"Okay, Mr. Lancaster. We're done for today."

Though his shoulders slumped and he'd stifled another yawn moments before, she caught a trace of disappointment cross his weathered face at her announcement. "That wasn't so bad. I hope you got what you needed," he said, giving her a nod. Using his cane for strength, he gradually raised himself from the chair. Once he was standing, he turned toward her. "You know, my son didn't want you doing this. Tried to get his attorney to change the judge's order. I guess some friends of his were talking—how these young people do…" He paused as a smile flitted over his lips. "Goes to show you money can't buy everything. But I'm glad now. Glad it didn't work." He held his shaky hand out. "It was a true pleasure to have met you."

She did her best to mask her surprise at his words. None of this had trickled back to her yet. She wondered at Keith Lancaster's motivation to try to have her removed from the case. Filing the information away to consider later, she shook the elderly man's hand. "Likewise."

After escorting him out to the lobby, where his driver was waiting, she was ready for a break herself. She ducked into the small kitchen area and prepared a mug of green tea before heading back to her office to begin the arduous process of scoring and interpreting the battery of tests she'd administered. Luckily, she'd received his medical records while she'd been in session. The more pieces of the puzzle she had in front of her, the easier it was to put them together to form a clear picture.

The interstate lights cast an orangey hue on the night

sky outside her window, signaling to her that she needed to wrap things up soon. She curled her finger around a tendril of hair while she pored over the remaining test scores and detailed her thoughts on specific findings. In any case, it was hard to witness an elderly person cope with a loss of functioning. In guardianship cases, these individuals lost a lot of personal freedom when they were assigned a guardian. Not that it wasn't necessary. Many could no longer care for themselves and would face personal and financial devastation if someone didn't provide for them. Be that as it may, it was still a humbling experience.

A car honked in the distance, jarring her from her thoughts. She sighed. It was possible that Mr. Lancaster was suffering from some type of dementia, but she wasn't ready to conclude that he was in need of a guardian. There were still other possible explanations—his grief being one of them.

She glanced over at her desk clock. It was already almost seven thirty.

Ugh, I'd better get out of here.

Earlier that day, she'd agreed to meet her two best friends and practice partners, Karen and Mike Conway, for dinner. Having all been close since they'd met in graduate school, the couple had grown accustomed to her tendency to put in extended hours at work. Whenever she became too deeply entrenched, they'd pry her away from the office with invitations like this one—invitations where there was really no choice to opt out, if she wanted to lay low and avoid any more well-meant attempts at an intervention.

She pushed the printed test reports and records onto the metal fastener and locked the reassembled folder in her file cabinet. If she hurried, she'd still be on time. Glancing at her reflection in the glass-covered prints hanging throughout the hall, she gave herself a once-over. Her dark hair was still held back in a tight ponytail at the nape of her neck, and her conservative navy-blue suit was free of wrinkles. Her work clothes would have to do for dinner, because there was no time to change.

On her way out, she noticed one lone door cracked open with light shining out. The ray traced back to their newest associate, Derek's, office. He hadn't been with them long, but he'd already become an asset to the practice, handling a fair share of the cases like a pro.

Sticking her head in the doorway, she found him hunched over his desk. She could tell from the mug shot that he was reviewing a police report. A lock of his wavy blond hair was resting on his forehead, as if it was about to cross the bridge carved out by the deep furrows in his brow. He looked like he could use a distraction.

"Hey, Derek. Hard at work?" She released her briefcase on the floor beside her.

"Just a few things I need to finish up," he replied. Then, with a smile, he added, "Being the new guy and all, I don't want to get a reputation as a slacker."

"Well, don't work too hard. Don't want to make the other partners look bad," she said, trying to affect a serious manner.

"I'm not sure that's possible when one of the partners never leaves during the daylight hours." He waggled his eyebrows at her. "Forget setting the bar, she defines it."

She cracked a smile while she rolled her eyes at him. He was definitely a charmer. When he'd first come on board, Mike and Karen had wondered if he and Jordan might even become romantic partners rather than solely practice partners, but it hadn't happened. She'd never felt attracted to him in that way and could tell he didn't feel it, either. She had no doubts now; they were better suited as friends.

He leaned back in his chair. "Then again, you are getting out before eight tonight. I should applaud you."

The corners of her mouth turned downward. "And how sad is it that?" In the six months he'd been there, he had her routine down. She tried not to think about what that meant. "But hold the ovation. I'm out of here—" she eyed the darkness outside his window, "—and I don't have a second to spare."

"Ah, don't want to be late to meet Karen, huh?"

She nodded. "You'd think it was her mission in life to get me out tonight. And I know her well enough to make sure I'm not late." She sprang to retrieve the handle of her briefcase as she remembered Karen's threat of a speed-dating event coming up if she couldn't make it to dinner. "No telling what she'd do next, but I'm not taking a chance," she said, throwing out a hurried wave as she left.

A rush of warm air hit her face as soon as she stepped outside. Despite the fact that it was early September and late, the temperatures in Orlando were still stifling throughout the day and offered little relief from the heat and humidity at night.

Humming the tune that had been playing through the surround sound system in her office, she made her way into the parking lot while reflecting on Derek's comment. It was true that she put in long hours, but she loved her job, and in all fairness, she put in more time than was necessary—

The sound of footsteps echoing behind her interrupted her reasoning.

As she attempted to spin around, a strong, slick arm wrapped itself around her neck, and another one locked across her waist. Adrenaline spiked her blood. She twisted back and forth trying to break away. The arm clutching her torso remained solidly in place. Who was he?

A scream surging from her throat was cut short as the hand digging into her waist relocated to crush against her mouth. His rancid breath warmed her neck. She thrashed within the hold, but her efforts were fruitless against the iron grip that encased her. He began to drag her across the parking lot. Heels bouncing off the asphalt, she tried in vain to grind them into the ground. It didn't work. She struggled to remain calm and remember the self-defense tactics she'd learned in a weekend college seminar. One thought kept popping back in her mind. If she let her captor take her to a second location, the odds would be stacked further against her.

In an act of desperation, rather than trying to anchor herself, she lifted her shoe and slammed it down on her assailant's foot. The three-inch stiletto heel sank into the top of his laces. His hold didn't loosen. Fighting panic that was creeping into her thoughts, she raised her foot again. This time, she'd go for his shin.

As she gathered strength to execute her counterattack, the man behind her groaned. Her lungs instinctively sucked in air as the grip around her neck loosened and then released her completely. Lightheaded and confused, she fell forward, scrambling to put distance between them. Her assailant hit the ground behind her with a loud thud. Chancing a look back, she saw Derek standing behind the crumpled figure with a baseball bat in his hands.

He moved in front of her, the bat now dangling in his right hand. "Are you okay?" He was shouting though he was right in front of her. "Did he cut you?" His eyes traveled down her body.

"What?" she asked. The word came out resembling a sea lion's bark as a result of the damaging pressure on her throat. She had no idea what Derek was talking about.

His gaze had shifted behind her, so she turned around. Only then did she see the knife lying on the ground next to the figure. A feeling of dread washed over her and she fought the nausea turning her stomach. Her legs wobbled like Jell-O. She glanced around for somewhere to sit before it was too late and she joined the man on the ground.

"I've got you." Derek placed her arm around his waist so he could support her weight. Then he guided her to his car.

After using his free hand to open the passenger's side door, he eased her into one of the Corvette's deep-gray bucket seats. She pulled her hands up in front of her chest and wrung them together in an effort to still her quivering limbs. The trembling didn't stop. Her whole body vibrated now.

Grabbing his cell phone from his front pocket, Derek dropped down in the seat next to her and began dialing. Jordan could hear the voice on the other end.

"Nine-one-one operator. What is your emergency?"

"Yes, my friend has been attacked." Derek rattled off the street address to their office. "We need an ambulance right away."

She looked over at the crumpled figure who lay on the ground not twenty feet from them. He was unmoving, still in the same position. Tearing her eyes away from the limp body, she realized Derek had ended the call and was speaking to her again.

"Everything is going to be okay. An ambulance is on its way to take you to the hospital to get checked out." He rested his hand on her shoulder.

Jordan closed her eyes. She'd mistakenly thought Derek had requested the ambulance for her motionless assailant. Forcing the thoughts to become words, she stated, "I don't need to go to the hospital. I'm okay. He didn't cut me, only tried to drag me away…" She trailed off. Nothing she said felt real. She'd worked with trauma clients enough to realize she was suffering from shock.

He gave a heavy nod. "I'm sure everything is fine, but it won't hurt to check."

She didn't have the strength to argue. She'd used up every bit of energy she'd had to fight her attacker.

It seemed like an eternity had passed when they saw the blue lights cutting through the darkness though, according her watch, it'd been only a few minutes. Two squad cars and an ambulance simultaneously pulled into the parking lot.

The officers exited the vehicles. One started toward them, while the other headed toward the figure on the ground.

"Hey. Is everyone okay?" the closest officer called out as he surveyed the scene around them.

Both she and Derek nodded as he came closer.

"Who's Derek—the guy who called this in?"

Derek lifted his hand up midway. "I am."

"Tell me what happened. What's going on here?" the officer questioned.

Derek provided a statement on what he'd witnessed, while the paramedics checked the vital signs of the unconscious man. Jordan turned the other way, as the sight of him made her stomach churn. On the other side of the parking lot, several more squad cars showed up, and officers began taping off the crime scene.

A new officer approached her and began to ask her questions. She was surprised at how calm she sounded as she answered him. It was as if her body were on automatic pilot and she were but a spectator. Watching from the safe place her mind had conceived, she saw her assailant being loaded onto a stretcher and into the ambulance.

"Do you need medical attention?" the officer asked. "I'll be glad to call another ambulance."

"I think that's a good idea," Derek said before she could reply, obviously done answering questions.

She shook her head. "I don't think that's necessary. I'm just a little shaken up."

"All right. Will you at least let me take you, then?" Derek asked, his voice filled with concern.

Giving in, Jordan nodded.

"That's about it for now, then," the officer stated. He turned his head to run through a few ten codes on the mic affixed to his shoulder lapel. "I'll be on my way to the hospital to interview the suspect. If he's regained consciousness by then. You gave him one whack on the head he won't soon forget." He looked at Derek.

"Yeah, well, I never thought our sports equipment for play therapy would be put to such good use," Derek replied grimly.

The officer gave a barely perceptible nod before turning his attention back to Jordan. "I'll be getting in touch with you to let you know the outcome of all of this and possibly to get more information. In the meantime, if you remember anything else, here's my card."

Jordan was relieved to see that the emergency room was almost empty. They waited only for a few minutes before being called back to an examining room. After undergoing a routine examination by a physician's assistant, she was pronounced clear for discharge. However, it was apparent she'd have some hefty bruises around her abdomen and neck.

All she could think of on the ride back was scrubbing herself clean in a long, hot bath. She wanted to wash the last six hours away. Wash away the feel of his sweat-soaked arms around her. The panic at being locked in his hold and struggling for every breath. The sour smell of his exhalations intruding into her precious air space. She knew it would never be possible. She hugged her arms tightly to her body.

"Are you cold?" Derek asked, reaching forward to turn down the air conditioner.

"No, not really. It's just been a hell of a day. Would you mind taking me straight home? I'll catch a ride with Mike and Karen in the morning. I don't feel up to going back to the office tonight."

"Sure. No problem," he said with a pensive expression. "I hadn't even thought of bringing you anywhere else. Your car will be fine. I'm more worried about you. Are you sure you'll be all right tonight? You're more than welcome to stay at my place."

"Thanks for the offer. Actually, thanks for everything. I don't want to think about what might've happened if you hadn't come along when you did. But I just want to go home, take a long bath, and try to get some sleep."

Derek looked over at her, sympathy marking his voice. "I get it. But promise me you'll call if you need anything," he said, easing the car into the circular driveway.

Jordan dipped her head in acquiescence then shifted to look at the familiar house in front of her. The pressure in her chest alleviated somewhat. She was home.

Waving goodbye to Derek, she made her way inside. The soft glow coming from her living room illuminated her path. Normally, she left the lamp on to help her see the obstacles around her, but tonight she was more thankful she wasn't walking into the unknowns born out of pure darkness. No telling what her mind would conjure up with no visual confines in her current state.

Her movements felt mechanical. She headed into the kitchen. Retrieving a drinking glass from the cabinet, she discovered her hands were still shaking. She grasped the glass tightly as she filled it from the refrigerator's dispenser. The cold water felt good on her parched throat.

Fighting the urge to submerge herself in a scalding-hot bath and then crawl under her comforter, she searched for something to eat first. She hadn't eaten since the energy bar she'd grabbed for lunch, so she should be hungry. Opening the freezer, she took out a dinner portion she'd previously frozen for occasions when she didn't have time to cook. It was usually one she liked, but tonight, her stomach rejected all thoughts of food.

The sound of her home phone ringing caught her by surprise. She automatically jerked back a step, hypervigilance from the night's events bleeding into her reaction. Taking a long, deep breath, she tried to calm her nerves before answering. "Hello."

"Jordan!" Karen's voice was filled with anguish. "Derek called and told us what happened. I've been worried sick since you didn't show for dinner. I kept calling but got no answer. My God, are you all right?"

"I'm fine. Just a little shook up. I must have accidentally left the ringer muted. I never even heard it ring." She strained to inflect some feeling into her voice. Her effort fell flat. The words came out sounding wooden and hollow, a reflection, she assumed, of the numbness that coated her from inside. "Actually, I'm glad you called. I was wondering if you and Mike would swing by and pick me up in the morning. I left my car at the office."

There was a momentary pause on the other line. Karen had recognized the deviation from her normal tone. "Absolutely." Another beat of silence followed. "Hey, are you going to be okay by yourself tonight? You know we can be there in a second if you want to stay at our place?"

She didn't want Karen to worry, but she needed time alone to even begin to process the events of the night. She tried to sound more like her usual self. "Thanks, but it's okay. To be honest, I only want to go to sleep. I feel like I've been up for days."

Karen released a sigh. "Okay, hon. We'll be there around seven, then. If you don't feel up to going in tomorrow, give us a ring in the morning. Work can wait. Taking care of you is more important right now."

Jordan pulled back the plastic wrapping from her dinner and stirred the sauce while contemplating her friend's advice. "I know, and I will, but I have so many open cases right now, and it'll help me to dive back in."

"I get it. But please don't feel pressured—you know, because of the practice—if you change your mind and need some time."

"I won't. I promise." Her tone was solemn.

"Good. See you in the morning then. And, Jordan—" Karen choked up, "—I'm so glad you're okay. I don't want to even think about…"

Jordan could hear the tremble in her friend's voice. "I know," she said softly, "but I really am okay. So try to get some sleep yourself."

Upon hanging up, Jordan felt lighter. The attack was still at the forefront of her mind, but the numbness that blanketed her emotions had eroded somewhat. She was fortunate to have such supportive friends. As she speared a piece of broccoli, she was surprised to find that she was starving. *At least something is back to normal.*

CHAPTER TWO

The parking area appeared undisturbed in the early morning light. Mike maneuvered his car into his reserved parking space while Jordan craned her neck around, scanning for anything out of the ordinary. But there was nothing. Even the crime scene tape had already been removed.

"You okay?" Mike asked, glancing back at her in the rearview mirror.

"Yeah, I'm good. It just feels weird, I guess. Looking around now, it's as if yesterday never happened."

Nothing that hinted of the horrible experience that had transpired remained. At the scene anyway. She tugged on the scarf she'd worn to cover the dark purple bruises scattered around her neck. Last night's attack had left its mark on her physically and emotionally.

Still deliberating on the motive behind the attack, she peered over at her car. It was there, exactly as she'd left it, the only difference being the addition of a few loose oak leaves as adornment. Karen's voice tore her from her thoughts, and Jordan realized she'd been speaking to her. "I'm sorry. What was it?"

Karen repeated her question. "I was wondering if you

ever found out who the guy was?"

"Not yet. He wasn't in any condition to answer questions when the police arrived," she said, shutting the car door.

"Humph," Mike interjected. "And I can tell you I didn't lose a minute's sleep over that fact, either. I wish I'd been here to help Derek out," he said in a harsh tone.

Jordan patted him on the back. Mike was mild-mannered in nature. His pitiless attitude now clearly stemmed from concern for her wellbeing. "Well, no worries. The officer at the scene said he'd be questioning him further when he regained consciousness." She switched her briefcase to her other hand. "To be honest, not knowing makes it even worse. I keep playing it over in my mind trying to figure out why—maybe because it's what we do."

"What are you thinking?" Karen's brows fused as she processed the comment.

"I don't think it was money, because he never once asked for my purse or keys. I don't ever remember seeing him before, so it wasn't an angry former client. Maybe it could've been a relation to someone in a case? Or worst-case scenario, he's a typical psychopath and I happened to be the victim he chose." The last suggestion triggered a chill that seeped through her body. Of all the personality types, this would be the last she'd want to encounter alone in the dark.

Karen put her arm around her friend. "I know it's difficult, but I think you should try to put any thoughts about motive out of your mind, at least until the police are able to provide more information. Otherwise, you'll drive yourself nuts trying to figure this out. You could be right on any of those, but for now, they're only educated guesses. You of all people know that sometimes, the motivations behind these kinds of violence are so twisted that no sane individual is able to ever fully comprehend them."

"You're right," she conceded. Karen had a valid point. They'd all worked cases in which identifying with the offender was an impossibility. She tried to take her friend's advice and shoved the thoughts aside. "Let's head in." She let Karen lead toward the back entrance to their office. "I have several calls to make before our staff meeting at noon. So I may be a few minutes late."

"Don't worry. We'll save you some of the rosemary focaccia rolls," Mike gently teased.

She perked up. "We're ordering Rosella's for lunch?"

"Yeah. We figured we'd let you choose today."

Jordan couldn't help chuckling. "And you didn't even have to ask me what I'd pick. You guys know how to cheer me up. Mama Rosella's cooking is exactly what I need right now."

"Yeah, well, whoever said the way to a man's heart is through his stomach never met you," he said with a grin. "A heads up though—it's going to be a busy meeting. We have quite a few more cases that need to be assigned. Referrals have been coming in one after the other."

Jordan tucked a loose strand of hair behind her ear. "Well then, I guess I won't have to try too hard to distract myself with work. Though I can't say I'm not grateful for the business. We've been fortunate."

"No argument here," Mike agreed. He hesitated before continuing. "Are you sure you're up to this?"

Her eyes softened at the concern etched on her friend's face. "I'm sure. I know you guys are worried, and I won't lie and say that I'm not still trying to deal with what happened. But being at work is therapeutic. It'll help put it behind me."

The trio entered the office together. Jordan checked her personal mailbox on the way in. There were a few case files, some psychological testing that had come back, and a message from a detective with the police department.

Hmm….so a detective is already assigned to the case.

18

She skimmed over the message that indicated he'd like to arrange a meeting as soon as possible. Turning to Nancy, the secretary, in the main office area, Jordan asked her to schedule a meeting with the detective during her first open hour.

"Actually, your eleven o'clock canceled a moment ago, so you're free then. Would that be too soon?" she replied, her hands poised above the computer keys, ready to fill the gap in Jordan's schedule.

"If that works for the detective, then it will be fine for me. Thanks Nancy."

At eleven o'clock sharp, her office phone rang, and she hit the speaker button.

"Detective Warren Larson is here to see you," Nancy's voice rang out.

"Please, tell him I'll be right there." Jordan made her way to the waiting room to meet the detective.

It was easy to pick the officer out of the clients who were waiting. He wore the traditional black uniform assigned to the local police department. His salt-and-pepper hair was cut short, and the lines around his face made him appear tired. Having to investigate these types of crimes would likely take its toll on anyone.

He stood as she approached him.

"Hi. I'm Jordan Clayton. Thank you for coming. We can meet in my office." She shook hands with the detective and led the way back to her office. "Just have a seat anywhere," she offered.

The detective glanced between the leather sofa and the club chair available. He sank into the chair. "Reckon I'd better sit here. Don't want to get too comfortable. But I'm sure many people are tempted to lie down on that couch. It only seems right when you're in a psychologist's office and all," he said, his tone amicable.

Jordan smiled. Over the years, many of her patients had made reference to the same stereotype. "Yes, it does."

Once they were seated, the light-hearted conversation dwindled away. He assumed a more serious expression, and she wondered what had caused the change. Shifting uneasily in the chair, he cleared his throat.

"Were you able to interview my assailant?" Jordan asked, trying to provide him with a lead-in.

"Yes. Well, the officer on the scene interviewed him last night at the hospital after he regained consciousness. He was trying to get basic information regarding the incident. Because of what was reported, I was assigned to the case." He glanced around the office and then continued on, meeting her gaze. "Guy's name is Henry Rigdon. He was arrested last night. I'm not sure if he'll make bond or not. He admitted to attacking you yesterday evening. Said he waited in the parking lot until he saw you come out alone."

Her chest tightened. "So, he was intentionally looking for me, but why?"

"Well, by his own admission—and we're still working on verifying this information—he was paid by an unknown source to commit the offense." The detective waited for her response before proceeding.

"Go ahead." Emotions tumbled inside her as she digested this last piece of information.

"It seems he was approached by a male via telephone. The man offered him ten thousand dollars to, in his words, 'remove you.' He was reportedly paid half of the money prior to the attack and was to receive the other half upon your death. The money was left at an agreed-upon location. Rigdon said he never got a look at the guy who hired him."

Jordan held her hand up. Her head swirled with questions and her turbulent emotions threatened her composure. Anger, sadness, and fear vied for a response to what she'd heard. Anger won. "You're telling me that this guy, Henry Rigdon, was hired to kill me for ten thousand dollars, money being his only motivator? And there's someone out there who intended for this to happen—no, intended isn't the right word." She paused, struggling again to wrap her mind around what she'd heard. "Someone who actively tried to make sure a plan to have me killed was carried out."

As wrath flushed through her body, her voice rose with each word. The reins on her normally well-modulated emotions went slack while she fought to make any sense of it all. It was callous, and unlike the many crimes she'd reviewed, it was personal.

She shook her head. *So ten thousand dollars is the going rate for a human life nowadays.* Disgust settled in the pit of her stomach.

The detective didn't seem put off by her reaction. He was in her position. She was the one who dealt with angry clients, who helped them deal with trauma and negative outcomes. And, as trying as some cases could be, there was a difference when the role was reversed.

He leaned forward, his hands steepled in front of him. "Unfortunately, yes. I know this is upsetting for you and there isn't much I can do to change that, but I can say that our agency will do our best to find the person behind this attack. We take this matter seriously, and it'll be a priority for both myself and the other investigators." The corners of his mouth turned down as he continued. "I hate to have to ask you now, but it's critical to the investigation that I get some additional information." He reached into his front shirt pocket and withdrew a notepad and pen. "Is there anyone you might suspect would do something like this? Or is there anyone in particular you know of who's angry enough or vengeful enough to consider resorting to this type of violence?"

It was all Jordan could do to suppress the bitter laughter caught in her throat. "If you're asking if anyone in my personal life may be connected with this, then the answer is no." She didn't feel the need to expand on her skimpy private life. "In regards to people in my professional life, you can take your pick."

She'd made enemies. It came with the territory.

"I'm involved in litigation on a daily basis. I regularly testify at child custody, competency to stand trial, criminal responsibility, personal injury, and sentencing hearings. Just to name a few." Even though the ultimate decisions were often left to the trier of the fact, as an impartial expert witness, the scientific information and opinions she provided during her testimony usually loaned support to one side or the other. "The findings I offer in some of these cases can make people very angry. Angry enough to do something like this? I honestly don't know. It would depend on the person." She let out a breath, her shoulders sagging at this admission.

"Have you received any threats lately? Perhaps by telephone, as it seems this is how our guy communicates," he persisted.

Her brow lifted. Truth be known, these types of calls were something she'd become accustomed to over the years, a regrettable indirect result of her role in the legal process. She often wondered if having an unlisted phone number only slowed them down a little. Searching her memory, she tried to remember the date of the last call. "It's probably been about three months, and I can't remember exactly what the caller said. I believe he spewed off a host of obscenities and references to, in his words, 'shrinks meddling in marriages.' It might've been related to a custody case. Those cases can be emotional for the parties involved."

"Good to know." The detective shook his head. "But that doesn't help us much at this point. From now on, if you receive any of these phone calls, please keep a record and notify me."

"I can do that," she said wearily. Discussing the details was making her all too aware of the challenges they'd be up against in catching this guy.

"Also, is there any way I can get a list of the cases

you've worked on and the individuals involved?"

Her eyes snapped fully open. "Now, that'll be a problem. I can give you the names that are already listed in public records. Usually, I've been appointed by the court to conduct assessments in those cases, but I don't want to reveal the identities of any other patients. They have a right to confidentiality, and I won't violate that."

He let out a sigh. "You are aware that, by not doing so, you're precluding us from fully doing our job."

"Right now, that's the best I can do," she said, her tone firm. "If we need to revisit this down the road, then I'm game. But I think the names you'll get provide the best starting point in terms of potential suspects with motive."

He hooked his index finger in the cleft above his chin as he considered the option. "Fair enough. One more question, then, in regards to your personal life. Are you currently having any type of relationship problems? I know it's an intrusive question, but we need to eliminate everyone."

"I'm not involved with anyone right now."

"What about ex-boyfriends? Any conflictual breakups?"

"No."

He looked at her, waiting for her to expand, his pen poised above the small, worn scratchpad.

"I haven't dated anyone seriously for a while, since my early college years to be exact."

The detective jotted down the information. She didn't know how many pages could possibly be left in the dilapidated note-keeping device, but her list of romantic entanglements wouldn't be the information to finally force it into retirement.

"My work keeps me pretty busy," she added before he could lift his pen.

Her spontaneous rationalization caused her cringe inside. She was proud of what she'd accomplished by dedicating most of her time to her practice, but spelling out her dating history—or, rather, the lack thereof—to this detective made it obvious that she hadn't developed much of a personal life outside of her work.

"Well, that's it for now." He pocketed his notebook.

He must have recognized he hit a dry well. She stood with him.

"We're going to follow up on the leads we have, and I'll let you know how the case is progressing," he continued. "Until then, be careful. We still don't know who's behind this attack."

Or if there would be any more. Although she could tell by the meaningful look he gave her that he was thinking the same thing, neither one said it aloud.

"I'd try to avoid going anywhere alone. Maybe have a friend go with you."

"Thank you. I'll be careful." As she escorted him out, she passed Mike and Karen in the hall.

The aroma of tomato sauce and rosemary wafted from the brown paper to-go bags they carried, but this was the only time Rosella's talents might be wasted on her. The revulsion that roosted in her stomach at the detective's news had stomped out any embers of an appetite she may have had left.

I'll be right there, she mouthed to them. They'd want to know the latest developments regarding the attack. If only she had better news to tell. This was worse than she'd ever anticipated. The event wasn't some random attack, and the perp wasn't a disgruntled relation to a previous case. Rather, it appeared it was the first in what might be a series of attempts on her life. No closure had come from the meeting with the detective.

As she entered the conference room, everyone was eagerly passing around the freshly baked bread and digging into the pasta dishes spread across the table. She grabbed her own order and sat down. Her colleagues' gazes drifted toward her, and she looked up to meet their questioning stares. She busied herself by removing the top from the foil container while she contemplated what to say. Steam began to seep up from the red sauce.

For a split second, she debated not telling them what she'd heard, but that wasn't the answer. If someone was truly out to get her, then they may be in danger too, even if by mere association alone. Besides, she had no idea how to cope with this type of situation by herself. She needed the support of her friends now more than ever.

"Well, don't keep us waiting. What did he say?" Karen asked, tearing a piece of the focaccia in half while she spoke.

How do I tell them someone was hired to kill me? Her mind raced, trying to think of how to share the information she'd received. It seemed surreal, the kind of thing that happened only in the movies. Finally, she decided to be direct. There was no way to sugarcoat the situation, and she didn't even want to try.

She took a deep breath. "That was Warren Larson, the detective who's been assigned to investigate my case. He interviewed the guy who attacked me yesterday. His name is Henry Rigdon. From what this guy Rigdon said, it seems he was paid to do it. Detective Larson still isn't sure who was behind it though. So, for now, he's investigating potential suspects and the leads he gathered from his interview with Rigdon."

Everyone sat frozen with stunned expressions. The room was so quiet that the whirring from the white-noise maker in the corner sounded more like a lawn mower. The contraption was normally discreet, serving its purpose by masking the conversation within the room. But today, there was no danger of private client details being overheard by someone beyond the closed doors. The threat was to someone within them.

Mike was the first to break the silence. The chair he'd been idly rocking back in prior to her announcement slammed forward to resume all four legs on the floor. "Who in the hell would do such a thing? Is the detective sure this Rigdon guy isn't making this all up?"

"Why would he?" Jordan asked him. "He's been caught in the act. He has absolutely nothing to gain from lying. He committed the crime either way. In fact, his admission will probably hurt him more than anything else. What's more, they found the money where he said it would be, a little under five thousand dollars in a black duffel bag under his bed."

Karen's mouth dropped open. "What are we going to do until he's caught? I mean, you aren't safe until this guy is off the streets. Whoever he is."

Her friend had abandoned her lunch. The torn bread pieces were steadily absorbing olive oil as they rested unattended in the shallow gratin dish.

"She's right," Derek said. "There's no telling what that thug would've done if I hadn't been there. It makes me sick, thinking about it." He cast his eyes downward before continuing on. "As it is, I keep telling myself that I should have been there sooner, or walked you out, just done something different."

Jordan patted his hand. "Hey, you don't need to second-guess a thing." Her voice was soft but firm. "You were awesome. I can never thank you enough for what you did." She tried to avoid thinking about what might have happened to her without Derek's help.

Derek gave her a curt nod, but the corners of his mouth remained turned down.

Mike spoke up. "Don't look at it like that, Derek. It's always easy to hash out the 'should haves,' but we're damn lucky you were where you were." He turned his attention back to Jordan. "Right now, we need to figure out how to handle this. Karen's got a point. You're not safe. Not with this maniac out there. And you definitely shouldn't be alone. Maybe you should move in with Karen and me for a while."

"Oh, Mike! I hate this. It feels like I'm trapped, waiting for something terrible and I have no idea what. I can't plan my whole life around this. You three won't be able to be with me every second of every day. Even though I know you'd try." She gave them a weak smile. "It wouldn't be possible, and it sure as hell wouldn't be fair to anyone."

Once again, the room was silent. Usually, staff meetings were filled with lively conversation and energetic debates. At times, it was hard to get a word in edgewise. Now, she could hear the sound of her plastic spoon scraping aluminum as she stirred her uneaten pasta around in the dish.

"Maybe if you took a vacation. You know, got out of town for a while until the cops get some idea as to who's behind this," Derek proposed.

"I don't see how that's possible. I have so many open cases and several court dates coming up. I can't desert my clients. Besides, I'd rather not run away. I don't think that would solve anything. I refuse to let this creep, whoever he or she is, win."

"But Jordan, there's too much at stake. You're risking your life!" Pools of water collected in the rims of Karen's eyes.

Mike took Karen's hand and held it in his own. "I have an idea," he said, his tone becoming more animated. "You're right about the vacation. Maybe it's not such a good idea. After all, whoever it is could just as well follow you. But there's no way around it. It's obvious this guy means business, and we need to figure out a way to keep you safe. I have an old friend I met during my undergraduate years at FSU. We had a few courses together and have stayed close ever since. He worked for the state police doing dignitary protection for a while, and now, he heads his own protection company. I can get in touch with him and have him select one of his close protection specialists to look after you until this situation is handled." He sat back in his chair and laced his fingers behind his head.

Jordan dropped her spoon and stared at him in disbelief. "Are you talking about hiring a bodyguard?"

"I think it's an excellent idea!" Karen exclaimed. "I'd feel so relieved to know that someone who's trained to deal with this type of thing is with you."

Jordan's jaw fell. "You can't be serious. How on earth could I do my job with some huge, overbearing powerhouse in a suit and sunglasses hanging over my shoulder?"

Mike laughed. "Oh, Jordan, you know as well as I do that the image you described is about as accurate as the ones out there of psychologists. I've known this guy for years, and he's as professional as they come. He's trained to blend into any type of environment and to stand out only when he needs to. I'm betting his team members are equally as good." He crossed his arms loosely over his chest. "I'm sure you two could work out the particulars."

She pinched her forehead around her temples where a dull ache had settled. Nothing about his solution sounded appealing to her, but she tried to approach it delicately. "Honestly, Mike, I didn't mean to be offensive. But in all seriousness, even if I agreed to the idea, which I'm not, I couldn't afford that type of protection. I have no idea how much it costs to hire a bodyguard, but I can imagine around-the-clock protection isn't cheap."

"I'll talk to him. I'm sure we can figure something out. Besides, we can always use the money we've put aside for the additional marketing costs for the practice. We don't need it. There's already over a two-month-long wait to get an appointment as it is. And even if there weren't, this is your safety we're talking about here. You can't even put a value on that."

Mike's last statement brought the reality of the situation back to her. It was ironic. Someone had assigned a value not on her safety, but on her life. Rigdon had tried to kill her for ten thousand dollars. Maybe she was being too hasty in rejecting Mike's idea. There weren't any better ones on the table. "I'll sleep on it tonight and let you know tomorrow. Okay?"

"It's a deal." He leaned toward her, his eyes filled with empathy. "Jordan, I know the idea seems strange, but it's the only thing we can think of that sounds reasonable," he said in a matter-of-fact tone.

Derek and Karen nodded in agreement.

I'm definitely outnumbered on this one.

She locked her bedroom door and checked that the window latches were secure before she crawled into bed. A feeling of uneasiness lurked within her, like something was about to happen but she didn't know what or when. She tossed and turned as she struggled to fall asleep, only managing to succeed in wrapping her sheets into a tight cocoon. As she straightened them out again, her thoughts led back to the staff meeting earlier that day. *A bodyguard?* Did she genuinely need a bodyguard?

Part of her wanted to laugh at the idea. On one hand, it sounded ludicrous. She'd always prided herself on being independent. She owned her own practice and her own house, and dealt with the related issues that came up for both. Although she worked long hours, she'd always managed to take care of herself. But would she be able to handle this threat alone? She remembered how close she'd come to being dragged away at the mercy of her attacker yesterday. The memory still made her queasy. There seemed to be no answer. Letting out a yawn, she finally felt herself being pulled into the gentle waves of sleep.

She was resting soundly when she heard a noise. Torn between her demanding unconscious and the escalating need to rouse herself from slumber, she struggled to pry her eyes open. Someone was in her room. She didn't see him, but she could feel his presence. Opening her mouth to scream, her panic increased when no sound emerged. She lay frozen as a figure emerged from the shadows and began to approach her bed. She could almost make out the profile of a man. And he was holding a knife.

Jordan sat up in bed screaming. Sweat poured off her body and the cotton nightshirt she wore was soaked. Taking in a slow breath, she felt her rapid inhalations become more regular. It was only a dream. *A dream that had felt so real.* In an instant, she'd made her decision. She'd have Mike call this friend of his tomorrow. She was used to making it on her own, but this was one time she'd have to admit she needed a little help, if not for her own sake, then for her clients. There was no way she'd be able to maintain her level of practice if she allowed herself to be in a continual state of fear or, at this rate, a constant state of exhaustion.

She sought Mike out as soon as she heard his voice in the main office the next morning. He and Nancy were hashing out plot holes from a popular television series they both watched when she walked in.

"Are you kidding me?" he said with exasperation. "You really think that could happen? The FBI isn't going to engage a college student in a situation like that."

"Mike, they use informants all of the time. Why not her?" Nancy countered as she slid the daily schedule sheets into the corresponding slots for each doctor. "Morning, Jordan," she greeted her without missing a beat.

"Good morning," she replied, dropping a letter into the mail basket. "I'm sorry to interrupt what sounds like a fascinating discussion—" she winked at Nancy, "—but I have an early client." She eyed her friend. "Mike, do you have a second to talk?"

"Sure." He grabbed his cup of coffee and began following her into her office. "I'll catch you later, Nancy. We aren't finished yet," he teased over his shoulder.

Nancy chuckled as they headed off.

Jordan turned her attention back to Mike. "I thought about what you said yesterday, and as hard as this is to say, I think you're right. Hiring a…bodyguard—" there, she'd said it, "—may be a good idea. At least until we find out who's behind this. Even if it's a little much, at least it'll give me peace of mind. Something I kind of need in this field." She gave him a weary grin.

"Yeah, I'd say so." He paused "Look, I knew you'd come around. I wasn't trying to overstep any boundaries." He looked at her with an earnest expression. "But I went ahead and called him last night."

Her eyebrows shot up. "You what? But I hadn't even... I wasn't sure—"

"Before you get upset, hear me out. I was simply getting some information in case you decided you needed his services. For all I knew, his specialists may have been booked."

She relented. She hadn't thought of that. "So, what'd you find out?"

"He's available to meet with you this afternoon at one, if you choose to, and yes, it's already on your schedule. I was actually lucky to catch him in between assignments. I'm sure any of his guys are competent, but I have to admit, I'll feel better knowing it's him looking after you."

She burst out laughing. "I should really get you for this. What were you going to do if I decided I didn't want to meet him?"

His face broke into a grin. "I'd have hounded you relentlessly until you came to your senses. But seriously, I'm glad you decided to go through with this. Even though you have my wife's stubborn streak, you're like a sister to me, and I don't know what I'd do if something happened to you." He pulled her into a bear hug.

"Oh, Mike. Thanks. I do appreciate what you've done. The whole idea was just a little intimidating." Jordan returned the hug, wondering exactly what she'd gotten herself into.

CHAPTER THREE

Chase Armstrong sat in the busy lobby of the forensic practice. He threw a casual glance around the room. Five other people were waiting for an appointment, one couple and three individuals. His friend's practice appeared to be doing well. However, the steady stream of clients meant it would be harder to identify the suspect in this case, assuming, of course, that the suspect was actually some type of business contact as Mike had indicated.

Mike had briefed him on the situation over the phone last night. The fact that the first act of violence had escalated to this point meant he'd have to be extremely cautious during the detail. These circumstances were a lot harder on his clients, particularly one who wasn't used to the presence of a protection specialist. It would mean more in-depth security measures, which, inevitably, equaled less autonomy.

He stood up when he saw his old friend walking toward him.

"Hey, my man." Mike grabbed his hand in a firm shake. "It's been a while since I've seen you. What country are you calling home lately?" he asked lightheartedly.

"Take your pick," Chase replied, matching his tone. "I

can tell you it sure is nice to be back here for a change." Protecting celebrities, corporate executives, and dignitaries who didn't fall under coverage by the Secret Service translated to plenty of frequent flyer miles and a greater appreciation of being home.

"I bet it is. Well, it's good to see you."

"You too." Chase shook his head. "I'm sorry we couldn't get together under better circumstances though."

Mike's lips formed a straight line. "Yeah. I won't tell you this hasn't kept me up at night. She's like family to Karen and me. Although, if anything can put my mind more at ease, it would be knowing that you're with her. I can honestly say I never thought I'd need your services, but boy am I glad you're here now."

"Neither did I. Still, I'm happy to help. You should've reached out sooner. I'd have been right over." He'd easily agreed to handle the case himself when Mike had called. Besides wanting to help out his friend, he was growing a little tired of living in the lives of the rich and famous. A change of pace would be nice.

"I know. It took us a little while to figure things out," Mike replied. "When you get to know Jordan, it'll probably make more sense. I'm actually surprised she agreed to this. It's not like her to ask for help much."

Chase raised his eyebrows. "But she's on board now?"

"Yeah. She's good now. Realized, like all of us, this was pretty serious. Nothing to mess around with for sure. Come on." Mike motioned for him to follow him. "I'll take you to her office so you can meet her."

They walked in silence until they reached her office.

"Hey, Jor." Mike poked his head around her open door.

"Hmmm," Jordan replied without glancing up. She was jotting down notes on a yellow legal pad. Her coffee-colored hair fell loosely just below her shoulders, the soft waves shimmering from the reflection of the overhead lighting when she moved.

"Detach yourself from your work for a minute." Mike laughed at her. "I have someone I'd like you to meet."

She raised her head as he and Mike entered, her blue eyes widening slightly when they landed on him. His body must've made a unilateral decision that the feeling was mutual, because his pulse shot up in response to her wide stare. Not that he was surprised. The woman was striking but in that rare classic—Vivienne Leigh or Audrey Hepburn—way. The way he'd always found extremely hot. With large round eyes, defined cheekbones, and full lips, she unequivocally embodied the type of beauty that transcended specific time periods or passing trends.

"Jordan, this is my good friend, Chase. Chase, Jordan." Mike's head moved back and forth between the two of them. "I have to go meet my next client," he said in a hurried tone, "so I'll leave you two to work out the particulars." He gave Chase a friendly slap on the back. "See you around. I guess this is one time you being busy with work means we actually get to catch up."

"Sure thing." Chase nodded, but his gaze was already back on his own client as he stepped farther into the office.

Jordan stood up from her desk. She was tall, about five feet eight inches, and her fitted slacks revealed a trim figure.

"Hi. Nice to meet you," he said as he extended his hand to her. When her soft skin met his, an unusual current zipped through him. It wasn't an uncomfortable one, like when he'd been tasered during trainings, but more similar to the gratifying burning sensation that came with a finger of Johnny Walker Blue. He'd experienced it once in a while with a woman before—never from a handshake.

"It's great to meet you as well. Please have a seat. Would you like anything? Coffee, iced tea, soda?"

He noticed that her voice faltered slightly. His ego

would have liked to think she'd felt something with the physical contact too but, in truth, her reaction was nothing he wasn't used to. Most people didn't interact with bodyguards in their everyday life, so a little uncertainty was commonplace. "Actually, iced tea sounds great," he found himself replying, more from the need for a second alone than from thirst.

She left the room, and a creamy gourmand scent settled in her wake.

Sinking down into one of her office chairs, he mused whether or not it was her physical beauty that was throwing him off a bit. Ultimately, he eliminated the explanation. He'd been responsible for protecting many gorgeous women during his work—actresses, singers, models—and touching them wasn't reminiscent of the heat from a velvety smooth blended scotch. He let out a long breath and told himself that she'd likely be his next client. The stark reminder had him abandoning the train of thought altogether. Whatever the cause, it would have no bearing on his interactions with her. He never mixed business with pleasure. In his line of work, those two could be a deadly combination. It was a rule he never broke—never even bent.

Jordan walked into the room carrying a tall glass. "Here you go," she said as she placed the tea on the small end table next to him. Condensation dripped down the sides onto the napkin she'd situated under the drink. "It's not sweetened." She watched as he took a sip. "I wasn't sure if you like it sweet or not, so here's some sugar if you want it." Her face flushed a bit as she set a few sugar packets beside the drink.

Her slight coloring likely meant she'd comprehended that sugar in the South could mean one of two things. He pressed his lips together to suppress a grin. Whether intended or not, she obviously had a way with words.

Rather than sharing that he normally would have no objections to either sweet or sugar—particularly if it was coming from her—he answered with a simple, "Thank you. This is fine."

She sat back down at her desk while rotating her chair around to face him. After fidgeting with the papers on her desk, she finally began speaking. "To be quite frank, I don't know where to begin. This whole situation still seems so unreal to me."

He sensed her discomfort and directed the conversation. "For starters, Mike has spoken to me briefly about the circumstances surrounding the attack, but it would help if I heard exactly what happened from you. After that, I can tell you the basics about my role as a personal protection specialist and we can discuss what your responsibilities as a client will look like."

She nodded and began to reveal the details of the past few days. While she spoke, Chase observed her. On the surface, she appeared cool and composed. She wore a tailored beige jacket that matched her slacks. Underneath the jacket, she had on a deep blue blouse that highlighted her eyes. He'd never seen eyes quite that color. They sparkled like tanzanite with flashes of violet.

It was when he was checking out her eyes that he noticed the darkness that defined puffy semi-circles below them. He could imagine it'd be hard for her to sleep with all of this going on. Though she appeared to be making an effort to sound unflustered, her body told a different story. He could see her muscles tense as she got further into the account, and her voice shook when she glossed over how he'd grabbed her from behind. His stare fell to the graceful hollow of her neck, where several bruises peeked out from the collar of her blouse. The sight caused a visceral reaction within his gut. Times like these made him miss being the one to put the cuffs on offenders who preyed on the innocent.

She interlaced her fingers in her lap when she finished and gazed back at him expectantly.

He considered everything she'd told him and what

she hadn't. "This is the kind of threat you should take very seriously," he said evenly. "The fact that whoever is behind this is resorting to violence indicates that he's determined to harm you."

"I know," she acknowledged in a resigned tone.

"As your protection specialist, it would be my duty to ensure your safety until the police are able to make an arrest. I've got a lot of experience with these types of situations. Many of the high-profile clients I've worked with are dealing with threats and stalkers, so it's not an unfamiliar scenario. As for my qualifications, I can give you a resume with my both my work and training experience as well as a reference list."

"That won't be necessary. Mike speaks highly of you, and that's enough for me," she interjected.

"Okay. Let me know if you change your mind." He stopped to take a swallow of tea before going on. This was the part of his orientation consultation he always reviewed thoroughly with each client. "Before we continue, you need to know that for me to be able to do my job, there are some sacrifices you have to be willing to make. The most obvious is privacy. I'm quite good at what I do, and whenever at all possible, you'll have space to yourself and time alone. However, there's been a direct threat to your life. This kind of situation calls for a high level of protection, which means a lot more caution. Unfortunately, being this cautious can be quite intrusive at times."

She nodded and crossed one long leg over the other, shifting her hips slightly during the process.

He continued, willing himself not to get distracted by the motion. "There will be times when you won't understand some of the procedures I follow. Yet it's still critical that you follow any instructions I give you. If you have questions during these times, you can ask them later. I'm not telling you this to discourage you from seeking protection. In fact, there are probably quite a few specialists out there who follow a less structured method of operation. But I don't take my responsibility lightly, and if I'm to do my job and protect your life, then I need your full cooperation." Upon finishing his usual spiel, he waited for her to accept or reject his terms. These were nonnegotiable.

Her eyes met his. She made no move to respond. The silence didn't seem to bother her.

He didn't say anything either, giving her time to think. It was her decision and one that she'd have to live with. There was no need to rush it.

§

Jordan tried to contemplate what Chase was saying and not focus on the fact that he was nothing like what she'd expected. She took in his chiseled features, olive complexion, and wavy brown hair. He wore a nondescript pair of khaki pants and button-down shirt. Though nondescript couldn't describe the clothes on this man. They fit snug in all the right places, displaying a broad chest that tapered down to a fit waist. It was apparent he was in excellent physical shape. Thankfully, he wasn't the hulking bodybuilder type she'd pictured. She told herself she was pleasantly surprised only because it meant he wouldn't stand out like a sore thumb when he accompanied her on business functions. She wasn't about to admit that she found his appearance appealing on a personal level as well.

Chase sat back in his chair, stretching out his legs in front of him. The shift made her office suddenly feel much smaller. His movement reminded her he was waiting for her response.

She thought about the drawbacks he'd mentioned. The points he'd brought up were the same ones she'd been deliberating herself. The thought of losing her self-reliance, not to mention her privacy, wasn't appealing. But what choice did she have? Going over the situation a thousand times in her mind, it all came down to one thing. She wasn't willing to try to escape from another attack by herself. She considered herself fortunate to have escaped the first attempt on her life. Her objective was to be better prepared should this guy make a second attempt. And, in this case, she was pretty sure she couldn't get any better prepared than she'd be by hiring Chase Armstrong.

"I understand what you're saying," she began, "and I did consider those issues before we met. I'm willing to cooperate with whatever measures you feel are necessary to ensure my safety. However, I'll admit that I have some reservations." She paused, looking into the green eyes staring back at her. The color reminded her of woodsy overgrowth in a garden landscape.

"By all means, let's address them. I want to make sure we're both clear on one another's expectations from the start," he said in a pragmatic manner.

"Well, I plan to continue working until this matter is resolved. I'm not quite sure how you'll fit into the picture. I see clients on a daily basis, which brings up the matter of confidentiality. I can't allow my clients' right to confidentiality to be compromised in any way." Her voice was firm. "Also, I often testify in court, attend board meetings, and teach classes." She chose her next words with care, trying to avoid being offensive. "I'm not sure what kind of impression it would make if everyone present knew I was being protected by a bodyguard."

He nodded. "I understand your concerns. I won't lie and tell you that I've dealt with them all before, because you'd be the first psychologist I've ever protected. But I can say that I've dealt with similar situations, and I'm sure we'll be able to find a way to work this out that won't compromise your safety or the integrity of your work. If there does come a point when I feel like something you're attempting to do could jeopardize your safety, then I'd have to ask you to refrain. There's no need to take unnecessary risks."

His last comment would have made her smile if he hadn't been so serious. She'd never considered herself any kind of a risk taker in the past. But the way things were now, going out of the house alone would be considered a risk. Based on this criteria, she'd be deemed an absolute thrill-seeker. The notion almost brought a smile to her face as the trait was so incongruous with her character.

"Thank you for expanding on that," she responded. "I really don't have any more questions about my specific situation. I do need to know what your standard fee for your services is?" She held her breath while waiting for his reply, hoping his charges were within her price range.

He quoted her a daily rate for his protection services. "In addition, you'll be responsible for paying any out-of-pocket expenses related to your protection. I'll cover the costs of my own meals." He shrugged. "From the way I look at it, I'd be eating either way."

She nodded, and the breath she'd been holding morphed into a sigh of relief. That wasn't nearly as expensive as she'd anticipated. As long as the police didn't take too long to make an arrest, she wouldn't have to dip into the marketing funds for the practice at all. "Then I guess that leaves us with one last question. When do you start?"

"Under the circumstances, as soon as possible," he replied. "I need to make a quick trip home to gather the things I'll need. How about I meet you here at five?"

"That sounds fine." Her smile became stiff. Did he say things? Exactly what had she gotten herself into? She'd always assumed moving in with someone would mean she'd found the person she'd share her life with in a romantic sense. Never would she have thought it would be a bodyguard, and an extremely good-looking one at that.

"Good." He dropped his chin. "Since we've gone over the basics, it's probably best that we start now." His voice took on a no-nonsense tone, and she could tell he was accustomed to giving out commands. "For starters, don't leave the building under any circumstances until I get back. Second, are you seeing any new clients today?"

She bristled at his commanding air.

"Don't feel pressured to give any names. I agreed to do my best to respect your condition to maintain client confidentiality, but I do need to know if you've planned to see anyone new today."

This arrangement was going to be harder than she'd thought. She'd forgotten how much it irked her to be ordered around by anyone, and her lack of sleep last night certainly didn't help her tolerance. She squelched her negative reaction and reminded herself that he was only doing his job. *And I'd better get used to it for now*, she conceded wearily. "No, I won't be seeing any new clients today. Actually, I have a heavy client load as it is. So, in light of the situation, I went ahead and told Nancy, our secretary, not to schedule any more for the time being."

"That was a smart move." He nodded toward her door. "I'd hate to have to search them for weapons before they're allowed to enter your office for their session."

Holy cow! There is no way he's going to search my clients. She lifted her carriage to full height as she prepared to inform him of this. Then she saw the grin that played at the corners of his mouth. He was joking. She swallowed the retort that had been on the tip of her tongue. Playing along instead, she plastered a smile in its place.

"I'm glad you caught on," he said, giving a crack of laughter. "For a minute, I thought I was about to lose my head before I could defend myself."

Somehow, the idea that he couldn't defend himself seemed at odds with everything she'd observed of him thus far. And she surely wasn't ready to admit she'd thought he was serious. "I knew you were probably kidding. I just figured I'd let you squirm for a while."

"Of course," he replied, clearly still amused.

They both seemed to know it would've been her left wriggling on the hook fashioned from her own overreaction had he not graciously accepted her flimsy excuse. So, maybe not the best start, but at least he had a sense of humor. Or at least she hoped.

Either way, the days ahead lingered in front of her like the winding line at a county fair. She didn't know how long it would take before she reached the end, but for now, she needed to be patient, moving forward a few steps at a time.

CHAPTER FOUR

At five o'clock, Chase entered back into the lobby to meet Jordan. He scanned the area, observing the three patients already seated. The number of clientele appeared steady through the workday. Walking up to the check-in window, which was ajar, he made a mental note to consider the opening as another possible means of entry.

"Hello," he said to the silver-haired woman seated on the other side. "I'm here to see Dr. Clayton. Chase Armstrong."

The woman gave him a quick once-over and then scanned the folders lined up on the desk. She frowned, not seeing a corresponding folder with his name.

Jordan walked up beside her. "It's okay, Nancy. You can buzz him in."

The door to his right buzzed, and he walked into the hall connected to the main office area. The security precautions already in place would be helpful. He headed through the open doorway to meet Jordan, who was still chatting with Nancy.

"Hi, Chase. I'd like you to meet Nancy. She's our secretary, and I'd be lying if I didn't say she also serves as my right arm here. Nancy, this is Chase Armstrong. He'll be working here with me to provide extra security."

Jordan didn't add anything regarding the recent attack, but it was clear from Nancy's understanding expression that she'd made the connection.

Nancy nodded. "It's very nice to meet you." She extended her hand.

"You as well." Chase responded, taking her hand.

"Sorry. I didn't recognize your name from the schedule earlier. I was wondering who the man was who was able to get Jordan to leave the office before sunset," she added with a chuckle.

Jordan froze for a second, then hurried to clarify the statement. "I usually work until later in the evening. It's the best time I have to catch up on dictation. But I wrapped it up early today so we could get started."

"Makes sense," he agreed.

It wasn't hard to conclude that Mike had summed up Jordan's current lack of a romantic life well. The part that didn't make sense was why she remained uninvolved. If she weren't his client and he had the settling-down kind of life, he'd try his damnedest to get her off the singles market. But, since neither was true, it was really none of his concern.

"I'll leave you two to work out the details," Nancy said, conveniently excusing herself from the conversation. "I'll see you around Chase."

"Sure thing," he replied. Then he turned his attention back to Jordan. "It's no problem for me if you need to work a little longer today. From here on out, I'll be with you twenty-four-seven, so it doesn't matter how late you are. I'll be happy to wait."

"Actually, I'm kind of beat. I haven't really slept well the past few days. It's probably just as well that I get out of here a little ahead of time for a change."

Her revelation drew him back to the circles beneath her eyes. The purplish shadows made her fatigue evident. "Okay, then. Let's go."

They exited the office and he walked next to her, scanning the area for any potential threat. He looked both above and below eye level for risks. As they approached the remaining parked cars, he turned to face her.

"Which one is you?" he asked.

"Right over there. The gold one." She pointed to the last car in the row ahead.

"Does your car have an alarm?"

"Yes. It has one the dealership installed when I purchased it," she answered.

"How sensitive is it?"

"What?" Her brows knitted together. "I have no idea. I've only set it off by accident a couple of times. You don't think someone might have tampered with it?" Her eyes widened as she waited for his response. In the remaining sunlight, they had even more flashes of violet.

Chase rested a reassuring hand on her shoulder. "You forget. It's my job to think someone could and would do anything and everything. Don't be alarmed. For the most part, it's a critical but entirely unnecessary effort." He didn't mention the times his efforts had saved lives; he wanted her to be cautious, not terrified.

Jordan nodded but still looked a bit unsure.

The sooner he had her out of the parking lot, where the whole thing had occurred and headed home, the better it would be for her. "Look, usually I will drive you to and from your commitments, but we need to get your car back to your house. So today, I'm going to have one of my guys drive you home in my car. I'll follow behind you in yours. If anyone is looking for you, they won't expect you to be in my car. That'll leave me to deal with any threats." His BMW was also equipped with ballistic protection, shatterproof glass, and an eight-cylinder turbocharged engine. Yeah, there was no question where she'd be safer. He waved to the man behind the wheel as they approached his SUV, which was parked on the other side of the lot.

"Has he been waiting this whole time?" Jordan's gaze

cut over to him. "I would have wrapped up more quickly if I'd known he was waiting out here."

"No worries. We're used to it. It's what we do ninety-five percent of the time. Everyone always pictures our job like Hollywood portrays it in action movies, but in reality, we spend a lot of time researching, planning, and waiting."

Upon arriving at his vehicle, he reached out to open the front passenger's side door for Jordan. Once she was settled inside, he introduced Jordan to his associate.

"Jordan, this is David. He's been with me pretty much since I started the business. David, this is Dr. Jordan Clayton, our newest client."

"Nice to meet you, doctor," David said, looking back at her.

"Please, call me Jordan," she said, clicking her seat belt into place.

"Can you open the back? Then give me a sec to check over her car and I'll follow you out," Chase said.

He'd already mapped out the route they'd take back to her house, and he and David had both rehearsed it. Unfortunately, though Jordan had an unlisted address, it had taken nothing more than a simple Internet search to locate her home. He grabbed a long-arm tactical mirror from the back of his SUV and carried it over to Jordan's car.

After establishing that the car alarm would have alerted had anyone attempted to alter it, he moved the mirror around the undercarriage of the car, looking for anything unusual. There were no tool marks on bolts, leaking fluids, or objects attached to the frame. Not seeing any evidence of foul play, he opened the hood.

Spending a large part of his childhood in his uncle's auto repair shop came in handy at times like this. He'd learned how to rebuild an engine before he'd graduated from elementary school. Always a daredevil, back then, he'd thought he'd use what he knew to become a racecar driver. His lips twitched at the memory as his gaze roamed over the remaining parts he was assessing.

Everything looked fine. He gave David the thumbs-up sign, and they were on their way.

After an uneventful ride to Jordan's house, Chase pulled into the driveway behind his SUV. David had left room for him to drive her car into the garage. Looking up to find the remote in the obvious place on the visor, he then eased the vehicle inside. By the time he exited, David and Jordan were waiting for him.

"Thanks, man," Chase said, turning to David. "Sure made things a lot easier." He shook his hand. "You still flying out in the morning?"

"Yeah. We're good to go for tomorrow. I'll see you around." David walked over to a black sedan parked by the sidewalk of her house.

"I guess I can see how you spend a lot of time coordinating all of this," Jordan observed.

"This wasn't anything complicated. Dignitary motorcades, speaking events in front of a coliseum full of people, children of VIPs—those can cause gray hair," he said, the corners of his lips turning up.

"Did you really just lump children in the same category as protecting someone speaking with thousands of people in an audience?" she asked with a grin.

"No, I said children of VIPs," he deadpanned. "Some of them would make the crowd screening of an entire coliseum look like the easier gig."

She shook her head. "I'll bet you have some stories from those times."

"I do. Fortunately for them, my lips are sealed. Client confidentiality." He smiled. "Something I know you can relate to. And, if I were to bet, I'd say you probably have some stories yourself."

"True," she agreed. "But like you, my lips are sealed," she said with a wink. Then she looked back toward the house.

It was a single-story craftsman-style home. Not one

of the common residential styles found in the area, but it blended in with the theme of the community.

She extended her hands out in front of her. "Well, this is home." Then her cheeks reddened at the pronouncement.

He knew what she'd meant, but she apparently didn't like the way the words had sounded when they'd come out. He had to fight to suppress a smile. She was certainly cute when flustered.

"Well, home to me…" she stammered. "I mean, please make it yours while you're here."

"Great. Thanks. Let me just grab my bags," he said, stifling the urge to chuckle.

Based on today's interactions, helping her out of the awkward conversations she got them into might become a habit for him. On one hand, she was adorable during these foot-in-mouth episodes. But on the other hand, there was some part of him that wanted to alleviate her discomfort. She appeared to be putting forth one hell of an effort to cope with the difficult and scary situation she'd been served. It'd feel good to take something else off her plate.

He'd already quoted her a rate that was less than half of his regular fee for services. He'd wanted to tell her that there'd be no charge as a favor to Mike, but he knew that wouldn't have been wise. Waiving his fee would make the detail personal—the kind of personal he didn't do.

§

As Chase gathered a few suitcases out of his truck, Jordan tried to move past her embarrassment over the latest awkward comments that had flown out of her mouth. She was on a roll today. *It must be this whole scenario.* It easily qualified as being one of the most uncomfortable situations she'd ever been in.

The worst part was, she wasn't used to feeling this unsure of herself. Her entire life she'd been more of a leader than a follower, her sights fixed firmly on the goal she was after. Dealing with this level of uncertainty was an unfamiliar undertaking. So far, all she'd learned was that she wasn't very good at it.

With a suitcase in one hand and a worn leather messenger bag in the other, Chase locked the SUV and headed toward her. "Once I get you settled, do you think you have enough room in the garage for mine also? I'd feel much better having it stored there and being able to come and go without being outside."

"Sure. There should be plenty of room. Yard equipment is in a shed out back, so there isn't much in the garage." Trying to let go a little, Jordan decided the most obvious thing to do next was to invite him in. "Why don't we head in so you can put those down?" She eyed the bags he held.

"Lead the way." His casual tone revealed a level of relaxation she didn't share.

She quickly opened the door. As they stepped in, she wondered what it would be like to be in his shoes, how it felt to continually move from one unfamiliar dwelling to another. Despite the long hours she put in at work, she always welcomed the comfort that engulfed her as she crossed the threshold into her home. She couldn't imagine letting go of that comfort to pursue a life of constant ambiguity and change.

"Wow. This is great." He dropped his bags while his eyes swept over the space.

She'd decorated the main living area in warm bronze tones and filled it with distressed wood furnishings. Connected to the living room was a spacious eat-in kitchen with a rustic pine table centered in the middle.

Many of the surfaces, including the fireplace mantel, were littered with pictures of her family or her, Karen and Mike. She was always the odd man out in the pictures with her friends. She wondered if he noticed.

"It's different from a lot of the architecture around

this area," he commented.

"Different in a good way?" She tilted her head to the side.

He ran a hand over the stonework surrounding the fireplace, his fingers dipping into crevices. "Absolutely."

"I know that a fireplace in central Florida seems superfluous, but I had the builder put it in the floor plans. I have always loved sitting around a glowing fire when it's cold outside. The few nights I actually get to use it are worth it to me."

He stared at her for a moment. "Sometimes, it's those times that don't happen often that we think about the most."

"Very true," she agreed, inwardly impressed with his insight. When it was clear he wasn't going to say more, she continued. "Do you want me to show you to the guest bedroom? I'm not sure where you're used to staying."

"That would be great. I'm not used to anything particular. I've learned to adjust to each situation as it comes along."

"Okay then, right this way," she said, guiding him into an inviting silver-and-sage-colored bedroom. "The desk in the corner has an outlet right below it for chargers or a computer." There was also a queen-sized bed, chest of drawers, and weathered wood nightstand that supported a lamp and small collection of well-worn books. "You can put your things in the chest of drawers if you want to. It's empty. Is there anything else you need?"

"No, it looks like everything is here." He nodded as he did a quick survey around the room. "We should probably discuss plans for dinner soon though. Do you usually dine out or eat in?"

Hmm. She hadn't thought about making dinner arrangements. He'd said he'd be responsible for his own meals, but it wasn't like he could leave to go get something.

"I usually fix something at home, but I haven't had a

chance to go by the store because of everything that's happened. How about we order in?" she suggested. Although she loved to cook, she was exhausted. "Do you like Thai? There's a place right around the corner that serves pretty authentic dishes. It's usually very good," she said, trying to stifle a yawn.

All of a sudden, she was struggling to keep her eyes open. For the first time in two days, she could put her defenses down. Without the constant outpour of adrenaline into her system, she was beat.

"Are you sure you're up for waiting? I'm good with anything and I can tell you're tired." His voice was soft and his eyes sympathetic.

"Sorry. The past couple of days have worn me down a little. But it'll do me good to sit down and eat tonight."

"If you're sure, then Thai it is. I haven't had good Thai food in a while," he said, reaching into his back pocket for his wallet.

With the movement, his shirt stretched tighter and the pronounced arches of his pectoral muscles rose up beneath the material. Her mouth went dry. He was the hulking, bodybuilder, powerhouse type she'd pictured— he merely hid it well. Like he was Superman masquerading as Clark Kent. She couldn't seem to tear her eyes away. The broad expanse of his upper body rippled with each progression, and her respiration increased with every swell. Had she really been worried about him being too muscular? She must've been out of her mind.

Commanding her eyes to move away from the spectacle, she looked up only to find he'd been watching her peruse his body. *Oh, no.* Heat crawled from her abdomen up to her face. But mercifully, he didn't say anything, choosing to hand her a twenty instead.

"That's not necessary. I'm using my debit card anyway." She waved the money off while purposefully keeping her gaze averted from his superb form.

Chase continued to hold the bill out to her. "Yes, it is.

I eat no matter where I am, so I'll cover the expense. It's part of the Chase package," he said lightly.

She almost groaned. The "Chase package" and what it entailed were the last things she needed to spend more time thinking about. Trying not to take his refusal personally, she gave him a small smile. "Okay," she relented, taking the money.

He was here on business, after all. It was probably best she remembered that.

Jordan called and placed the order, while Chase unpacked his suitcase and moved his car. Then she settled into one of the reclining chairs in her living room and began lazily leafing through her most recent clinical journal. As she turned the pages, her mind wandered back to her bodyguard. Her stomach dropped at the thought that he'd be temporarily living with her. For the life of her, she couldn't figure out why he elicited this sort of reaction. Not to mention the blunders she'd made when she'd been around him. She couldn't deny that he was extremely attractive, but she'd met many attractive men who hadn't made her foot take up residence in her mouth.

And she hardly knew anything about him—the actual man behind the calm demeanor and methodical behavior. She stifled another yawn. Maybe she was simply sleep-deprived. A good night's rest would give her much better perspective.

The doorbell sounded and she moved to get up, but before she'd made it out of her chair, Chase was standing behind the door. Rather than opening it, he turned to her.

"Stay put until I say it's okay," he instructed.

Her breathing stopped for an instant until she realized his actions were probably standard procedures for a bodyguard. She perched on the edge of her seat and observed him cautiously. Her heart hammered even though the rational side of her knew it was likely only their dinner.

"Who is it?" he called out.

"Thai Spice. Delivery," the respondent answered in a heavy Asian accent.

Chase glanced through the peephole and then slowly opened the door to the man standing on the other side. He took the bag of food, setting it down on the entry table. His eyes never left the deliverer. "I appreciate it. Have a nice night," he said, handing the guy another twenty-dollar bill. He would have a generous tip. Chase closed the door, but then he waited by a nearby window until he saw the delivery man drive away. "Coast is clear," he announced. "The food smells delicious."

It was only as he looked for a place to relocate the food that Jordan noticed the small handgun in his right hand. She gasped.

Chase searched out the source of her distress. He followed the direction of her gaze to his weapon and shoved the gun back into his side holster. "I didn't mean to startle you," he said, still holding their dinner.

"I'm fine. It's just that I hadn't thought about you needing your weapon here. I mean, I know it only makes sense, but…it surprised me. That's all." She stood up. "And really, a warning that I won't be answering my own front door would have been helpful," she snapped.

He watched her face closely. "I know it feels unnatural to have me answer the door in your home, but under the circumstances, it's best that you don't. You're right. I should have given you instructions prior to his arrival. I have to keep reminding myself this type of security is entirely new to you." He pinned her with stormy green eyes. "But I can guarantee this won't be the only time that you're caught by surprise. In our initial meeting, I told you that you might not understand all of what I do, but it's critical that you follow my instructions just the same. This is an example of what I was getting at. In fact, you did well tonight. If the guy at the door was our man, you wouldn't have been anywhere near his line of fire."

Jordan turned away from his stare as she considered

what he'd said. She knew he was right. He was trying to protect her, and she was giving him a hard time. Her shoulders slumped and she let out a sigh. How could she explain that she wasn't upset with him, that it was the idea of having to place her life in his hands? She'd taken care of herself for so long that she now found it difficult to let someone else take over that responsibility. On top of that, she had to admit that when it came to fighting bad guys, she was out of her realm. For a woman who was accustomed to consistently providing help to others, she now felt utterly useless to help herself.

"I'm sorry. I do realize you're doing what you need to do. It's going to take some time for me to adjust. That's all. I can tell you I won't stand in your way though, no matter how strange it feels. I know this is your area of expertise," she conceded.

"No worries. We'll get it down," he said, his voice reassuring.

She gave him a quick nod. He was more certain than she was that she could adjust to this type of routine. Not wanting to debate it any longer, she changed the subject. "The food does smell delicious, and I'm starving. Why don't we get started? You can set the food on the kitchen table. I'll get the plates and silverware."

Over the tantalizing aromas of fresh lime, spices, and lemongrass, she told him more about her work.

"So how often are you out of the office?" he asked conversationally while he squeezed another lime over his Pad Thai.

She watched his long fingers make quick work of extracting the juice. "Quite a bit, though it sometimes comes and goes in waves. Between going to jails, prisons, or hospitals to perform evaluations and testifying in court, I can sometimes be gone more than I'm there."

"What types of evaluations do you go to the jails

for?"

"Competency and sanity—" she paused, not knowing if he was familiar with the latter, "—sanity at the time of the offense are probably the most common. Sentencing or sexual offender evaluations are some of the others." She tried a bite of the red curry.

He leaned forward like he was about to say something, but stopped himself.

She titled her head. "What is it?"

"I'm curious about your perspective. To be honest, I find it kind of aggravating when a criminal commits some horrible crime and then claims that he didn't know what he was doing. How do you deal with that?"

"You aren't the only one," she replied, shaking her head. "The public perception of the insanity defense is mostly negative. Some speculate it's because of the media. But the truth of the matter is, the defense is rarely used in real life— less than one percent of the time—and out of the times it's used, it's successful less than one percent of those."

The corners of his mouth turned down. "I didn't realize that."

She gave him a wry grin. "Most people don't. It's a common misconception."

"But how do you know the right answer? These are criminals, after all. How do you know which ones are telling the truth?"

"There's a lot of science behind the methods we use. We have tests with normative data that provide useful results. I'm not saying it doesn't happen. But it's something we often catch when it does. I've diagnosed defendants with malingering when they were using the system to avoid jail or for some other gain."

"You can tell when they're doing that?" He looked at her with interest.

She nodded. "I was evaluating a defendant once who had all kinds of mythical creatures in the room with us. Unicorns, dragons, even a miniature mermaid. It was something." The corners of her mouth turned up as she shared the memory. "He was trying very hard to appear impaired, but his symptoms weren't consistent with any real mental illness. It made for an interesting morning though."

Chase chuckled, and Jordan felt herself laughing lightly with him. It was so easy to share things with him. She couldn't help but think that he probably made a wonderful date. He could teach the men she'd been set up with on rare occasions a thing or two.

"So what about you?" she asked between forkfuls of broccoli and bell pepper. "Mike said you were with the state police before. I'm sure you've been to the jail a time or two."

"I'll say. When I first started, I couldn't seem to stay away from the place." He shook his head. "I remember a buddy telling me I needed to learn how to drive home with blinders after my shift ended—this was after a week of barely sleeping between arrests and court appearances." His tenor became somber. "But I could never do it. I'd see a driver ping-ponging back and forth between the road lines, and all I could think about was preventing anyone from getting hurt. Getting home was the last thing on my mind then."

"That's a hefty responsibility." Jordan rested her chin on her fist. "I can't imagine being able to ignore it either."

"Yeah, well, I've had to tell enough parents they've lost a child…husbands they've lost their wives or the other way around. If there was anything I could do to save someone that unwanted visit from one of us, I did it."

She felt her heart constrict at his confession. "That must've been hard. Having to be the one to tell the family members."

Chase didn't say anything. He nodded, then took a long swallow of his water. "Sorry I got into that. It's not exactly dinner talk."

"I don't mind," she responded softly.

"Well, I'm glad those days are behind me. That's one part of the job I don't miss." His tone indicated he was done discussing it.

She didn't pursue it any further. It was apparent the death and loss he'd encountered had weighed on him. But she'd also seen a determination to protect others in what he'd shared. She wasn't surprised he'd ended up a bodyguard, given his inclination to want to shield others from danger. The setting might've changed, but he was still doing the same thing he was those late nights on patrol.

CHAPTER FIVE

After finishing dinner, they retired to the living room. Jordan settled into a recliner, and Chase took a seat across from her on the couch. He debated going straight to his guest bedroom, but he decided to sit with her for a few minutes instead.

The sleeping setup wasn't what he was used to. He purposefully didn't tell her this when she'd asked earlier. Most of his employers had specific quarters designed for security personnel. When he traveled, he generally requested a hotel room adjoined to his clients. He couldn't remember a time when he'd stayed in such close quarters.

Letting out a breath, he reminded himself that this was part of the reason he'd taken the assignment. He'd wanted a change from the ordinary. And the physical proximity wasn't the only difference. Most of his clients could afford an army if they needed one, but Jordan was facing this difficulty while living alone. And though she was putting up a strong front, it was clearly wearing on her.

"I usually watch the news or read a little then turn in for the night. If there's something you'd like to watch, you're welcome to change the station." Her voice was groggy with sleep.

"No, the news is fine." He settled into the soft cushions on the back of the couch.

"Chase." Her voice was almost a whisper.

"Yes?" He strained to hear what she was saying over the anchorwomen droning on about another heat wave approaching.

"I'm really sorry about my reaction earlier. That's not like me. It's all just a lot to take in."

Chase wrestled with how to respond. Earlier, he'd started to apologize when his gun had startled her, but then he'd caught himself. He would have his weapon wherever they were. As much as he wanted to shield her from all of this, that wouldn't be smart. She needed to be aware of what was going on, not kept in the dark. Although the darkness would prevent her from seeing the demons around her, it would make her blind to the danger.

He tried the middle ground. "It is," he said with a nod of understanding. "And I'll try not to blindside you next time. That was my bad."

"Good idea," she mumbled sleepily. "At least it was just dinner…" Her voice drifted off.

Despite the shaky start, he'd enjoyed their dinner together, far more than he usually did while on assignment. Her ingenuity and wit impressed him. He'd found himself intrigued as he'd listened to her describe her work. He hadn't meant to get into his days with the patrol and certainly not the death notifications. That wasn't like him at all. There was something about the compassion she'd shown when she'd identified with his obligation to act. She got it. And the connection made him want to tell her more. He needed to watch that.

"Yes, just part of the routine," he assented.

When she didn't reply, he glanced over at her and discovered her sound asleep. She'd drawn her legs up around her and turned her head so it rested on the back of the chair. Although he could tell from her heavy respiration and peaceful expression that she was sleeping contently, the position she was in looked terribly uncomfortable. Not to mention, she was still dressed in her suit. Pushing himself up from the couch, he decided she'd thank him tomorrow if he woke her up now. Sleeping like that would lead to cramped muscles and maybe a pinched nerve.

"Jordan," he said softly, not wanting to startle her.

No danger in that; she didn't even stir.

"Jordan, wake up," he said a bit louder. He was rewarded with an unintelligible sound as she settled deeper into the chair. He jiggled her shoulder. Once again, he got no response. *Oh well. At least she's able to find sleep tonight.*

He picked the remote control up and clicked the television off. As he went to turn the light off, he gazed back at his stunning new client. Her long soot-colored lashes were splayed across the top of her cheeks, and her chest rose and fell steadily. But he could still see the dark circles beneath her eyes. There was no way he could, in good conscience, let her spend the night in that chair.

"Oh, to hell with it," he mumbled under his breath. Then he walked back over to her and scooped her up into his arms.

She murmured something he couldn't decipher and settled in against his chest. The movement caught him off guard, and he inhaled deeply to steady his heart, which was now beating at an erratic pace. Instead of the calming effect he'd intended, the breath only intensified his feelings of restlessness as he took in her soft, feminine scent. She smelled like something sweet. And vanilla? Whatever it was, it didn't help matters. Heat spread through his body. He hastily deduced the faster he got her into her bedroom, the better, so he made a beeline in that direction.

Although he hadn't been in her room, he'd seen it at the end of the hall when she'd walked him to his. He pushed the door open with his foot and carried her through the entry. A small table lamp illuminated the room. Unlike the décor in the remainder of the house, which had a simplistic rustic beauty, her bedroom was more luxurious and elegant. His feet sank into plush carpets covering the hardwood floors as he moved forward. He wondered at the differences in style. She was certainly an enigma. From her tailored suit and professional demeanor, he might have pictured her entire house this way, but it was only this room.

Looking down at the beguiling woman he held in his arms, he almost regretted that he had to put her down. The feeling lasted only a few seconds before rational thought smothered it away. She was a client—that was all. He'd never again become personally involved with someone he was hired to protect. The two didn't mix.

He leaned forward, pulling the covers back from the tall, velvet headboard. After easing her on to the mattress, he positioned a pillow beneath her head. Her hair fanned out around her face, framing it in a dark silky cloud. Tearing his eyes from the exquisite sight, he cupped the bottom of each calve and removed her dress shoes. While he was slipping off the second heel, it dawned on him that he was putting her to bed in her conservative linen pantsuit.

The suit will have to stay. This is where I draw the line. Taking a last look around, he saw a large sitting window in the corner of the room. He made sure the lock was securely in place then treaded lightly toward the door. When he realized what he was doing, he switched back to his normal gait. Probably nothing could wake that woman short of an explosion.

§

Jordan awoke to sunlight streaming through her window. She couldn't remember the last time she'd slept so soundly. Taking in the beautiful morning, she moved to stretch her arms out over her head. About halfway up, something hindered her movement and she looked over to identify the culprit. Seeing the sleeve of her suit jacket, she sat up straight, now entirely awake. She was dressed. *But how?*

She didn't remember going to bed. The last thing she could recall was watching the news with Chase… Then understanding crept up on her as she grasped what had happened. Chase must have carried her into the bedroom last night. She found herself a little self-conscious at the thought of such an intimate interaction, particularly one for which she had no recollection. *He was only being considerate,* she reminded herself. Still, she couldn't help but be moved by the gesture. She was certain it wasn't part of the "Chase package."

Wondering if he was up yet, she hurriedly took a shower and threw on a gray-blue silk dress. The vision she saw of herself in the mirror looked significantly less tired than the one she'd seen yesterday. Her skin was more vibrant, and the purplish hue beneath her eyes had faded. What a difference an uninterrupted eight hours made.

On her way toward the kitchen, she could hear the water running in the guest bathroom and gathered that Chase was taking a shower. There was no need to rush now. She poured herself a cup of coffee and then hunted around the fridge for a suitable breakfast. Her foraging resulted in little that was still edible. A container of sun-dried tomato cream cheese and a package of bagels appeared most promising. She needed to get to the grocery store soon.

While toasting the bagels, she heard the water shut off. She pictured him getting out of the shower. Wet hair combed back, muscles glistening with beads of water… A streak of desire shot through her, leaving a warm sensation in its path.

Chase's deep voice intruded into the way-too-appealing image. "Good morning."

Even his voice is freaking sexy.

He walked into the kitchen, dressed casually in a

green-striped button-down shirt and khakis. Still wet, his hair looked strikingly close to how she'd imagined it.

Jordan's cheeks grew warm as she echoed his greeting. "Morning."

He raised a quizzical eyebrow. Her blush was probably giving her away. She was glad his investigation talents didn't include mindreading.

"You sleep like the living dead," he said, taking the cup of coffee she held out to him. He took a big gulp then lifted the cup and nodded his appreciation.

Jordan laughed despite her embarrassment. "I should have warned you. I'm a pretty deep sleeper. But I generally make it into bed myself."

Chase snorted. "Deep sleeper, huh? I'd say that's putting it mildly. I don't think a live Bon Jovi concert at a venue next door would wake you up."

"Oh, I don't know about that. Jon is pretty cute. Hearing his voice next door may be worth leaving wherever I am in dreamland." She handed Chase a plate with a toasted bagel. "There's cream cheese if you want some." She gestured to the container on the counter.

"Careful now. I know all the words to 'Livin' On A Prayer,' and I'm not above using them." He spread cream cheese on the bagel and paused before he bit into it. "You might not want to fall asleep on me again," he threatened.

Jordan felt her stomach tingle at his teasing warning. She didn't tell him that his threat held little weight for her. Even if he couldn't carry a single note, the deep tenor of his voice alone would probably make anything he uttered sound sexy as hell.

Their lighthearted repartee continued throughout breakfast and during the drive to the office. As they neared her building, Jordan, more relaxed, asked him some of the questions that had been swirling in her mind.

"So, what will you do all day? I mean, while I see clients."

"I'll find an inconspicuous spot to observe you from

and watch for any threats."

She furrowed her brow. "Is that how it is on most of your other jobs?" she asked, not comprehending why he'd choose to pursue such a career.

"It depends on the job. But like I said yesterday, there's a lot of waiting around."

Bewildered, she tried again to understand his position. "May I ask what the attraction is, then?"

The corner of his mouthed turned up slightly. "I know. When you think about the amount of time spent observing, researching, rehearsing, and waiting, it's easy to see how people wonder why on earth anyone would choose to make this a career. But there's a lot that's good about it too. I enjoy traveling to different countries and meeting new people from different cultures. There's a level of excitement that goes with never knowing where you'll be sleeping from day to day. I could be guarding a dignitary in Afghanistan one day and escorting a well-known actor at the Oscars the next. Those parts of the job are pretty enticing, at least initially."

"When you look at it that way, I can see the draw." She nodded. "Not to mention you seem to have an aptitude for it."

"How do you mean?" His gaze left the road and darted over to hers.

"Well, we haven't worked together long, but you seem to be in your element. You know…aptitude, as in you appear to be a natural at what you do."

A flash of sorrow crossed his features. What was it about her statement that would have elicited that type of reaction? It was so unexpected that she almost thought she'd mistaken it, but when he replied, he seemed preoccupied.

"I like to know I'm using my skills and training to do something good," he said, checking the rearview mirror before pulling into her office parking lot.

Though she was sure that he meant it, his reply

sounded detached. Jordan didn't press him any further. Still, she questioned why what she'd meant to be a compliment had troubled him instead.

At six thirty she decided to call it a day. She'd been relieved to find that Chase's presence didn't disturb anyone's work. He'd decided to stake out a place in the main office, at a spare desk that offered a view of her doorway. True to his word, he was able to blend in so that no one really noticed him.

Well, that wasn't entirely true. She'd seen some of the female clients eyeing him through the glass window where Nancy was usually stationed, but she didn't think that had anything to do with his job. He looked striking today in the shirt that matched the color of his eyes. She was surprised at the stab of jealousy that had moved through her when she'd overhead one of the women grilling Nancy about him. Fortunately, Nancy had been quick on her feet and had smoothly explained that he was a temp hired to help out in the office.

She dictated the report she'd been working on and gathered her things together. Thankfully, it was Friday and she could use the weekend to get back on track. She'd been scheduled to instruct a court-mandated anger management class on Saturday, but Karen had volunteered to take her place and she was grateful for the reprieve.

She tried to recall everything she planned to get done. Going grocery shopping topped her list along with catching up on things around the house. Not to mention she'd missed her regular workout sessions this week. Sessions she sorely needed for her own mental health right now. Chase would be accompanying her on all of these errands. For some reason, the thought of his company during these mundane tasks made them seem slightly more appealing.

Heading toward the main corridor, she overheard Chase and Mike bantering back and forth. She couldn't hear what they were saying, but Chase's laughter echoed down the hall. Mike was animatedly adding to the conversation when she got closer.

"And when that canoe started heading down the river with our clothes, I thought I was going to die."

"Yeah. Well, from what I remember," Chase shared, "it was ten times worse when we had to race naked down the river trying to catch the damn thing with the entire cheerleading squad rooting for us to reach it."

"I still blame you for that, you know," Mike said. "The whole thing was your idea. Somehow, you always pulled me into your outrageous escapades."

"Hey, that wasn't my fault. How was I supposed to know it was their annual canoe trip? The place is usually deserted during the week," Chase said innocently.

Not wanting to eavesdrop any longer, Jordan made her presence known. "I must be missing something good," she said, entering the room.

Chase looked over at her and instantly sobered. His reaction wounded her a little. Though he'd initially been reserved, after last night and this morning, she'd thought some of the professional distance between them was starting to dissipate.

"Oh, Chase and I were recalling the good old days," Mike said. She knew he'd noticed Chase's reaction and was trying to spare her feelings.

Jordan tried not to let her hurt show. She reminded herself that he and Mike had been friends for years, and she and Chase had only met yesterday. The close proximity they shared and their unusual relationship—employer and employee, bodyguard and target, close friend of her best friend—only confused things. *And on top of that, why does it matter?* After all, this was only a temporary situation, and he was solely her employee.

"Sounds like you two must have had some fun," she said lightly.

"Yes, those were good times," Chase said, his tone

conversational.

If she hadn't heard him talking to Mike two minutes ago, she never would have noticed the difference in his voice. But she had. Sticking to her resolve to keep from making her interactions with Chase more than they were, she tried to sound nonchalant when she replied. "Well, if you're ready, I was hoping to stop by the grocery store on the way home. I don't think I can survive on what's left in my fridge." She grabbed her briefcase.

"Ready when you are," Chase replied, getting up to leave.

Mike looked at them intently. "I'll see you two later."

"See you in the morning," Jordan said with a wave.

"Later, brother." Chase gave him a pat on the back then followed Jordan out.

Jordan began taking the grocery items out of the brown paper bags stacked on her kitchen counter. Chase came in behind her, carrying the last of the bags. He caught her by surprise when he started helping her unpack them.

"You don't have to do that," she said.

"It's no problem. I'm quite at home in the kitchen." He pulled a plastic sack of tomatoes out of one of the brown bags.

In truth, he did look quite at home in her kitchen, just as he had in the grocery store. She'd expected he'd want to get out of there as soon as possible, but he'd walked with her as though they had all the time in the world, watching as she'd inspected vegetables and scanned the shelves for her favorite items. There was no doubt he was good at what he did. Although he'd been attentive the entire trip, he hadn't at all been overbearing.

They finished unloading the groceries, and Chase volunteered to help her fix dinner. They diced vegetables side by side and fell into an easy conversation. Nothing very personal, but she enjoyed it nonetheless. They spoke of their favorite hangouts and places to go. Chase's experiences far outweighed hers, having been on numerous protection assignments in the area. Her mouth watered as she listened to him describe the maple crème brulee he'd tried at Disney's California Grill. The restaurant was one of her favorites too, but she hadn't tried that particular dessert yet.

"Stop! I can't take it anymore!" she said, holding a hand up and feigning anguish. "I think I'll starve before we get dinner done." She adjusted the temperature beneath the pot.

"Oh. You'll survive," he said playfully.

"And what is that supposed to mean?" she asked, sounding indignant while trying to keep a straight face.

"Only that you had lunch about six hours ago. I think you may live," he said, his eyes twinkling. "But what are we making anyway?" he asked, watching her combine finely chopped mushrooms, onions, and tomatoes with cream cheese, spinach, and cooked pasta into a pot.

"Tortellini primavera and grilled chicken. Though, it's clear from what you've told me, this is not the type of gourmet fare you're used to being served while on assignment." She grinned at him as she stirred the ingredients together. "Do you think you'll be able to get by?"

"Well, it smells awesome. But if you insist I provide you with a verdict now, I'll have to give it a good ol' American try," he said, reaching a spoon into the mixture.

"You can't. It's still not done!" she said much too slowly.

Chase was licking his spoon by the time she got the words out. "Delicious," he said after swallowing the last bit.

"It probably isn't even heated yet," she admonished, though she couldn't help the smile that spread across her face.

"Then it'll only get better," he said in mock

seriousness. "Actually, I think I need to try it one more time."

He started to grab another spoon, and she lightly pushed his hand away. "Oh, no you don't. If you're going to offer a verdict, I'm going to make sure it's not raw."

He propped himself up against the kitchen counter and folded his arms in front of him. With the shift, he was now only a couple of inches away from where she stood. "Wait a second, you can't change the rules in the middle of judging."

Her heart picked up as she tried unsuccessfully to ignore the effects of his nearness. "That was the judging for the 'before' round. You'll have to wait for the 'after' round to judge again." She pointed her mixing spoon at him. "Which begins after everything is actually cooked."

A chuckle escaped as she took in his expression, which now closely resembled a child who'd dropped his ice cream cone. She liked this side of him. His humor and roguish grin made him even more appealing though. Add that to the fact that he seemed to have lowered the guard he'd erected earlier, and he was much less like a paid protection agent and more like a friend she was hanging out with. Albeit an incredibly sexy friend who had a penchant for undercooked pasta and an uncanny ability to raise her blood pressure with his mere presence.

"So many rules to remember." The end of his mouth quirked slightly as he reached past her to put the spoon in the sink. His forearm brushed lightly across her stomach. The touch launched tingles that raced through her body. Her eyes jerked up to witness his reaction. She tried to decipher if he'd felt anything similar. But he'd begun scrubbing a dried patch of tomato seeds from the countertop, so absorbed in the task that he didn't seem to notice the contact. She let out a long, silent breath. His touch had made tingles run down her spine, but he was totally unaffected by hers.

Just my luck. I had no interest in anyone until this moment, and I find someone who has no interest in me.

"I feel much better now," Jordan declared, sitting back in her chair. She'd polished off the last bite of pasta from her plate. She looked over to find Chase working on his second helping. "Looks like I wasn't the only one who was hungry," she commented.

"I don't know if it's hunger or the fact that it tastes so good. I couldn't stop at one serving. My compliments to the chef."

"And the sous chef," she added with a meaningful look his way.

She was glad the uncomfortable moment at the sink had passed. Dinner had initially been quiet, and she could sense that Chase had withdrawn again. She prayed it wasn't because he'd noticed her response to their brief contact. She didn't see how, since he'd been absorbed in cleaning the counter, but what else could it have been?

She looked at him intently, trying unsuccessfully to read into his thoughts. He had an unfair advantage. While she had trouble finding the motivation to mask her emotions in situations like this, he had no comparable difficulty disguising his. Her train of thought was distracted by a pair of green eyes looking back at her. Too late, she realized she'd been caught once again unabashedly staring at him.

"Sorry," she said. "I was lost in thought."

"Care to share them?"

Absolutely not. Instead, she replied, "It was nothing important. I think I'm just getting sleepy."

"No Friday night plans?"

"Not tonight. Truthfully, I don't stay up very late. Even on weekends. I guess I'm more of a morning person. I usually go jogging first thing on Saturdays."

"Sounds good to me. I have some bookkeeping to do tonight, and that'll keep me plenty busy. Another one of the not-so-fun parts of the business."

"Yeah, that one I can relate to," Jordan said as she began to clear away their dishes.

Chase tried to help, but she insisted she had it covered. He took a seat in the living room and removed his laptop from its case. The subtle glow from the screen illuminated his features: the hard line of his jaw as he studied a spreadsheet, his shirt unbuttoned just enough to expose a smattering of dark hair at the top of his well-defined chest.

Realizing what she was doing, she stopped herself. *It's a working relationship, not a date.* Although the statement made sense on a logical level, she knew enough about underlying thought processes to know that emotions weren't always rational.

She finished loading the dishwasher and turned toward him. "I'm turning in. I'll see you in the morning."

He looked up from the screen. "Night. Oh, and Jordan?"

"Hmm?"

"I should be awake, but if I'm not, make sure to get me before you go running in the morning."

She raised an eyebrow. "Do you think I'd take off without you? Kind of defeats the whole purpose of you being here, right?" She wouldn't pretend for a second that she liked relinquishing so much of her independence, but she wasn't naïve to the fact that someone wanted her killed and the job wasn't complete.

He wiped a hand across his mouth. "Okay, so I take it that was a completely unnecessary request. But you'd be surprised by how many times I've been ditched at inopportune times. Good to know you aren't going to add any to the list."

"No worries there," she said matter-of-factly. "I'm much too reasonable to throw away my protection detail on a whim." She paused, thinking more about his revelation. "No, I'm definitely not the girl in the horror film who makes you bite your fingernails off because she insists on going down the dark staircase to check it out herself. That drives me nuts. So rest easy on that one."

Chase appeared bemused by her confession. "Sometimes, I forget what you do until you make comments like that. Takes the old aphorism 'know thyself' to a whole new level."

"Yeah, well, wait till you hang out with all four of us psychologists at the same time. Conversations are interesting to say the least."

She left it at that. Increased self-awareness was kind of a rite of passage in her field. Probably at least partially related to the host of personality tests they took before they were taught to administer them. Whatever the cause, she didn't think it was a bad thing. Most of the time, anyway.

She was half asleep by the time she got to her bed. *If nothing else, at least I can sleep in peace with him here.* But as she laid her head down on her pillow, her thoughts drifted back to him. She let herself wonder for a moment what would have happened if his arm across her stomach tonight had led to more intimate contact. If instead of going on like nothing had happened, he'd snaked his arm around her waist and pulled her close to him. Her pulse quickened as she imagined being encircled in his hold, pressed up against the solid planes of his chest… The sound of her kitchen cabinet shutting echoed into her room. She let out a groan and pulled the pillow over her head. *I'm pathetic,* she thought wryly. *I've reduced myself to having stolen thoughts about my bodyguard. I definitely need to get out more when all of this is over.*

CHAPTER SIX

Chase was up early. After lying awake for hours, he'd finally decided he might as well get out of bed and try to do something useful. He'd powered up his laptop, but thoughts of Jordan kept intruding on his efforts to finish the work on his books. He'd felt like a jerk yesterday when she'd walked in on his conversation with Mike at the office. He could tell he'd inadvertently hurt her.

He ran a hand through his already-disheveled morning hair. It wouldn't surprise him if his hair began to grow in rows commensurate with his finger widths, he found himself raking through it so much lately. It wasn't that he didn't enjoy talking to her—it was more that he tried to reveal as little about himself as possible while on the job. Disclosing too much led to becoming personally involved, something he was determined not to do.

What was worse, Chase knew Mike hadn't missed the interplay between them. He was sure he'd hear about it next week. Mike had stipulated that Jordan was hands-off when he'd contacted him. He wanted her safe from her assailant but with her heart left intact.

Chase had laughed at his friend's nerve and immediately assured him he didn't get involved with the clients he protected. And nothing would alter that. He'd meant it then, and his feelings on the matter hadn't changed. He wouldn't jeopardize her safety.

He could hear Jordan moving around in the living room, so he shut his laptop down and headed out there. He'd gotten dressed in his workout clothes when he'd woken up so he'd be ready to go when she was.

When he walked in, Jordan was pulling on her running shoes. He took in a sharp breath as he laid eyes on her. He'd grown accustomed to seeing her in conservative clothing that only hinted of her svelte form beneath the layers. Her choice of garments usually left his quite-willing imagination to fill in the curves of her figure. But as she stood in front of him now, wearing spandex shorts and a tank top, he realized his imagination hadn't done her justice.

Holy hell. She had a body straight out of a fitness magazine. Her arms were cut with well-defined triceps and biceps, and her long legs were shapely and toned. Yet, despite her powerful physique, she possessed an hourglass figure that was utterly feminine. The swell of her chest and gentle outward curves of her hips were all woman. A perfect blend of softness and hardness.

"Lord have mercy," he mumbled to himself. If he didn't know Jordan better, he'd have thought she was testing his resolve to keep their relationship strictly professional. But from what he did know, he was convinced she had no idea how she was affecting him. Nevertheless, that was what he was—affected. And not at all pleased by the fact.

"Morning," she said, oblivious to the reaction her attire had elicited. "I can't tell you how happy I am to get outside. It's been too long for me. Are you ready?" she asked, her sentences rushed together in her excitement. Her dark hair was fastened into a secure ponytail that bobbed around as she stretched from one leg to the other.

"Ready when you are," he said with a scowl.

He'd thought it had been bad last night when he'd lost himself in the process of scrubbing a counter so he could gather his composure. Composure he'd lost over the briefest of contact with her. The touch had been totally unintentional, but his body hadn't cared. And a new day hadn't changed much in that regard.

"Not a morning person, huh?" she replied, noticing his glower. "Are you sure you're up for this?"

"I'm fine," he said more neutrally as he headed for the door. He was trying not to be unreasonable. It wasn't Jordan's fault her mere presence threatened his long-term resolve.

They jogged side by side through the streets surrounding her house. It was a beautiful fall day, and the view through her neighborhood was gorgeous. The sun was reflecting off the lake, and the air was still crisp. In Central Florida, it was almost impossible to jog during the day because the temperatures were stifling. That left mornings or nights for running, and despite the misimpression he'd given Jordan, he most definitely preferred getting out early.

"Have you always been a runner?" she asked, breaking the companionable silence.

"I've enjoyed running since high school. I started training in martial arts, and the sensei was big on physical conditioning. I never really minded though."

"What type of martial arts?"

He could tell from the expectant expression she gave him that she was genuinely interested. "Shorin-Ryu. It's an Okinawan martial arts form. One of the older styles of karate."

"Did you stick with it?" Looking both ways, she led him onto a different street. She was keeping a nice pace despite the steady conversation.

He fell back into step next to her. "I still practice when I can. It's kind of hard to explain, but I draw from it a lot in what I do now. The practices and philosophies have become a foundation." He didn't mention the tournament trophies or the black belt hanging in his closet. Those were the less important things he'd gained from his training.

She pursed her lips, and it was evident she was thinking about what he'd said. "I can see that." She nodded in agreement.

He watched her facial muscles relax as she comprehended what he'd been trying to say and his strides lightened in response. It was incredible how well she could extract the underlying meaning in the things he shared with her. For a few seconds, he felt like he was running on air. Until the dawning crept upon him that he was divulging parts of himself again. Damn. It was like she was a neodymium magnet with a pull so powerful he didn't even detect the divide. He ignored the gratifying stirring her acuity had generated and steered the conversation back to less personal ground.

If she noticed the shift, she didn't let on, and before long, she was telling him about a prank she and Karen had played on Mike while they were working on their doctorates.

"So, you know how he is about football?" She shot him a glance, checking for confirmation as they headed up a small hill.

He tried to focus, pulling his gaze away from the small dimple in her left cheek that accompanied her mischievous grin. "Yeah, saying he's a fan is a bit of an understatement," he said dryly.

Jordan's brow rose. "A bit?"

"Okay. In your world, it might even be diagnosable," he conceded.

"Hmmm, you're probably right." She looked up like she was considering his suggestion.

He lightly elbowed her in the ribs. "So get on with it. I want to hear this." She'd piqued his curiosity when she began laughing before the first words of the story even left her mouth.

"Well, when they lost the big game against Florida, he was devastated. Moped around the entire night, like it was the last game they'd ever play. Karen and I had early clients at the counseling center the next morning. While we were there, Karen came up with the idea to fill out a fake client intake form for him. We listed the presenting problem as grief related to FSU's loss the night before. We even got the secretary to go in on it with us, and she completed the form so it'd look authentic down to her handwriting."

"Did he buy it?" Chase wasn't sure if he was smiling about the prank or because she looked so cute completely lost in the funny memory.

"I didn't think he would. I mean, that would be pretty ironic. But sure enough, he drifted in later, still looking like he'd lost his best friend, and pulled the intake form out of his box. When he read the client description, he got this look of panic." She stopped for a minute to catch her breath, not from the running but from her laughter. "Turned on his heel and was about to run to the secretary to say he couldn't see the client. He was sure there would be too much countertransference."

"He said that?"

She nodded. "Oh, yeah. In his own words, 'There'll be so much countertransference, I won't be able to tell if it's his issue or mine.'"

"What stopped him?"

She pressed her lips together but her eyes were still lit with amusement. "My face. Later, he said I reminded him of the cat who'd eaten the canary."

Chase snickered. "I can see that."

"Yeah. I'm sure I did. A joke like that is something I never would've done on my own. Karen and Mike are good for me in that way."

They circled back toward her house. The jog had done wonders for his mood. Looking over at Jordan, he felt sheepish about his behavior earlier. He wasn't a moody guy. Maybe he needed something more than a change. Maybe he needed a vacation from work. Days lounging around outside and nights spent without his laptop within his reach. He couldn't remember the last time he'd done that.

Jordan flipped through the mail she'd retrieved from her mailbox. A few wisps of hair had escaped from her ponytail, and small beads of sweat dotted her hairline. If possible, she looked even hotter than when he'd first laid eyes on her this morning.

"I completely forgot to check it yesterday," she said without looking up as she tore open an envelope.

Her eyes widened when she unfolded the bottom half of the paper. A car whizzed by them, but she didn't seem to notice. The contents of the envelope had her full attention. She inhaled a sharp breath. Whatever it said couldn't be good. Her focus continued to move back and forth across the page. With each return, her face blanched until the color had completely drained from her complexion.

He was immediately by her side. She shifted her weight against him, and his eyes dropped to the letter she clutched in her hand. The message was printed on plain white paper.

> *Did you get your run in this morning? You know you need to. I can see it on your face when you leave. You move with such purpose. Setting a steady pace until you've completed your route. It's how you do everything. Like you're ticking items one by one off a never-ending list. You make it so easy for me to study you. I've often wondered if you don't enjoy it? Knowing I'm out there. Feeling my eyes on you. Speculating as to what I'll do next. Maybe I've made this better for you than I'd intended. In truth, I've grown so used to watching you that my life will be dull when I finally get the justice you owe me. After all, you'll be gone. But the end will be worth it. You don't deserve to be here. And don't worry, I'm going to make sure you get everything you deserve.*

There was no signature or anything else that would indicate the identity of the author.

Chase surveyed their surroundings while positioning his hand on the small of her back. The road was empty now. He caught a hint of movement from a neighbor across the street. She was putting gas into a lawn mower, her back toward them. No danger there. Oftentimes, these jerks got off on seeing the victim's reaction to their threat, but he didn't see anything out of the ordinary. Keeping his weapon holstered, he urged her toward the door.

Once inside, careful not to touch any more of the surface, he had her put the letter and envelope on the entrance table. "It'll be all right," he said, helping her to the couch. Her body was quivering so fiercely, he could feel his hand bouncing alongside the concave arch of her spine.

"I know." She wrapped her arms around her midsection. Her eyes were moist. "I feel like such a coward. It's just…I'd thought maybe…"

Chase saw the emotions play across her face. He knew she'd thought the danger might've passed. It was wishful thinking on her part, but he hadn't tried to dispel the notion. There was no reason to. Despite her denial, she was following his instructions completely. He didn't need to constantly remind her that her life was in jeopardy. She needed to maintain some semblance of normalcy in her life. Unfortunately, that would be even harder to do now. Her protective shield had been shattered, and it incensed him. He wished he could get his hands on the bastard who was responsible. There'd be no more need for threats. No, only one encounter.

"Jordan, look at me," he said, taking her hand. "You're not being a coward. Truth be known, you're handling this situation better than a lot of the people I've dealt with. But it's okay to be scared. It doesn't make you a weak person if you admit that."

Jordan shot him a look of gratitude. "Thanks. I guess I'm not used to admitting that something is beyond my control. I'm usually pretty independent."

"I never would have guessed." He gave her a sympathetic grin, then squeezed her hand before letting it drop into her lap.

The corners of her mouth lifted shakily.

"Why don't you stay put while I go call Detective Larson. He'll want to collect the letter so they can try to lift fingerprints and DNA from it."

She nodded, leaning back into the couch and closing her eyes.

Chase came back carrying a cup of hot tea. "Here. I thought this might help," he said, handing her the cup. "Larson said he's on his way over."

"Thanks," she said, taking the steaming cup from his hands.

She brought the warm liquid to her lips and inhaled the peppermint fragrance. Her hands had finally stopped shaking, and the color was back in her face. It didn't make him want to catch the bastard any less. Maybe he should have made himself a cup too.

By the time the detective arrived, Jordan had composed herself enough to speak frankly about the letter.

"You got it today? Regular mail?" he asked as he placed the letter and accompanying envelope into an evidence bag.

"Yes, I'm sure it came today. And there's a postmark, so I don't think someone just stuck it in there."

"Yeah, I saw that too. That'll give us the postal receiving facility it was processed at. Not much to go on. I'll send it to the lab and have it checked for fingerprints and DNA. Unfortunately, we haven't uncovered anything new related to your case. Maybe this will offer us a better lead."

"So, what happens next?" she asked.

"Well, we'll continue to investigate. I'll be honest with you. At this point, we don't have any strong leads." His gaze moved to Chase before continuing on. "You were an LEO, so you know the drill."

Chase nodded, encouraging him to go on.

"We acquired a court order to search Henry Rigdon's cell phone records, but the calls he received to coordinate the attack and payoff were all made from throwaway cells. You can purchase those almost anywhere. Wal-Mart, groceries stores, even gas stations, and they aren't traceable. I'll continue to investigate people you've had contact with. Maybe we'll be able to lift some prints or genetic material from the letter. I'll let you know. If you think of anything else, no matter how remote it may seem, don't hesitate to call."

"Sure. I'll call you if I think of anything," Jordan said distractedly.

"You still okay?" Chase asked her as he closed the door behind the detective.

"Yeah. I have no doubts the department is doing the best they can." She massaged circles into her temples as she spoke. "I've reviewed thousands of pages of criminal investigative reports for evaluations, and I know things don't always come together as easily as they do in the half-hour crime shows we all watch. I'm just racking my brain trying to make sure there's nothing I've missed that would help."

"You're right on all accounts. If there is something, it'll come to you. One of the problems, no offense—" he looked at her ruefully, "—is that in your case, there are quite a few potential suspects. Maybe not as bad as a needle in a haystack, but enough that it's going to take some time."

"Do you think this letter was written by the same person?" she asked.

"I don't know. Your guess is as good as mine. The modus operandi is vastly different. I mean, typically, these guys don't go down in their level of threat—from hiring a hitman to writing a threatening letter. Seems the reverse would be more logical if it was the same guy. But who knows. You've been inside the heads of them too. Not everything is logical."

"That much is true. Damn it, it's frustrating to feel like I'm sitting back and waiting for him to make the next move." She brought her hands down on her knees with the last word. "If it weren't in the heat of the day, I'd probably go for another run. But since it is, I'm going to go clean the bathtub. Maybe I can scrub out some aggravations."

Watching her go, he decided now wasn't the best time to tell her that Saturday morning runs were a thing of the past until they caught this creep. Anger had apparently chased away some of the fear that had initially struck her. He hadn't heard her curse since he'd been around her. Though he didn't fault her. Seeing her struggle with this and being unable to stop it were causing a few expletives to run through his head as well. He heard a bucket hit the floor. Yeah, best bet was probably to wait and let the bathtub take the brunt of her frustrations first.

Fortunately, the remainder of the weekend was uneventful. He tackled the rest of his books, while Jordan spent the majority of the time catching up on work, bills, and stuff around her house.

On Monday morning, she was dressed and ready to go earlier than usual. The purple shadows beneath her eyes were absent, and a plate of steaming eggs and bacon greeted him as he joined her in the kitchen. The distraction method obviously worked for her.

He was more on guard. Whoever was out there had sent them a message to make sure they both knew he was watching. What he didn't know was what the perpetrator planned on doing next.

.

CHAPTER SEVEN

She and Chase entered through the back door of the practice. Catching a whiff of freshly brewed coffee, she made a beeline for the conference room. Chase took his place at the vacant desk, and Nancy began ribbing him about taking up too much of her workspace. Jordan sputtered over her first sip of joe as she listened to Chase kid back with her. In his own defense, he was relaying the countless merits of his company. *Oh, geez. Someone to keep a watchful eye over her candy dish?* She snorted as she carried her steaming mug back into the main office. He'd made a mistake when he'd volunteered that one. Nancy hadn't spotted that all of her mini-chocolate bars had disappeared into said company. Knowing that the woman relied on chocolate as her afternoon pick-me-up, Jordan waited for the fallout.

Nancy squinted her eyes when she saw the half-empty dish. Chase tried to distract her with more dubious advantages, but the damage was done.

Jordan took a few more swallows from her mug, not wanting to interrupt their jousting. It was quite entertaining. Her usually decorous secretary was now threatening to oust Chase from the office. He responded to her threat by hanging on to the desk while he promised to replenish her dwindled supply.

But although he participated in the amusement, he remained alert to his environment. When the door opened and a client walked in, he was all business, surreptitiously observing the new arrival. Nancy, on the contrary, wore a broad smile as she opened the glass window and passed the sign-in sheet through.

When the client sat down, Jordan had Nancy print out a copy of her schedule for the week. Scanning the names printed in the hour blocks, she was surprised to see her collateral interview with Bradley Lancaster's son scheduled for today. She'd reviewed the statement he'd provided to the court, but today, she'd be able to gather more information directly from him.

As she walked down the corridor to her office, she couldn't help but feel a little guilty. She'd intended to present the case and her working conceptualization at their last staff meeting, but addressing the detective's news had taken precedence. Given the high stakes of the case, she planned to bounce her theory off her colleagues and hear their thoughts on it. She resolved to make time for the consultation before the day's end.

The day wore on, and she was relieved to find she was able to focus on her work despite the anxiety that nibbled at her stomach. After an individual therapy session, she moved on to complete an assessment battery on a twelve-year-old for a custody evaluation. Though the case was going to court, the parents were on amicable terms with one another, and the approach was evident in how much more relaxed their child was during the testing process. She wished most of her custody work fell under this umbrella instead of the contentious canopy that sheltered more than its fair share.

The custody evaluation consumed the rest of her morning and by the time twelve o'clock rolled around, she was looking forward to eating with her colleagues. Every Monday, they made an effort to get together for a working lunch. Sometimes, things would come up that made it impossible. But, according to her schedule, everyone was available for consult today.

She popped her head into Karen's office to find out where they were going. Mike was already in there. He was laughing at Karen as she struggled to pry his hand off her car keys.

She shook her head. Between Nancy and Chase this morning and Karen and Mike, now she was beginning to think half her day would be spent playing referee to her boisterous crew. She had to admit though, the comic relief eased some of the tension that had gripped her unendingly since Saturday.

"What's going on here?" she asked Mike, her tone light. "Are you causing trouble for my best friend?"

"I thought we were both your best friends." With an exaggerated frown, he gave her his finest attempt at a pout. His hand didn't loosen from the keys though.

Oh, boy. She'd walked right into that one. "Of course you are." She rolled her eyes skyward. He really was a terrible actor. "But since you appear to be the guilty party, I'm temporarily disowning you."

A grunt escaped him. "Oh, you're the model therapist. I do something you don't like and I'm no longer your best friend. What ever happened to unconditional positive regard?" Mike waggled his eyebrows at her.

Jordan couldn't stifle the smile that had been trying to form on her lips. "All right. You win. You know I have a soft spot for Carl Rogers," she said. "But you still haven't told me what you two are up to."

"Mike said he won't let me drive anymore after what happened this morning," Karen said.

She was almost afraid to ask. "What happened?"

Karen's driving performances were historically frightening events. Karen drove on the Orlando

Expressways like she was in the Indianapolis 500 and had a tendency to take "shortcuts" that were actually opportunities to get lost in unfamiliar neighborhoods. She gathered that siding with Karen on this one wasn't the smartest thing to do. They were all riding to lunch together, and she'd prefer that anyone other than Karen drove. She was still having flashbacks from the time Derek had let them borrow his Corvette.

"You need some help holding on to those keys?" The familiar voice came from the door.

Jordan spun around on her heel. She hadn't even heard Chase walk up, but he'd obviously been standing there long enough to take in most of the conversation.

"I think I have it under control," Mike replied. "But thanks for the offer." He'd succeeded in getting the keys into his pocket, and Karen graciously refrained from pursuing them.

"Actually, it'd probably be best if I drove anyway. Sorry, Karen. I hope you're not too disappointed," Chase said. He looked her way. One side of his mouth was kicked up with just a hint of a grin.

Jordan regarded him as if he'd grown wings and donned a halo. She couldn't help herself. He might not have made the suggestion to spare them from Karen's driving, but he'd inadvertently rescued them by making the proposal.

"So, where are we going for lunch?" Derek asked, entering Karen's office.

"How about Books, Butter, and Bagels?" Mike suggested.

"Never been there," Chase said. "But I'm up for something new, if that's the consensus."

Karen filled him in, already having forgotten her quest for the keys. "It's an antique bookstore with a café in the center. The food is usually pretty good, and they have the best bubble tea around."

"Sounds good to me. Let's go." Chase led the way out

of the office.

Jordan followed him out. Although it was a spacious room, the presence of the three sturdy men had suddenly made it quite cramped. Chase's broad shoulders almost spanned the entire width of the door. It was a mystery to her how someone with such a significant presence managed to blend in so unobtrusively wherever they went.

Chase held the door for her as they entered the bookstore slash restaurant. The building itself wasn't very large, but the interior was quaint. The walls were made up of cedar shelves lined with aged books on all subjects. In the center of the room were worn wooden tables for the patrons who came hungry. From the business attire the customers wore, it was apparent they weren't the only ones who'd escaped the fast-paced office environment in exchange for a relaxed lunch in the cozy café.

Jordan trailed their hostess as she zig-zagged through the maze of tables. The place was packed. When the hostess stopped short, she felt herself being crushed back against Chase. The sharp smell of cedar from the bookshelves mixed with the familiar scent of sandalwood. Her pulse quickened as she felt his warm breath on her neck, and then they were inching forward again. She exhaled slowly and distracted herself with the titles on the shelf next to her.

"How is this?" their hostess asked, pointing to one of the few unoccupied tables now in front of them.

Jordan peered over her shoulder at Chase for direction. They'd be at a table adjacent to the wall. The table appeared less exposed than the ones centered in the room, but it was his call.

"This is great." He nodded to the woman.

They all got situated with Chase choosing to sit with his back to the bookcases behind him. Jordan was seated next to him, feeling a weird combination of relief and disappointment that she could no longer feel him pressed up behind her. The hostess passed around leather-bound menus that resembled antique books.

"This is a cool spot," Chase said, unfolding his menu in front of him.

"Yeah," Mike said. "Karen came across it one day by accident. We'd all assumed it was only a bookstore. Now, it's one of our usual places for lunch." He glanced around the room. "But I think the secret's gotten out."

"I'll say," Chase agreed.

After they'd placed their order, Jordan brought up the guardianship case. She relayed what she knew of the case so far, careful to avoid mentioning any identifying information and making sure she couldn't be overheard by the other restaurant patrons.

"So, do you think he's suffering from some type of dementia?" Derek asked.

Her brow furrowed as she considered his question. It was the same one she'd asked herself at different points in the evaluation process. "I'm not so sure. It's certainly a consideration." Problems in thinking and memory related to some type of brain dysfunction were common symptoms of focus in guardianship cases. "In the court documents, the son is reporting memory issues that are interfering with his dad's day-to-day activities. And the tests do reflect some level of cognitive impairment, but the deficits appear most centered around attention and concentration. His recent and remote memory weren't notably impaired. No problems recalling names or uses of objects."

"How about insight? Is he concerned about his current problems?" Mike asked.

She shook her head. "Not really. He did dismiss his cognitive problems, but he didn't present with the lack of concern or denial we can see in dementia cases. He relied more on rationalization—it's a big responsibility, a lot of money—that type of thing."

"Mood?" Mike asked.

She nodded, following his line of thinking. These types of observations were essential in determining a patient's current mental status. "I think his mood is an important component to consider. He seemed pretty apathetic about life in general, but expressed a lot of guilt and regret related to the past."

"He's depressed?" Karen asked.

She sat up straighter. "Yeah, that's more what I'm leaning toward. The timing doesn't necessarily match up with the death of his wife, but bereavement doesn't have to follow a predictable course."

"True," Derek agreed. "Losing someone like that…he's spent most of his life with…" His voice trailed off and he stared past them to the array of hardbound books on the shelves. Eyes glazed over, he appeared lost in thought for a moment. Then, shaking his head, he returned his attention to the group. "Anyway, I know from experience that kind of loss is hard to get past."

"I'm sorry." Jordan clasped her hand over his. "What happened?"

He hesitated but eventually continued in a low voice. "It was my brother. I lost him years ago." His shoulders slouched and his face was solemn. "He was murdered."

Her free hand went over her mouth. What a terrible way to lose someone you loved. "That's awful. I had no idea," she said, the words coming out in a rush. "I can't even imagine what you went through."

"Yeah, it was a tough time. We were very close. He was a lot older than I was, so I looked up to him. He was the person I wanted to be. I got to know a therapist during that time, and that's what led me to pursue this career. I already had a bachelor's degree in business. I took a few additional perquisite courses, aced the Graduate Requisite Exam, and was accepted into a doctoral program. She—the psychologist—was definitely an inspiration to me. I keep meaning to contact her and let her know how much of an influence she's been, but I haven't taken the opportunity yet. Someday soon, I will…" He looked around the table then shook his head. "I'm sorry. I didn't mean to monopolize your consult."

"Oh, Derek. You know we're here for you any time." She squeezed his hand and then let go.

"I know. I can't tell you how lucky I feel to be in practice with all of you." He shot the three of them a look of gratitude, and then his eyes landed on Chase. "And that you came along to keep our girl safe," he added, lightening the moment.

§

Chase lifted his glass and gave a nod.

Jordan and his friend had apparently created a group of practitioners who not only worked well together but also supported one another in the process. Being a business owner himself, he recognized that wasn't an easy feat to accomplish. It'd taken him a lot more trial and error to get it right. He'd hire someone, only to find out the employee enjoyed the partying more than the protection part of the work, or that the person could meet the physical demands but not the emotional ones.

People weren't all what they seemed. He was glad he didn't have Jordan's job of trying to figure them out. Keeping them safe was much less complicated.

At least, it used to be.

CHAPTER EIGHT

Every hour block on her schedule was filled after lunch, but she welcomed the pace. Anything to keep her mind focused on where it needed to be.

She removed the Lancaster file from the stack. Her eyes skimmed down the photocopied pages in preparation for her meeting with Keith. As she'd remembered at lunch, Keith acknowledged his father had been experiencing cognitive problems for over six months.

Her office phone rang. "Jordan, your three o'clock is here." Nancy's voice came over the line.

"Thanks, Nancy." Jordan got up to retrieve him from the waiting area.

A solidly built middle-aged man advanced toward her as soon as she entered the room. Dressed in a checked blazer and coordinating chinos, he looked like he'd walked in straight from a Thomas Pink catalogue shoot.

"Good afternoon," she greeted him with a handshake. "It's nice to meet you." Close up, she could see that he resembled a younger version of his father, though he carried himself with more reserve.

"My pleasure." He gave a curt nod, but the greeting didn't reach his pale blue eyes.

They made their way back to her office, and she caught a glimpse of Chase as she walked by. He gave the appearance he wasn't paying her any particular mind, but she could feel his eyes tracking her as they proceeded down the hall. She tried to ignore the warm tingles that instinctively spread down her spine in response. *It's his job to observe*, she reminded her deluded subconscious once again.

Once Keith was settled in her office, Jordan went over her role in the evaluation process and how the information he provided would be used. She then began to discuss his father.

"I've read the information you supplied to the court in your petition, but I wanted to hear more from you on what you have observed and the reason you filed a petition for guardianship on your father."

"Uh…I'm not sure where to start." He hesitated then continued. "At first, I didn't realize how bad things had gotten. I mean, it was a missed bill or meeting here or there. Then I started to notice he wasn't paying attention at all to the company quarterly reports. Someone would ask him a question, and he didn't even acknowledge it, or if he did, he didn't know the answer. He was never that way in the past, so I knew something was wrong."

"Was there anything specific that led to you file when you did?"

"No, not really. I think I just finally realized I needed to do something to help him. I've tried to take over as much of the business as I can, but he still holds the controlling shares. And he said he's not ready to turn those over to me." He edged to the end of his seat. "Yesterday, he forgot the password to his accounts, and the secretary had to call me to get it. I know it sounds trivial, but he's had that password for over thirty years, and he's never forgotten it once."

"Is there anything you're worried about happening as a result of what you're seeing?"

"Hell yeah." His response was forceful. "I'm worried he's going to end up in any number of bad situations. He stands to lose a hell of a lot of money if someone takes advantage of this. I'm not the only one who's noticed." He ran his fingers through his hair and sighed. "I can't believe something like this could happen. He was always the strong one and sharp as a tack. You should've seen him after Mom's death. I never would've thought."

"I can imagine it's hard," she replied, watching his demeanor.

He shook his head slowly, casting his eyes downward. "Yes, it is." After letting out a long breath, he lifted his head. "And I also feel guilty about being the one to initiate this whole process. I mean, I know I'm doing it for him, but I don't know if he'll ever understand that."

She nodded. "The process can be very stressful." She proceeded to try to gain more specific examples of the alleged impairments before moving toward the main area she needed to learn more about. "You noted that your father was remarkably strong following your mother's death. How did he grieve?"

"What do you mean?" Keith eyed her warily.

She treaded forward cautiously, not missing his guarded stare. "How did he cope with her death? Did he ever talk to you about his feelings? Did he seek support from friends? See a counselor?"

"Not really any of those things." His tone was deliberate and he appeared to be evaluating each statement he made. "He hurled himself into what needed to be done. At first, it was her funeral. When everything was settled, he immersed himself back into the business. His knee surgery and the complications forced him to take a break from the office, but he still stayed on top of things from home. I always came by and briefed him. I had to get his advice on how to handle things." He threw his hands up. "I mean, he's been at this longer than I've been alive."

She wrote out some brief notes on his interpretation

of the events. "Did you notice anything out of the ordinary during those visits?"

"Yes. That's when I noticed he was more forgetful, and he always said he was tired. He didn't seem very interested at times, just told me to make the decision myself. He was never like that before."

"You noted he wasn't on any pain medications then?"

"No, he took them right after the surgery, but not for long. He wasn't big on medications. He always soldiered through. Kind of a tough-guy approach."

She nodded then paused a beat before continuing. Bradley's emotional state following his wife's death was key to the case, but given Keith's earlier response, she wasn't sure how receptive he'd be to discussing it further. Deciding to be delicate but direct, she broached the subject again. "Did he ever seem sad when you visited?"

Keith sat up straight. "What are you asking? I mean, yeah, he was down about the surgery and getting sick afterward, but anyone would be. Especially someone like him, who's used to running nineteen to the dozen all the time."

"Did he talk about it? Feeling sad?" She raised an eyebrow.

"Of course not. It's not like he was depressed or anything like that." His voice rose, and he narrowed his eyes at her. "What does this have to do with anything, anyway? It sounds like a waste of time to me and—" he glanced down at the stainless steel Rolex wrapped around his wrist, "—I don't have time to blow on nonsense like this."

She softened her tone in an effort to deescalate his reaction. "Depression can sometimes result in cognitive symptoms, such as difficulties in concentration, memory problems, impaired judgment and problem-solving," she explained. "The positive aspect is, with treatment, these symptoms can be alleviated. The deficits are only temporary, as they're not caused by a neurological disorder." The conclusion remained unstated. If this were the case, there'd be no need for a long-term guardian.

"Dr. Clayton, I get where you're going now, but my father is a strong man and in our family we support one another. I would've known if he was depressed. In fact, I resent this entire line of questioning." Pointing a finger in her direction, he leaned forward in his chair, closing the distance between them. "I'd heard you were a busybody when you were assigned this case. My friend, Dave Buckman, told me you sided with his wife in their custody case. Did him in good. I tried to request someone else, but it seems you have an in with the judge here." He shook his head and mumbled under his breath, "Knew something like this would happen if you weren't removed."

She was a little taken aback at his quick change in attitude, but she remained calm. "Mr. Lancaster, I can't discuss any other cases I have or haven't worked on. However, I can assure you that I conduct a thorough and ethical evaluation. I'm sorry if I've offended you with the questions, but the information you've given me has been helpful in assessing your father's current condition. An accurate opinion on his current state and need for a guardian is all I'm providing here."

Keith stood up and glared down at her. "Well, I think you're barking up the wrong tree in this case. My father is as far from depressed as you can get. I'd think twice before I'd go putting that kind of thing in a report," he said. "Now, are we done here?"

"We are." Jordan got up to walk him out, but he was storming out of her office before she even got to the door. She followed behind and watched him exit without a word to anyone.

Chase was already heading toward her. "Hey, do you have a minute?"

"Sure. Come on in to my office." Her voice wavered slightly and her heart rate was still beating to eighth notes. She was baffled from the unexpected turn the interview had taken. He'd been reserved and then defensive as the interviewed had progressed, but the underlying anger and resentment had caught her unaware.

As soon as they were behind closed doors, Chase rested his hands on her shoulders. "Are you okay?" he asked, his eyes reflecting concern.

"Yes." His apprehension touched her. She squeezed her small hand over one of his large ones and gave him a wan smile. "Did I mention that sometimes this type of work can get pretty emotional?"

The gesture didn't assuage the worry evident from the deep creases on his face. "What happened? Did he threaten you in any way?" He didn't release her from his hold but stepped back while he scanned her from head to toe. His gaze settled back to her eyes.

She struggled with how to respond. "Not really. He did mention that I shouldn't put something in a report. And he was very angry. But he didn't threaten me directly."

He gently released her. "It sounds like enough of a confrontation to report to Detective Larson," he said. "Any potential leads need to be examined so we can track this guy down."

"But this only happened today—" She stopped herself, Keith's words echoing in her head.

He hadn't wanted her on the case. She concentrated in an effort to remember the date she'd been assigned the case. It'd been the week prior to the attack. The timeframe fit. Her chest tightened.

Chase squinted his eyes. "What is it? I can tell you thought of something."

"You're right," she acquiesced. "The petition is public record anyway. I'll give him a call when I get done today. Right now, I have to get to my next eval."

"Okay. I'd rather sooner than later though. You don't finish today until six, and he may be gone by then."

Jordan almost asked how he knew, but then she

remembered that Nancy always gave him a clean copy of her schedule without any client information on it. "Good point. Let me get going here, and I'll call him while this next client is completing some of the independent testing." A sinking feeling took root in the pit of her stomach. She didn't relish the idea of discussing any cases with the detective, even if the information was public record.

"Hey, don't look so glum," Chase said, opening the door for her. "This is only temporary." He rubbed her back as she walked by.

"I know. But this is one of those days where six p.m. can't come fast enough." She couldn't wait to curl up in a pair of PJs and relax tonight. Maybe even uncork one of her better bottles of wine. But until then, she still had one more evaluation and a call to the detective to complete.

"I guess I shouldn't mention that it's only Monday?"

She looked over her shoulder to see him raising his eyebrows at her, his expression innocent. She threw a smirk back at him, not fooled for a minute by his chaste appearance. "Don't even go there. Or my PJ night may involve a continuous stream of Lifetime Movie Specials."

The corners of his mouth turned down. "That sounds bad. I think I'll heed your warning."

"Smart man." She was now genuinely smiling despite her earlier disappointment. *Damn, he's good.*

True to her word, while her client completed the self-assessment portion of the evaluation, she left the testing room to call Detective Larson.

"Detective Larson," he answered.

"Hello, Detective. This is Jordan Clayton."

"Hello, Dr. Clayton. What's going on?" he asked.

"Nothing else has happened," she said, grateful that wasn't the purpose of today's call. She informed him she'd been assigned to a guardianship case recently. "Though it's not unusual to have emotions running high in these cases, I did have contact with the petitioner today. He seemed very angry at both my assignment to the case and the questions I asked him. Again, I'm not even sure it's relevant, and it certainly isn't unusual, but I wanted to let you know, just as a precaution."

"Sure. What's the name?"

She let out a breath. "Keith Lancaster is the petitioner. Alleged incapacitated is Bradley Lancaster."

A momentary pause followed by a chair squeaking into a new position ensued. "Do you mean Bradley Lancaster as in Lancaster Incorporated?" the detective asked.

Jordan massaged her temples with her fingers as she fought off the tension building in her forehead. High-profile cases were treated like any other at her office, but unlike other cases, name recognition would always be a factor in these. Of all the cases she had right now, this was the only one in which it was guaranteed that the identity would be immediately recognizable. And it was the case she'd had to make the call on. "That's the one. Do you know him?"

Detective Larson whistled. "Enough to know there's money involved in that one. Bradley Lancaster is a huge supporter of local law enforcement. Always has been. He's also well respected. A stand-up guy from what I've heard."

"Well, again, I'm hoping this call was unnecessary."

"Gotcha, but it's a good thing you gave me the information. Anything you've got can end up being helpful. Don't hesitate to call if you think of something else, as trivial as it might seem."

Jordan sighed contently, now curled up in a fleece blanket on the couch. The soft material of her favorite sweatpants just might have been more comfortable than the PJs she'd been dreaming of as the stress of her day had escalated. Chase had suggested they watch a movie and have dinner delivered. It ended up being a perfect idea. After polishing off a pizza with extra cheese, they were settling in to watch the movie they'd agreed on.

"Hey, you're not going to sleep on me, are you?" Chase said as he threw an accent pillow her way.

She caught it deftly and put it behind her head. "Of course not. The movie hasn't even started yet."

Chase was sprawled out in her recliner. He had his feet elevated and appeared most at home. For a fleeting moment, she wished the appearance was a reality. But even though she'd admitted to herself that she was somewhat attracted to him, he'd done nothing to indicate that he harbored any similar feelings. On occasion, she entertained thoughts of flirting a little to see if he might reciprocate. However, despite her feelings toward him, they still had to continue working together. She didn't want make it awkward between them, particularly when it seemed he wasn't interested in her in that way and was finally relaxing around her.

"I know the movie is just starting, but you do have a history to consider." His comment broke her away from her thoughts.

Jordan laughed when she grasped that he was referring to the time he'd had to carry her to bed. The fact that she was such a heavy sleeper had been the subject of a great deal of teasing since then. Before she could come up with a witty retort, the phone rang, interrupting the exchange. She jumped up to grab it, but she tangled herself deeper into her blanket and fell with a thud into a pile on the floor.

Chase was rolling with laughter.

"All right. You can stop laughing now."

Her comment didn't even phase him. She couldn't blame him though. She was having a hard time catching her breath between bouts of laughter and the tight confines of the cover.

"Chase, could you get that for me? I seem to be a little tied up," she pleaded with him.

"Maybe… What's it worth to you?" He waggled his

eyebrows at her.

"Chase!" She was now struggling to free herself from the wrapper she'd created.

He grabbed the phone. "Hello. Clayton residence." A brief pause ensued as Chase listened to the caller. He shifted his weight and looked over at Jordan with an unreadable expression.

His silence piqued her curiosity. She'd assumed it was Karen, as she always called around this time, but Chase's face showed no signs of recognition.

"One moment, sir." Chase covered the receiver and turned to Jordan, who was finally loose from the entanglement. "It's your father."

"Oh, no." She groaned. So much for it being Karen on the line. What on earth was she going to tell her parents? She sure as heck wasn't going to tell them the truth. They'd be worried sick. Not to mention they'd immediately want to fly over from Texas.

Realizing she couldn't put it off any longer, she took the phone from Chase.

He considerately walked out of the room. However, with the minimal insulation in her house, she knew he'd still be able to hear most of the conversation clearly from his bedroom.

"Hey, Dad. How's everything going?" A distinct echo when she talked signified he had her on the speakerphone.

"Same ol' stuff here." His deep Southern drawl was tinged with excitement. "Sounds like your life's more interesting though. Who's the young fella who answered the phone?" To her father, anyone under forty was a "young fella."

"Oh, Dad, he's just a friend." Even as she said the words, she knew she didn't sound one bit convincing. Though her parents were proud of her accomplishments, lately they'd been more vocal in their desire for her to begin a family of her own. She recognized that hearing Chase answer the phone probably gave them false hopes she'd have to remedy.

Her mother chose that moment to chime in. "Darling, he sounded quite handsome. We've been hoping you'd meet someone soon. You know, Rose has four grandchildren now! Can you believe it? She's always showing me their pictures, and I get so excited imagining being in her shoes."

"Four! Mom, I'm not so sure about having four children," Jordan said.

"Well, of course not, my dear. You know Rose has two children and you're our only…but even one would be such a blessing," she said wistfully.

"Mom, I'm not even married yet. It may be a while. Besides," she said, realizing this was not where she wanted to go with the conversation. "Like I said, Chase is merely a friend."

"Of course, honey." Her mother was not to be dissuaded. "How long have you two been friends?"

"Not too long. I met him through Mike. They were friends in college." As soon as she said it, she knew it was a mistake. Her mother adored Mike and Karen, and there was no doubt that the idea of Chase as a potential husband had become even more appealing.

"Really? That's wonderful," her mother said, warming to the topic. "And what does he do?"

Jordan hadn't anticipated the question. *Oh Lord, how do I answer this one?* "Well, he actually owns his own company."

"Must be nice," her father said, joining back in. He began telling her of an old friend of their family who'd recently opened up a business.

Letting out a breath, she figured she was safe for the moment. They spoke for a few more minutes about happenings in their small Dallas suburb until her mother halted the conversation.

"Well, we don't want to keep you too long, seeing as you have company. Do we, Ted?"

"Yeah, right. Maybe we'll be meeting the young fella sometime soon," her father managed to get in before her mother hung the phone up.

Jordan stared at the receiver for a second. Despite her intentions, her parents thought she and Chase were dating. Hopefully she could rectify the misconception later on. But by then, she thought ruefully, the news would probably be all over the Lone Star State.

Chase walked in behind her. "You still up for the movie?" he asked, his brows knitted together. From the look on his face, he'd heard at least part of the phone conversation.

"Yes. That was my parents…but I guess you already figured that out." She felt like she should explain, but she didn't want to make a huge deal of the comments. "Anyway, they can be a riot sometimes. My mother gets an idea in her head and runs with it. She's…tenacious."

"Well, that explains a lot," Chase said.

"What do you mean?" Jordan stared at him, an eyebrow arched while waiting for a reply.

"I was wondering where you get it from." The lines around his face became more pronounced and the end of his mouth quirked slightly.

"You'd better watch what you say," she said, reaching for the pillow he'd thrown at her earlier. "Being tenacious means I won't give up easily." She grasped the pillow like she was considering when to throw it back at him, but she was inwardly relieved to change the subject.

"Okay, I surrender." He held his hands up in jest, making his sculpted biceps project out from the sleeves of the casual T-shirt we wore. His green eyes twinkled mischievously, and her breath caught at the sight of him. "And for the record," his tone softened, "your tenacity is kind of admirable."

She examined his face for any indication that he was still playing with her but found none. He looked completely sincere. "Thanks, I think," she said, her voice husky.

He gave her a wink that released butterflies in her stomach, and then his gaze swung back to the television. "You ready?"

"Sure." She directed her attention on the screen in front of her and was eventually successful in focusing her thoughts away from the drama that had become her life and back to the fictitious one playing on her television. It was a nice reprieve, and she was almost sorry when it was over. As the credits rolled over the screen, she looked over at Chase. A lock of his wavy hair fell into his face as he leaned forward to read something off the screen of his phone.

"I think I'm going to turn in." She stood up, this time careful to separate herself from the blanket first.

"Night, Jordan." He pulled his laptop out.

Though she was tired from the stress of the day, she took her time before heading off to bed, straightening the kitchen up and setting the timer on the coffee maker. There was a part of her that couldn't help but wish Chase would give her an indication that he wanted her to stay.

The glare from the screen in the room reflected on his face. His brow was furrowed, and he had a spreadsheet pulled up. Seeing him already immersed in work, she abandoned the foolish notion and strode toward her bedroom.

In less than half an hour, she was showered and tucked into her bed. She looked up at the ceiling and listened to the whirring of the ceiling fan. The white noise helped lull her to sleep, but it wasn't working tonight. She flipped over to her other side and readjusted the comforter that lay across her. Taking a deep breath, she tried to concentrate on the rise and fall of her abdomen with no luck.

So much for the relaxation exercise. Her head was cluttered with thoughts she couldn't seem to escape.

Whenever she closed her eyes, images of Bradley and Keith Lancaster faced her, along with the horrible image of the man who'd attacked her.

And then there was Chase. A man who made her laugh when she was on edge, feel strong when she felt anything but, and feel safe just by his mere presence. There was honestly nothing simple about his presence though. Or about him period. Complicated—that was what he was. What the whole situation was. Or was it only complicated for her?

A flickering of florescent-green light caught her attention. Those block numbers glowing on the digital clock indicated that another hour had passed. If she didn't fall asleep soon, she'd be exhausted in the morning. She started to roll over again, but a faint noise caught her attention. It sounded like someone was scraping something. She listened closely. The noise was coming from outside. She looked toward the window, and that was when she saw him. Silhouetted against the night sky was the figure of a man gripping something in his raised right hand.

Fear rendered her immobile. She commanded herself to run, but her limbs were glued to her sheets. She had to do something fast! Something to stop him from getting to her. Forcing herself to sit up, she screamed until her throat burned. The attacker was momentarily stationary, and then he sprinted away from the window. She peered into the black velvet of the night, trying to make out where he'd gone.

Focused on the window, she almost didn't hear it when someone began to jiggle the doorknob to her bedroom door. Was it possible that he'd made his way into her house? In a state of terror, she let out another scream as her bedroom door turned into splinters.

CHAPTER NINE

Chase's heart pounded as he stormed into the room. He kept his center of gravity low and his gun trained in front of him. The unfamiliar throbbing in his chest was a nuisance. His experience had taken him long past the adrenaline rushes he'd encountered as a rookie. Or, at least, he'd thought it had. Keeping his breathing modulated, he methodically searched the room for any immediate threats. Seeing none, he moved next to Jordan.

"What happened?" There was no emotion in his voice, and he knew the question sounded more like a command. He positioned his back to the wall behind her while he continued to scan the room.

She pointed toward the window, and before she could utter a sentence, he was travelling along the perimeter of the room. He ended up standing slightly to the left, beside the curtains. Making sure there was no light behind him, he advanced to the window but saw nothing from his restricted view.

"I saw someone out there, trying to get in. He had something in his hand."

He took a few seconds to consider his options. Instinctively, he wanted to go after the bastard, but if he did that, he'd be leaving Jordan alone. If there was more than one perpetrator, that would leave her vulnerable. He decided it wasn't worth the risk and instead headed for the telephone on Jordan's nightstand. With his attention back in her direction, he noticed she hadn't moved at all since he'd come in the room. She was sitting completely motionless and still staring toward the window.

After setting his gun on the table, he called in the incident and then eased himself next to her onto the edge of the bed. "You all right?"

She nodded then turned her head toward him. "Can you please just tell me that this will be over soon?" Her question sounded more like a plea for help. Her voice was filled with anguish, and though he could barely make out her features in the darkness of the room, he could see her lips were quivering.

"You have no idea how much I wish I could." His own voice was hoarse with emotion.

Against his better judgment, he took her in his arms and held her so her head rested against his chest. Her heart beat wildly next to his chest through the thin fabric of her nightshirt. He promised himself the gesture was only because she had no one else there for support, but even as he rationalized his behavior, he knew it wasn't true. He wanted to be there for her, and although it shouldn't have, holding her at that moment felt completely right.

He could feel her muscles loosen as she relaxed into him, finally loosening her grip on the sheets beside her. Her heart rate began to settle into a more regular pattern. But as the fear seemed to drain from her body, the intimacy of their contact became strikingly evident. The scent from her shampoo surrounded him, while the heat from her skin melded with his own. He'd known, no matter how he tried to rationalize it away, that he was drawn to her before, but with her skin alongside his now, the attraction between them was undeniable.

Her warm exhalations against his bare chest reminded

him he hadn't even had time to grab a shirt. All he'd thought about was getting to her, and now she was right here in his arms. He sucked in a ragged breath as her fingers traced their way around his waist and splayed across his back. If he didn't do something fast, he knew he'd give in to the urge to explore every square inch of her in return.

"The PD is on the way. Hopefully, they'll be able to find some trace of the guy. They usually leave behind something," he said thickly.

He waited for her to respond by moving away, but she didn't. He looked down and his gaze met hers. Their lips were only inches apart, and without thinking, he gave up the fight within him and bent down to kiss her. He brushed his lips lightly across hers several times at first, reveling in the feel of the caress. But it wasn't nearly enough. He cradled her head in his hands and kissed her again, this time leaving his lips pressed to hers. Using the tip of his tongue to gently coax her lips apart, he delved further into the warm softness— getting lost in the way she tasted, the tender strokes of her tongue against his. His hands slid down her back and slipped underneath her nightshirt. In the recesses of his mind somewhere, he knew he had to stop, that it shouldn't—couldn't—be this way. But his exploration of her satin skin continued, as if he was acting on reflex. He gently cupped her breast in his hand and kneaded the small, hard nipple.

Jordan let out a low moan in response to his touch and arched toward him. Her reaction triggered something inside him, and the realization of what he was doing slammed into his conscience. He was crossing a line that could lead to deadly consequences.

He dragged himself back from her, with every centimeter feeling like he was trying to escape a raging rip current. Nothing about pulling away from her felt natural, but he had no choice. "Jordan, I'm sorry."

She didn't say anything. He leaned forward and

snapped on the lamp. A soft glow illuminated the room, and he could see confusion reflected in her eyes. He loathed what he'd done to put it there.

"I hadn't intended for this." He motioned between them.

She briefly closed her eyes, but she still didn't respond.

He let out a slow breath. "I can promise you that it won't happen again. I'm sorry." He grabbed his gun and left the room before she could reply. He didn't want to hear it.

Minutes later, the police were at the house. Jordan emerged from the bedroom and gave them an account of what she'd seen. She barely looked his way. Her reaction wasn't unexpected, but the torn feeling in his gut was foreign to him. He told himself that it was better this way. She would be safe.

"I'm going to head around back where the window is," one of the officers informed Jordan.

"I know which one it is. I'll go out there with you." Chase accompanied the officer to the area outside the window.

The officer shone his flashlight along the edges of the window and the ground in front of it. The grass was dry, and there was no sign of any footprints or anything else that could provide any clues as to the identity of the shadow at the window.

"Nothing to see here," the officer commented.

Chase nodded. "Yeah, figured as much. Worth a try though."

They walked back to the front in silence. Every muscle in his body was strung with tension. He wasn't sure if he was more irritated because he wasn't able to chase down the jerk who'd had the nerve to show up at her window or at himself for being the jerk who'd let go with her when he shouldn't have. Either way, he felt like crap.

The officer shook his head at the other one,

indicating the search hadn't turned up anything.

The second officer turned toward them. "Well, thanks for calling. We'll be sure to let Detective Larson know. Glad you guys are okay."

"Thanks for coming out," Jordan said, her voice tired. Without a backward glance, she went straight back to her room when they entered the house.

Chase focused on the rush-hour traffic as he drove Jordan to the office the following morning. The tension in the car was so thick that, if it were fog, he wouldn't be able to see one foot in front of him.

Jordan shuffled through paperwork on her lap. She was making an attempt to appear lost in her work, and she probably would've pulled it off with most people, but not with him. He could see that, despite her concerted effort, she was accomplishing nothing other than to re-sort the pages once again. She'd been this way since they'd met in the kitchen that morning. After the requisite "good mornings" and brief small talk, she'd grown silent, focusing on menial tasks around the house until it was time to go. Not that he blamed her after last night. It was his fault for putting her in this position in the first place. He knew better. And though he couldn't take back what had happened, he would sure as hell make certain there was no repeat.

Wondering how long her silence would last, he glanced over at her. "What time do you have to be in court today?" He already knew she had to be there later that morning, but he was hoping to get her talking to him again.

"Ten o'clock," she replied without making eye contact. She leaned forward to put the papers back into her briefcase.

He inwardly grimaced at the indifference in her tone. There had to be a way a forward from here, but he damn sure had no idea what it was.

§

Jordan looked out the window as they approached the office. She needed to maintain some semblance of a working relationship with Chase, but she was still frustrated and confused after last night's events. She was unable to stop her stomach from fluttering as she remembered him holding her, his bare chest pressed against her. Though calming at first, his nearness had brought forth feelings that were anything but calm.

She knew he'd been attracted to her in that moment as well. But what she didn't understand was his abrupt end to it all. When he'd stood to go, he'd seemed repulsed by the whole incident. And then today…Chase might be able to continue on as if nothing had happened, but she wasn't ready or able to do that yet. She needed some time to process her own feelings before she could tend to their relationship, professional or otherwise.

"Here we are." His words were subdued.

She couldn't tell if he expected a response or not. Either way, she wasn't giving him one. He put the SUV in park, and safety issue or not, she had to restrain herself from jumping out of the car. Instead, she grabbed the handle on her briefcase and smoothed her skirt down while waiting for him to check the area and then open her door.

They walked into the office in silence. As soon as she had the day's files in hand, she broke away from him and fled to her office. She sat down and grabbed the case she'd be testifying on later that morning. Reviewing her notes would be a welcome distraction from her thoughts.

As she attempted to skim the first page, she could hear Chase talking in the background. His presence was usually comforting to her, but at the moment, her attention was reduced to that of a student during the final class hour before college let out for spring break. Every time he spoke, it served to remind her of the details she was trying to block out. She leaped up from her chair and shut the office door.

Back at her desk, the quiet reprieve lasted a mere five minutes before the door to her office flew open and Mike popped his head in. "Hey. What's with you? You're all holed up in here like a recluse. You okay?"

"Yes, I'm good." She gave him a wan smile. "Just prepping for court."

"Chase called me last night and told me what happened." He walked in farther and gave her shoulder a gentle squeeze.

Jordan stiffened with his revelation. She stared back at him, her mouth too dry to speak.

"I can tell you're not good. I don't know who would be in your shoes. Waking up to find someone trying to break into your bedroom had to be scary."

Jordan let out the breath she'd been holding and swiveled her chair around to face him. Inexplicably, talking about the man at her window seemed less threatening than revealing what had happened—or almost happened—with Chase. "It was. Seeing him at my house, it brought back those same feelings I had the night of the attack. The only difference is, this time, I felt immobilized. Before, I'd been able to fight back right away."

"Does that worry you?" He took a seat on the couch across from her.

"In a way. It makes me wonder if I'd be able to do it again. I should have run from the room, but all I could bring myself to do was scream."

"Jordan. What you did worked. You got Chase's attention. Don't second-guess yourself too much. There's no right or wrong here. Well, other than for the creep who showed up at your bedroom window. I hope to God they catch him soon."

"Me too," she said quietly.

"You want me to leave you alone now so you can get back to work? I don't have a client for an hour, so if you

112

need to talk some more, I can stay. Karen would be here too if she hadn't had an eval to do at the jail first thing."

"No. I may not actually be good." She tried to make a better attempt at a full smile this time. "But I'm dealing with everything okay. And I know you both are here for me. I'm grateful for that." She hated to lie to him, but she wasn't ready to talk to anyone about Chase, let alone a good friend of his. "With everything that's been going on, I've gotten a little behind. Hence my retreat into the cave." A half truth, not exactly a lie.

Mike smiled. "Nice analogy." He gave her a curious stare before standing to leave.

Her excuse hadn't completely flown with him, but she was relieved when he didn't question her any further.

§

Chase saw Mike leaving Jordan's office shaking his head. His chest tightened. Had she told him everything about last night?

"Hey, brother," Mike said, walking in Chase's direction.

Chase didn't sense any anger from him, so he'd bet she hadn't shared the full reason she'd holed herself up in her office.

Mike motioned him into an empty office to talk in private. "What's up with Jordan today? I asked her, but she seemed evasive. Nothing else has happened, has it? I mean, since the guy at the window."

Chase had given him the rundown on the events of the night before over the phone. Well, the part he'd wanted him to know about. He was pretty sure his good friend would have his head if he heard everything. "No, not since then. Though it was pretty scary for her. Me too, for that matter. When I heard her screaming, I thought…oh, I don't know, man. I was just worried I wasn't going to get to her in time." Chase rubbed the back of his neck as he made the last statement.

Recognition registered on Mike's face. "Dude, you have to give yourself a break sometime, you know. It wasn't your fault."

Chase immediately knew where he was going with the discussion. "I don't want to talk about it. It's in the past," he said, crossing his arms over his chest as he leaned his shoulder against the wall.

"Yeah, well, maybe you should. You haven't been the same since it happened. I haven't said anything before...I knew you needed space. But I'm saying this now, and it's probably long overdue. You couldn't have done anything differently that would have changed the outcome."

Chase clenched the fists that were anchored under his biceps. "You mean I couldn't have prevented him from dying? Isn't that supposed to be my job?" His voice rose with each word, though he was careful not to disrupt the office staff.

Mike didn't back down. "There's no disputing you're good at what you do. But if a client tells you to leave, you don't have much choice."

"You don't get it. It was my fault." He winced at the memory. "We'd become friends. I let that wall drop, and even though we disagreed half the time, there was something about us that worked. I got him, and I got why he did the crazy, screwed-up things he did."

"Then do you honestly think, if you had no personal relationship with him at all, you'd have been able to talk him out of it?" He shook his head.

Chase dragged a hand through his hair and let out an exasperated sigh. "I don't know, but I guess that's the problem...that I don't know. So I can continue to critique everything that happened that night and how many ways I could have changed the ending."

"Hindsight is always twenty-twenty. You can't live life asking the what-if questions all the time or you'll find that, somehow, you missed out on the 'what truly is' parts."

"Buddy, you'd better watch it. You're starting to

sound like a shrink or something," Chase said with a faint trace of a smile.

"Well, as long as you're acknowledging that I sound like a good one, then I won't complain," Mike said, grinning.

"Okay, you win," Chase said. "There may be a grain of truth in there somewhere."

"Well then, the next question would be, what are you going to do with it?" Mike looked him directly in the eye.

Chase met his gaze. "It doesn't change what happened."

"But it should change what will. You need to lower the wall a little. You don't have to take it down, but you have to let people you care about in again," Mike said. "I'd tell you I've missed you these last five years, but it may go to your head." He tapped his fist to Chase's shoulder.

Chase didn't have to read between the lines. He ought to make more of an effort. Now, Jordan was still his client. She was a whole other ball game. Or was she? He dismissed the thought as soon as he was aware of it.

Mike seemed to be reading his mind. "You don't have to sleep with her. Actually, better stated, you'd better not sleep with her. She's not into casual flings, and you aren't the settling type." He shot him a stern look. "But it wouldn't hurt to be a little nicer. Damn, you're running hot and cold so much when she's around that even I never know which Chase to expect. She's not the governor."

"Yeah, I kind of noticed," Chase said with a wink.

"Yeah, well, it stops at noticing in that regard," Mike replied lightly.

"Message received." He knew his friend was only half-joking. "Let's get to work." Chase opened the door and ran right into Jordan as he and Mike were leaving the office.

Mike gave her a nod and headed back down the hall.

Jordan started to move forward, but Chase reached out to stop her. He gently placed his hands on her shoulders. "I'm sorry," he said gruffly. "And not only for almost running you over."

Jordan tilted her head to the side. "Yeah, I heard that part last night. Please tell me. What exactly are you sorry for?" She pinned him with her glance.

There was no easy way to answer her. He was trying to be honest, but he had no desire to hurt her any more than he already had. "Jordan, I'm sorry for everything. It shouldn't have happened. I wasn't really thinking then."

Her shoulders sagged beneath his touch, and she looked down the hall before turning back to him. "Then I guess that answers that." She paused. "I don't want it to be awkward between us. I'm trying to move forward. Just please don't 'stop thinking' around me again. This—" she pointed her finger back and forth between them, "—whatever this is…was, isn't as easy for me."

Chase swallowed the words he wanted to say. They'd only confuse her more without sharing the whole disturbing story. "You have my word." His tone was tinged with regret. He regarded her for a moment. "What time do you want to leave for the trial?"

"In about half an hour? It's downtown," she answered.

"I'll meet you—"

"At the back entrance." She gave him a small smile after finishing the sentence. "I've pretty much got the drill down now."

Chase sat in the back of the courtroom while Jordan testified. Despite the tension in the room, she remained calm and answered each question succinctly. He stifled a yawn and tried to readjust his position again. There were only so many ways to sit in the stiff benches, and his body had grown tired of them all several hours ago.

Jordan sipped from a glass of water as the prosecutor approached the stand.

"Dr. Clayton, tell me some of the things you saw in

the police report that would suggest to you that this wasn't an impulsive act related to an inability to reason or control his behavior."

"If you look at the timeline, the action didn't occur in one night—as you might see when an individual gets angry and kills someone while involved in a lover's quarrel or drug crime. The timing of the murder suggests it was carefully planned out so no one would notice the victim's absence for several days. In addition, the crime scene was cleaned with materials the defendant brought with him to the house, and the disposal of the bodies was conducted in such a manner that would involve advanced preparation. For example, he dug the holes he'd use as grave sites earlier that week."

The prosecutor took a few more steps forward. "Are the actions you described suggestive of a brain injury?"

"No, they're not." She shook her head.

"Tell me why."

"The actions are more indicative of characterological traits that have been present over a long duration of time. The nature of personality issues is that they're long-standing." Her demeanor was relaxed as she proceeded to explain her conclusion. "In looking at the defendant's past history, he demonstrated behaviors that reflected a general disregard for the welfare of others and any negative consequences of his actions. He'd manipulate people in order to fulfill his own desires, establishing relationships with women so they'd assist him in his crimes or befriending his clients in order to gain access to their personal banking information or credit cards…"

Chase listened to her expand on the characterological traits of the defendant and speculated that at least a few would apply to the perp who was threatening Jordan. But despite the stress she'd been dealing with, she presented the same now as she had when she'd first taken the stand almost seven hours ago—appearing self-assured but not arrogant or defensive. His chest swelled a little as she neatly sidestepped a trap the defense council set up. He'd done his share of testifying with the state patrol, so he had to give it to her. She was much better than he'd ever been.

Like he needed one more reason to admire the woman he was assigned to protect.

"Finally," he said when she headed toward him after meeting with the prosecutor one last time. "I was beginning to think we might be sleeping here tonight."

She laughed, seeming too tired from the long day to do anything else. "Yeah, I kept thinking we'd continue into tomorrow, but I think the judge was ready to wrap it up."

She motioned for him to follow her, and he gladly followed her out of the courtroom. He was ready to move on from this day in more ways than one.

§

Jordan watched Chase's forearm muscles flex as he steered the SUV onto the expressway. As soon as they'd shut the doors, he'd promptly pulled his tie off and rolled the sleeves of his button-down dress shirt up. His olive-toned skin contrasted with the light-blue material.

She reclined back in her seat and closed her eyes before her thoughts led her places she didn't want to go right now—not ever, really. She'd stopped herself from telling him exactly how she felt, knowing the entire staff was around the corner. There was no point in risking being overheard and creating unnecessary drama at the office. So far, they'd managed to keep everything running smoothly, despite the frightening threats made toward her. Besides, Chase didn't seem interested in her response. He'd clearly drawn his conclusions without her. His first apology last night had left her confused and hurt, and the second one today had made her as glad as he was that they'd stopped when they had. Being someone's regret wasn't something she ever wanted. She shoved the unpleasant memory out of her mind and tried to focus on the present. Moving forward, she reminded herself.

"You going to sleep on me?" he asked.

She opened her eyes part way and slid her gaze over to him. "I wish. I'm so ready to crash, but I'm also starving." Her stomach chose then to rumble in agreement.

Chase lifted the corners of his mouth. "Sounds like it. I'll swing by and grab us something to go. Do you have a preference?"

"Couldn't care less. Whatever you want is fine with me." She still hadn't bothered to adjust her seat upright. It felt good to simply sit back for a moment and let him make the decisions. Between court today and the events of last night, she was done thinking.

After several minutes, Chase pulled into a deli and parked the SUV directly in front of the glass door. Through the slits of her eyelids, she could see there was only one other car in the parking lot. Not registering anything as a potential threat, she let her eyes drift shut again. But even with them closed, she could feel him staring at her. She shifted toward him.

"Sorry. I didn't know if you were actually sleeping this time. Your stomach didn't seem to have any input either way."

The evening sun was just bright enough to illuminate his sexy grin as he teased her. Ugh. Truth be known, her traitorous stomach was busy doing somersaults as if an Olympic gold were at stake. It must have forgotten the need for food. But there was no way she was letting him in on that.

"No, I'm good. Still awake."

"Okay, then. "Do you want to wait here while I run in? I'll be right in front of the door while they fill the order."

She nodded absently. Sitting in the car and watching the sun sink behind the tree line, she tried to maintain her resolve to keep her mind still. She didn't want to think about the hit on her life, or her bodyguard. Before long, she saw Chase push open the door carrying several bags, his confident stride showcasing his muscular physique now illuminated by the early moonlight.

She grabbed the bags from him as he jumped in the car. They were quite heavy, considering he was supposed to have picked up only two meals. "Seriously? How much do you think I eat?"

He arched an eyebrow at her. "Do you really want me to answer that? Because I'm not sure there's a good one."

"Yeah, you should probably scratch that question. My parents used to joke that I had hollow legs and that's where all of the extra food goes."

Chase's eyes grazed over the length of her legs to the hem of her skirt, leaving a trail of heat along his path. When he reached her upper thighs, she realized her skirt had ridden up since she'd been reclining in the seat. Several inches of nylon-covered upper thigh was now on display. A flush crept into her cheeks as she did her best to balance the carryout bags while tugging at the wayward hem.

Chase shifted in his seat and abruptly directed his attention to merging into the oncoming traffic.

After deciding that her hemline had returned to a respectable position, she looked over at him. "So, what are we having?"

"Hmmm?" He muttered distractedly, checking the rearview mirror.

"You know, the ten-pound bags you have for dinner, what's in them?" She wondered where he'd disappeared to.

Surely, her bare legs hadn't left him that unnerved. From the way he'd won over the women on her staff his first day, she was pretty sure he'd seen more than his fair share over the years. She shook her head in an effort to brandish the thought away. After their recent encounter, she had no desire to picture him with a woman he'd chosen to be with. It would only leave her questioning why he didn't pick her. She looked out her window as they drove by the turnoff into her neighborhood.

"Chase?" she said in an uncertain tone.

He still hadn't answered and was glancing in the rearview mirror again. She checked her side mirror, noticing a car approaching them from behind.

"What is it? Are we being followed?" she asked. Her chest tightened as she gripped the bags in her lap.

"It would seem so. He's been behind us for the past five turns," he said. "And I made sure a couple were just around a block a few miles back. I need you to hang tight while I try something."

Chase entered the right turn lane and turned on the right blinker. The car eased in behind them, though it was too dark to make out the features of the driver. When the light changed to green, Chase gunned the engine and sped into the adjacent lane going straight instead. He was able to get ahead of the other cars on the road.

Jordan looked back, hoping the car following them wouldn't make it. Then the screeching of brakes tore through the night, and a car swerved over to avoid being hit by their tail. She held her breath until she saw that the other driver was safe.

"Damn it, this guy is an idiot." In the dim moonlight, Jordan could see that Chase's jaw was clenched tight as he concentrated on trying to stay ahead of their pursuer. "I'm going to head to the police department. You call nine-one-one and report our location now. Maybe there's an officer in the area." The driver was gaining speed behind them, but Chase's voice was steady and his tone calm.

Feeding on his strength, Jordan reached down to grab her phone from her purse. She fumbled around for a second until her hands wrapped around the familiar device.

"Hang on." Chase barely got the words out before the SUV took another sharp turn and centrifugal force plastered her against the center console.

The phone she'd just retrieved flew out of her hand and hit the floorboard. Ironically, the three bags on her lap stayed put. As the scenery flew by her, she noticed they'd turned onto a less crowded side street that would lead them downtown. But they were still minutes away from the station. After hoisting the bags over her shoulder into the back seat, she began rummaging around the floorboard again for the lost phone. Headlights growing brighter behind them let her know the driver of the other car was almost caught up to them.

"Sit up," Chase instructed. "I think he may try to hit us."

She popped up right as the car swerved around to their left. A hard jolt charged through her and she grazed the side of her head on the window beside her. *Did we collide?* Gravel hit the undercarriage of the vehicle as the BMW spun onto the shoulder of the road. Turning the wheel in the same direction, Chase wrangled to gain back control. The edge of the woods came looming toward them. She squeezed her eyes shut and braced herself for the crash. But there was no impact. Instead, they jerked to a sudden stop. She peeked out to see that they were now perpendicular to the line of trees. The vehicle had rotated enough to avoid hitting them head on. She craned her neck around to look for the other car but saw no hint of movement.

"Are you all right?" Chase asked. She could hear the concern in his voice.

"I'm fine," Jordan said, her breath catching. She felt disoriented, but other than some pressure from the seat belt, she was relieved to realize she was okay. Physically, anyway. "Where'd it go?" She didn't see the other car, but she didn't trust that the maniac was truly gone.

"It's okay." He rubbed her shoulder. "He passed us after he ran us off the road. I tried to get a tag number, but there was no way from our position." His hands returned to the steering wheel, and she immediately missed the comfort of his touch. "You sure you're okay?" He looked over at her as he put the vehicle in reverse and eased the SUV back onto the road. "I thought your head hit when we turned."

"It was only a bump." She rubbed the spot that had grazed the window. There was no wetness that could be blood. Only a small knot. Verifying her head wasn't injured, she abandoned her assessment in favor of monitoring their surroundings as they began driving. The BMW seemed no worse for the wear, and she was thankful his car offered more protection than hers would have. "You don't think he'll come back, do you?" Her voice shook as she asked the question.

"I don't think so. But I'm not sure. I have no intention of sitting here and waiting to find out. I'll call Detective Larson once we're back at your house. I'm sure he's gone for today, but I'll leave him a message with the gist of what happened and fill in the details tomorrow. He'll want to file a report so the incident will be on record."

"We aren't going to the station?"

"No point now. Larson can file the report tomorrow. There's no evidence to preserve tonight that won't be there in the morning. I'd rather get you home."

She didn't argue. Being at home sounded much better to her. The sooner she was off of the roads, the better. Would she ever feel safe again?

Jordan hadn't gone into work that morning. Between the events of last night and the nightmares that followed, she was in no shape to be there. She'd briefed Karen over the phone, and she, Mike, and Derek had all come over to her house during their lunch hour.

"I'm sorry. You've been through so much. I can't believe this is really happening." Karen gave her a tight hug, tears glistening in her eyes.

"Me neither," she said, shaking her head. She pulled a

chair out and motioned for her friend to sit.

Everyone else followed suit.

"I feel terrible about being out today, but for the first time since this all started, I don't think I should be at work." Her voice cracked and she fought back tears of defeat. "I'm not sleeping. I can't concentrate. All I can think of is what this guy is going to do next. It's consuming me."

Karen grabbed her hand and held it in her own. Jordan was grateful for the gesture.

Mike rubbed his chin thoughtfully. "What about leaving town for a while?" Jordan began to protest, but Mike raised a hand to stop her. "Hear me out. Not for long. Maybe just until the cops have made an arrest or even have a suspect."

"Weren't you the one who said that wasn't a good idea because he could follow me?" She wasn't trying to argue. In truth, she didn't have the strength. But it felt like they were going in circles, or more like this creep had them jumping through hoops in an obstacle course with no endpoint.

"That was then. It's gone too far now," Mike said, his voice firm. He'd torn the label from his bottle of water as he spoke and was now shredding it into a pile in front of him.

"I agree with Mike. There are too many unknowns," Derek said. "It's hard to figure out what to do when we don't have much to work with. This guy has managed to evade being caught at every turn. It's uncanny, really, that he's left nothing for the cops to trace back to him."

"Yeah," Chase said. "Makes me think he may be involved in some type of law enforcement or investigative work."

"But why hire the hitman then? If he could have carried his plan out better himself?" Derek looked at Chase for an answer.

"Don't know. If I did, maybe we'd have a better

handle on who he is." Chase shoved his chair back and stomped over to her fridge to refill his glass.

Jordan looked over at Derek. He opened his mouth then closed it as if he thought better of saying what he'd intended. Probably a smart move. She could tell by Chase's forceful movements that he was frustrated. He hadn't shared that theory with her before. She wondered if he'd given Detective Larson his hypothesis. Not that it changed anything about her current predicament. Nausea turned in her stomach as her friends continued to debate suggestions.

"That's why I think she needs to leave," Mike said. "We can't stop something or someone we have nothing on. We still don't even know what this creep is after. It just pisses me off." He slammed his hand down on the table, sending the slivers of paper fluttering into the air.

Jordan flinched.

Karen squeezed her hand, offering reassurance while giving Mike a stern look.

"I'm sorry," he muttered. "I think we all feel pretty helpless right now." He used the side of his hand to scrape the bits back into a pile.

Jordan looked across the table at him. "Don't worry about it. If it were one of you, I'm sure I'd feel the same way." She gave him a weak smile.

"So, what do you think, Jordan?" Karen asked. "I know before that you believed it would be letting him win if you left town. Do you still feel that way?"

Jordan remembered making the comment back then. So much had changed since that conversation. Before, worrying about the hit and who'd ordered it had been more of a nuisance to her. Now, it still felt like she would be letting him win by leaving, but the feelings of defeat were nothing compared to the worry over what might happen if she stayed.

"It sounds like an option. But where would I go? I'm not putting anyone else in danger. My parents, family and friends… No, he could follow me, or worse, he may have some of this information already."

"What about our condo in Panama City Beach?" Mike volunteered. "If you've got to get out of town, might as well get away to somewhere beautiful."

"Hmmm. That could be a workable option." Jordan considered his suggestion. It would mean leaving her house, her business, and her clients with little notice. But her ability to work was compromised anyway.

As if reading her mind, Karen said, "I realize it's hard to leave everything like this, but Mike's right. If you have to do this, the condo is the perfect spot. No one would associate it with any of us, because the deed is still in my maiden name. Plus, it's a good distance away from here." Her forehead lifted and she pinned her friend with a stare. "You're a great asset to this practice, but we'll handle everything while you're gone. No worries about that part, okay?"

Derek turned to Chase. "Are you going, too?"

Jordan's eyes widened at the question. She hadn't thought of that. When they'd first entertained the idea of hiring Chase, it was so she wouldn't have to leave the practice while all of this was going on. Now, she'd be generating no income and the practice would still be paying for Chase's protection. Though, given how reasonable his rate is, she was hoping to cover the cost herself.

Karen weighed in before Chase could respond. "I think he should. It would be crazy to leave her alone." She turned to Jordan. "No offense. You're smart and tough, but you aren't trained for this like he is. And I've felt one hundred percent better since we hired him."

"I agree. Not even a question as far as I'm concerned," Mike said.

"Absolutely," Derek said. "I just wanted to make sure we're all on the same page. Chase? Does the trip work for you?"

Chase looked around the table. "I hate the idea of leaving, too. But at this point, until the PD is able to learn more about who it is we're dealing with here, then I think it's the best option." His eyes met Jordan's with an unspoken apology. "I know it isn't what you'd wanted, but the objective is to keep you safe, and I think it's the best way to do that. I can take precautions to make sure we aren't followed, and Karen's got a point about the lack of association—our current names aren't documented anywhere in connection to the place."

Jordan nodded at him and then looked at the others. "Well, I guess it's the best decision, then. I'll pack up today, have Nancy rearrange my schedule, and we can leave any time after that."

There wasn't much else to say. In a way it felt like she was running, but she trusted Chase's judgment. She just prayed that the ordeal would be over soon.

CHAPTER TEN

Chase observed Jordan as the elevator rose to the fourteenth floor. A piece of her hair was falling into her face as she stared down at the lighted pushbuttons on the control panel. She was dressed casually in a cobalt-blue sleeveless dress made from some type of airy, gauze-like material. The outfit suited the warm weather they'd driven into that day.

It had taken the good part of the previous day to rearrange her schedule and pack what she needed for the trip. Wanting to leave in the daylight when visibility was better and he could see any tails, Chase had made the decision to drive out early the next morning. He was glad her colleagues had decided to keep him on board because it had stopped him from telling them that he wasn't going anywhere. He was involved now, and fee for services be damned—there was no way he was leaving Jordan before this guy was locked up for a long time.

The elevator stopped at the tenth floor, and a young woman pushing a cleaning cart stepped in, mashing the button for the eleventh floor. Though he sensed no threat, he remained alert as they climbed up one floor. He'd taken numerous precautions to make sure no one had followed them up there, even checking his SUV for tracking devices. He could almost say with certainty that the perp hadn't followed them by car.

"You folks enjoy your stay," she said, pulling the cart out behind her.

"Thank you," Jordan said, pushing the loose strand of hair out of her eyes. She chewed on her bottom lip as they continued their way up.

He watched her worry on her full pink lip. She'd been restless and on edge until they'd hit the turnpike, then he'd seen her posture relax a little. *Does she feel better since we left town?* Jumping inconspicuously over the nonexistent button for a thirteenth floor, the number fourteen lit up and the bell dinged, signaling they'd reached their destination.

As they exited the elevator to the front balcony, the winds caught Jordan's dress, causing the skirt to swirl around her ankles. The material was no match for the wind tunnel, and the dress was now pressed tight against her entire body, accentuating every curve. His pulse revved up at the sight of her sexy silhouette, and dots of perspiration beaded along his forehead. Sweet Jesus. Prying his eyes away from her body, he hurried through the six-digit code and threw open the door. He tried to forget that it was now only the two of them. Maybe he was a masochist and never knew it?

Shutting the door behind them, his heart rate became more regular as he fell into the comfort of his routine. "Wait here for a second." He kept Jordan at the door as he cleared the first room, and then he took her with him to clear the master and the guest bedrooms. He didn't find any targets, nor did he intend to, but he never took chances. Re-holstering his gun, he gave Jordan the all clear.

"Wow!" Jordan exclaimed as she walked toward the view of the surf.

Chase eyed the sparkling, crystal waters and white-sand beach when she spoke, but the woman standing in front of the expansive glass doors was the more breathtaking focal point to him. "Yeah, it's beautiful, all right."

Her long hair fell down her back in waves, and her face was flushed with excitement as she looked out at the ocean. To him, her radiance rivaled the Florida sun reflecting off the waters below.

"Have you ever been to this part of the coast before?" he asked, trying to keep his voice level.

She looked back at him over her shoulder. "No. I had no idea what I was missing. Mike and Karen have had this place for several years, but I never took them up on the offer to stay here. They even suggested I come up with them a few times when they drove. Really dumb move, huh?"

He sensed there was more to the story. "I'm sure you had your reasons," he said, walking up to stand next to her.

"I guess I thought I did." She paused to watch a pelican swoop down to the water's surface and swallow his thrashing catch. "Busy with work some of the times. Other times, I felt they needed the time away together. With everything that's happened lately, I'm beginning to change the way I look at things…relationships, time, priorities." The tenor of her voice was pensive. She turned toward him. "What about you? Doesn't doing this kind of work ever make you want to reevaluate things?"

Chase cleared his throat. She was a little too close to home. "Yes, I suppose it does. I probably haven't given it as much consideration as you have. What is that called in your field? A lack of insight?" He gave her a crooked grin, but he hesitated before going on.

Jordan nodded, returning his smile.

He didn't expect an answer. It was a rhetorical question. But the momentary silence that followed gave him time to contemplate his response. "I guess, hearing you say it now, I know that it happens. Or maybe that it should. Though the same hazards apply to this line of work as they do to yours—spending more time addressing your client's needs, dealing with the crisis of the moment, you know…"

He was tempted to say more. To tell her about his uncertainties and questions surrounding how long he wanted to live this lifestyle, but he stopped himself. Too many lines were getting blurry as it was. Lines he needed to be visible, if not for his own sake, for Jordan's.

"But enough about me," he said in a more relaxed tone as he clasped his hands together in front of him. "It's your first time on Florida's Gulf Coast. What do you want to do to begin with?"

§

"You make it sound like I'm here on vacation," she said, conscious of his evasive response but choosing to let it go. She didn't want to push him. Better a few slow steps forward than going back to where they'd begun. "Are you sure it's safe?"

"You'll be fine." He didn't give a direct answer again. Though, if she were in his shoes, she probably wouldn't have either. Neither of them seemed to be able to predict this guy's next move with any precision.

"I'm thinking about it," she said.

"Jordan, I'm here to protect you. And since I'm working, one of us needs to enjoy this place as much as possible under the circumstances. Or we can just hang out here all day if you'd prefer," he said, the corners of his mouth twitching.

He was obviously joking with her, but she inwardly groaned at how appealing she found the thought of spending the entire day with him in this condo…sans clothing, of course. A shiver of raw desire ran the length of her spine. Needing an immediate distraction from her fantasy, she opened the sliding glass doors leading to the balcony. A gust of wind sent her hair flying away from her face, and she was greeted by the salty smell of the ocean. She inhaled deeply, relishing the distinctive scent.

"I can't be this close and not out there," she said, eyeing the shore. "Are you up for a run?"

Chase leaned sideways and bumped his arm to hers. "With an oceanfront backdrop? For future reference, you never have to ask me that again," he said with a wink. "Just tell me when."

She could still feel the tingles in her arm from where he'd touched her. Having him so close to her in this incredible setting was doing things to her she hadn't anticipated. It was as if her body was hyperaware of his presence. She took a step back and reminded herself that the location was the only thing that had changed as far as she and Chase were concerned.

"I'd better slip into something else first," she said, looking down at her dress. "And I guess we should probably put away our luggage."

Chase gave her a nod and grabbed her suitcase from the hall. "I'll carry this in for you." Not bothering to pull the handle out to roll it, he lifted it effortlessly and led the way back into the master bedroom.

Jordan tried not to be impressed, but she wasn't one to pack light. His defined muscles flexed as he laid the suitcase across the luggage rack. Her mind wandered back to how it had felt when those arms had been wrapped around her and his competent hands had left a trail of heat across her bare skin…

Gracious, she had to get him out of the bedroom. Out of the condo, period. Space. That was what she needed. "Thanks. I appreciate it," she said, her tone clipped. She began unzipping her suitcase as she waited for him to leave.

"Are you hot?" he asked as his eyes searched her face.

"Hot?" Her hands froze on the zipper, now only halfway around. Had he somehow read her thoughts?

"Yeah, hot. You look a little flushed," he said, his

voice laced with concern.

"Oh, like without the air on?" She unconsciously fanned herself and then stopped as soon as she realized she not only sounded but also looked ridiculous.

"Well, yes. What did you think I meant?" He didn't attempt to hide his grin.

Jordan shook her head. "Sorry. My mind was somewhere else. I'll be fine." She resumed unzipping the suitcase and purposely avoided eye contact with him. She was sure "flushed" wouldn't even begin to describe the color of red her face was now. "Besides, we're leaving soon anyway."

"Yeah, I was thinking the same thing. I can turn the air on, but you might be cold when we come in off the beach." He regarded her with a perplexed expression.

"No, you're probably right." She pulled out her shorts and a tank top, thinking Chase would leave, but no such luck. Even without looking up, her body hummed with the tension his nearness created.

"Mike and Karen did a nice job on this place," he said, looking around the room, oblivious to her need for space.

She exhaled with relief at the change in subject and followed his gaze around her new quarters. The walls of the room were a pale aqua, and the bedding was the color of sand. It wasn't overdone with palm trees, fish prints, and the bright colors often used to decorate beachfront condos; instead, the only real art was a beautiful coral fan centered on one wall. She walked over to get a closer look.

"I remember Mike telling me about a friend of theirs, a boat captain, who gave them this coral," she said, gently touching the delicate extensions. "A couple of tourists pulled it up on their line when he'd brought them out to fish. They gave it to him, but he lived on his boat and didn't have anywhere to keep it. Mike and Karen took him out the next night to celebrate his birthday, and he surprised them with it. It's amazing how nature gives us some of the most awesome creations."

"Yes, it is," he said, watching her. There was a thickness in his speech that made her pretty sure he was no longer talking about the coral. His words incited a flurry of activity in her chest. Before she could respond, he was turning toward the door. "I'll give you time to change," he said on his way out.

Still rooted to her spot, she let out a frustrated sigh. He'd chosen now to leave. How he could send the blood rushing through her body with one comment both annoyed and astounded her.

And he throws those comments out and then leaves as if he'd remarked on the weather. No wonder I'm a hot mess right now.

She pulled the sundress over her head and replaced it with the tank top and shorts. Next time, she wasn't going to let him off so easily. If he could dish it out, he could learn to stick around for her response. In truth, she'd never been good at these types of flirtations, always more content to say what was on her mind. Maybe that was how she would turn the tables on him. She smirked, imagining his reaction if she was brave enough to tell him what she was thinking in return.

"You almost ready?" His voice came from the living area.

She must have spent more time lost in thought than she'd realized. "Just a few more seconds," she said. She threw her hair into a ponytail and grabbed her favorite running shoes. "Let's go," she said, walking out to meet him.

After only a short walk down from the condo, they were standing in front of the ocean. The fragrant salty water was so clear she could see tiny schools of synchronized minnows darting in one direction and then the other. She and Chase set an easy pace, and she basked in the sound of the waves crashing down against the smooth sand shore. Every so often, a larger wave would break. Then a pool of water would creep up, dampening the dry, powder-like sand and expanding the shoreline. The entire process reminded her of clearing an Etch-a-Sketch. When the ocean drew the water back, the footprints and valleys in the sand were all erased, replaced with a pristine sand canvas. She found it soothing on some level, mimicking how the vast expanse of the ocean seemed to be wiping away the strain of the past week. *This is truly heaven.*, she thought. *If everyone could do this on a daily basis, it might put therapists out of business.*

"So, you never told me if you've been here before?" she asked him.

"Not here exactly. I've been to St. George Island not too far from here. Actually, Mike and I used to go a lot when we were at FSU in Tallahassee. It was close, and the beach looks exactly like this. It was our getaway place."

"Oh, I keep forgetting you both were there at the same time. I can't imagine the two of you together. Mike is an awesome guy, but he can be pretty adventurous all on his own."

"Yeah. We were a pair." A smile crossed his lips. "We've tried to stay close over the years. The times we've drifted apart were probably my fault. I was busy with work, circumstances similar to the reasons you gave as to why you never came here until now." He changed their course to avoid a family building sandcastles in front of them. "Anyway, I'm going to try to be a little better about it. He's a good friend."

After passing the family, Jordan looked up the shoreline and saw that it was deserted. They'd have the beach to themselves for the next stretch.

"Do you think it'll be easy? Sometimes, learning to be less busy is more difficult than people think. Myself included. You'd think, being a psychologist, I'd practice what I preach, but just because you know what the right thing is to do doesn't mean you always do it."

"Hmmm…is it kind of like this?" he questioned, his

eyes sparkling.

"Like what?" she asked. Before she knew what was happening, Chase had swept her off her feet and was carting her toward the ocean.

"I know I probably shouldn't, but I'm going to do it anyway," he replied as he carried her, one arm around her torso and the other supporting her legs.

"What are you doing?" She attempted to sound firm, but from her current position the effect was lost. Then she felt the icy spray of the waves. "Chase, you'd better put me down!"

He continued to trudge out farther. "Maybe you're right."

Then the cold surf engulfed her as he stood her upright. She was waist-deep in the ocean in her running clothes.

"Seriously, I cannot believe you just did that." She tried to be indignant, except he was laughing so hard that she found herself unable to resist joining him. There were tears gathering in the corners of her eyes before she was finally catching her breath. "You should have thought this through a little more."

He managed to stop laughing long enough to reply. "And why is that?"

"Because, my fearless protector, you're as soaked as I am." She eyed his running shoes through the clear water.

"So maybe it wasn't the best-laid plan," he acknowledged, following her gaze down to his shoes. "But I think we were both long overdue for some comic relief." He was clearly still amused, but his eyes grew serious as he spoke. "You've been through so much lately. Now is the first time I've seen you this relaxed."

"To be honest, it does feel good. Well, except for the water and sand in my tennis shoes. My favorite tennis shoes, might I add." She directed a mock frown at him and shook her head. "You're right though. Being here, I can see that I needed to get away from everything more than I realized," she said.

"So, how about we focus on more times like this while we're here? *Carpe diem*. Are you in?" He raised an eyebrow.

She slowly nodded. "I'm in," she said in a decisive tone. "And in the spirit of seizing the moment, I will suggest we get dinner. All of this *water play*—" she gave him a look of admonishment, "—has made me ravenous."

"Did you actually just say ravenous?" He cocked his head to one side.

"Yes. What's wrong with that?" she asked, skimming the tops of her fingers along the water while she spoke. "It's a perfectly legitimate word."

"Plain hungry wouldn't do?" He pressed his lips tightly together in an attempt to restrain a grin.

"No, because I'm more than hungry."

"Uh-huh." He pretended to consider her explanation. "For some reason, I'm not surprised." He let out a chuckle.

"Hey," she said, pretending to be offended. "This is no laughing matter." Enjoying the moment, she used the side of her palm to send a spray of water his way.

He jumped back as the wave of water landed inches in front of him. "Okay, I get it. Back to our very *serious*—" he emphasized the word, "—dinner planning." He stepped forward. "Why don't we check out the restaurant we passed before our condo? It's only a few buildings down from here, and it overlooks the water. In case you haven't gotten enough of the ocean yet," he said, snickering even as he reached to steady her when a strong wave rolled over them.

"Uh-huh. You can laugh now. Just know that I'm like an elephant," she said.

"Oh, really." His eyebrows raised, while the corners of his mouth twitched slightly. "So, I'm guessing you're not going to forget this anytime soon?"

"There's no way I'll forget this." She winked at him.

"You'd better watch your back."

Chase leaned forward until they were only inches apart. "You realize we haven't even made it out of the water yet. You might want to save the threats for retaliation until you're safe on land."

Jordan swallowed as his nearness made her heart jump. He was so close she barely had to speak above a whisper. "And what else is there for you to do? I'm already soaking wet." Belatedly, she realized the double entendre in what she'd said.

Chase's expression changed from playful to one of pure desire. He stared longingly at her for a moment. Then, with a pained expression, he backed away. "There's so much I could say to that…and a huge part of me wants to say, but I'm going to do the right thing this time." He gently took her hand. "Let's get back to the condo. Maybe we can make it to the restaurant in time for the sunset."

Jordan silently followed him out of the water. Neither of them spoke, but he didn't drop her hand until they'd made it back to shore. So maybe that didn't actually count as being brave and sharing her true feelings. After all, she hadn't intended for the words to come out like they had. A Freudian slip, maybe. But the consequences were the same. She'd unintentionally laid it out on the table, and he'd walked away…again.

CHAPTER ELEVEN

The crash of the ocean was like a melody in the background as they sat on bar stools, perusing the menu at a local hangout. Chase could smell the warm salt air mixing with the seafood cooking on the grill. Every once in a while, a lone sound from the mic would break in as the band tested the equipment for their upcoming show.

"This may be one of the worst places I've ever had to work in," he said, leaning back and interlacing his fingers behind his head.

Jordan put her sunglasses back into her purse and then turned toward him. She wore a white sleeveless blouse that dipped down into a V in the front with a turquoise skirt. A delicate turquoise pendant hung from her neck by a thin silver chain. His heart sped up as he took in how the outfit highlighted her hourglass figure and her long legs.

"Yeah, this is pretty rough, all right. Couldn't imagine having to put up with all of this—" Jordan gestured around them, "—every day."

Curved lines formed around her mouth as she tried to restrain her smile, and he noticed how the dimple on her left cheek became more pronounced. For a split second, he wished he could pull his phone out and use his camera feature to capture how beautiful she looked tonight.

A waitress made her way to their table, carrying a tray of empty glasses balanced on her hip. "What will y'all be having to drink tonight?" she asked.

Chase turned to Jordan and raised his eyebrows.

"Hmm." She stared down at the menu, her finger running down the drink descriptions. "How about I try one of your specials? The Sunset Serenade?"

"Good choice," she said with a nod of approval. "And for you?" She directed her attention to Chase.

"I'll have a club soda and lime."

"Great. I'll be right back with those drinks." Then she maneuvered the tray from her hip to her shoulder and treaded toward the bar.

"You know, I don't mind if you drink," Jordan said, leaning forward. "I mean, I can understand why you aren't, but it wouldn't bother me."

"I appreciate that. But it's no bother. I'm used to situations like being in a bar and not drinking. Minor hazard of the job, I guess," he said with a shrug. "Though, now that you mention it, I can't remember the last time I was in a bar to actually have a drink."

"I'm no expert. Well, maybe I am." She smiled again. "But that probably means it's been a little too long."

"You could be right. I may have to remedy that soon," Chase said.

"Seriously?" She tilted her head. "Or are you merely caught up in the ambiance of this place?"

Chase hesitated. He'd already told himself that he wasn't going to confide in Jordan about this, but it struck him how much he'd come to respect her opinions. She was logical yet also resourceful. A good listener but honest and objective in her feedback. And she was a client, and eventually, all of his clients would know if he altered his services. Having rationalized his concerns away, he decided a brief overview of his potential plans wouldn't be too much. "Actually, it may be time for a change for me. All work and no play has begun to feel more like too much of what was once a good thing. Now, I'm wondering if it's time to scale back a little."

Jordan paused before responding to take a sip of the orange-and-red frozen concoction the waitress had set in front of her. "Is that a real possibility for you? I mean, would it be feasible for you to remove yourself somewhat from your own company?"

"Good question. I've considered that one, too. Frankly, I've got some great guys. I've built a top-notch team over time, and I'd trust my life with any one of them. And let me tell you, that's saying a whole lot, because there aren't many people I'd say that about. In or out of the field. Though we stay pretty busy, I'm not pompous enough to think that my guys couldn't handle the details as well as I can. So I guess the answer to your question is yes, it could be a real possibility."

"So, this is something you've thought about before?" she asked.

"For a while. Maybe more often these days. I enjoy the work, but lately it seems I've let it consume me. I'm not so much worried about how the business will fair without me, as how I'll fair without the hands-on part of the job," he said, staring out toward the gulf. He stopped himself from saying more and turned back to her. "I'm not sure how I got started on that. It's more of a question on what direction to take the business in."

Jordan didn't comment, but he could see that he had her full attention. She was perched on the edge of her chair, leaning toward him, her eyes locked on his.

A part of him liked that she'd taken her time in considering what he'd said without needing to jump in with her comments as soon as he was through talking. But her silence was also a little unnerving, given that he hadn't intended to share the bit about his personal worries.

"You aren't analyzing me, are you?" he asked, only

partly joking.

"If you aren't paying me, I'm not working," she said in a matter-of-fact tone. "Though…" She placed her index finger on her chin. "Maybe we could arrange some type of bartering system, like free protection for ongoing therapy?" She gave him a grin.

"I think that may cross some ethical lines," he responded, his tone light-hearted.

She let out an unladylike snort. "More like obliterate them. You're right. No good for either of us," she said. "So I guess we can go back to you just talking and I'm a friend listening."

The word *friend* sobered him instantly. "Jordan, I know I've done this wrong before, so I'll try to do it right this time. I really do like you and I'm probably enjoying this detail more than I should."

Her eyes widened slightly and her lips parted, and he fought like hell to keep from kissing her.

"But there can't be anything more than friendship between us. Not now. Our friendship alone is more than I planned for and probably not the smartest move. I'm not the kind of guy to lay everything out there, so I'll just say this. I've made some mistakes in the past. One of them happened when I was protecting someone. I can't open the door to that type of mistake again… And most of all, I can't risk anything happening to you because of something I missed. Something I missed because I was distracted."

She was silent for a moment. "I like you too, Chase. Probably more than I should," she said, using his own words against him. "And I understand where you're coming from. I wouldn't want to do anything that would compromise the services I offer my clients either. It wouldn't be fair, and I get that." She sighed. "So where does that leave us?"

He looked over at her and gently grasped her hand across the table. "I don't know. Right now, I'm focused on keeping you safe. It's where my mind has to be. And to be honest, that's quite a challenge when it comes to you."

Jordan leaned farther toward him. For a second, he thought she was going to disregard everything he'd said and kiss him. And God help him, he knew he wouldn't even stop her. But instead, she whispered, "Up for a dance?"

"That's it?" He gave her an incredulous stare.

"I guess it is for now." She lifted the corners of her mouth in an attempt to smile, but her eyes reflected regret.

Chase realized she was right. There wasn't anything more to say right then. Wanting to see her happy again, he grabbed her hand. "Then let's dance." He led her onto the small dance floor in front of the stage.

The band was playing Jimmy Buffet hits, and they found a quick rhythm together with Chase whirling her around. He tried to ignore the fact that he felt like the luckiest guy on the dance floor, even though she wasn't even his.

§

Jordan surprised herself by letting go on the dance floor. They were so close to the band that she felt like she was part of the music. Though the timing saddened her, Chase's admission caused the events from earlier in the week to come together for her. If anything, his honesty made her respect him even more.

Ducking under Chase's arm and curling into him, she laughed as he pulled her hand and she spun out from him. She had to hand it to him. He might feel like he was all work, but he'd learned how to play at some point and he was pretty good at it. After dancing to several songs with him, she felt almost giddy.

As the band played the final notes of a song, Chase placed a hand on the small of her back and steered her back toward their table.

"What is it?" she asked, moving in closer to him. She scanned the restaurant, trying to make sure nothing seemed amiss.

"Nothing bad," he clarified quickly. "But we're about to view a spectacular sunset, and I don't know about you, but I'm kind of missing the dinner we seem to have forgotten about. Particularly seeing as how you're ravenous." He gave her hand a squeeze then pulled her chair out for her.

"Oh my gosh, you're right. That's very unlike me," she said, wide-eyed. "Being out there was so much fun though! I haven't danced liked that in a long time." She was almost breathless with excitement.

"Me neither," Chase said. "And…" He stopped to clear his throat. "Friend to friend, you looked absolutely beautiful out there. Well, and here. Really, all night."

Jordan was taken aback by his compliment. Her chest fluttered. "Thank you."

Chase gave her a wink, and her stomach dropped like she was descending down a steep hill on a roller coaster. Though she didn't say so, he looked gorgeous tonight as well. The simple white polo shirt he wore accentuated his dark hair and dark olive skin and showed off his muscular arms. She took a deep breath and reminded herself of their conversation earlier.

"Look. The sun's about to set." Chase pointed out over the water.

They watched in comfortable silence as the sun set into the ocean. Shades of gold, amber, and crimson reflected both in the sky and off the water. It was spectacular. In truth, the entire day had been pretty spectacular.

She sucked down the last of her second Sunset Serenade. "These are good," she said appreciatively. "But I should probably eat some actual food soon." She was already feeling the effects of two drinks on an empty stomach.

"So, what are you having?" Chase asked her. He glanced around the entire bar before coming back to her.

Though his attention was on her, he was also aware of their surroundings wherever they went. His ability to remain alert while he appeared relaxed made her feel more secure when they were out.

She took one last look at the menu spread out in front of her. She'd already been over the entrees several times. "I don't know. All of it sounds good. Do you want to order a few things to share? Maybe some lobster chowder, smoked tuna dip, fried shrimp . . ."

"Okay, okay," he said, displaying a wide grin. "So basically, a little of everything on the menu?"

"Sounds good to me."

When the waitress came, Chase ordered an appetizer sampler, a bowl of crab chowder, and a seafood platter, which all turned out to be heavenly. They enjoyed trading dishes and savoring the different coastal flavors while listening to the band in the background.

When their plates were nearly empty and she couldn't fit another bite into her stomach, she leaned back and let out a contented sigh. "This has been one of the best days I can remember in a long time. I know that seems weird to say—I mean, under the circumstances—but getting away from Orlando was definitely a good decision."

"I agree on both. This has been an awesome day," he said softly then continued in his normal tone. "And I think getting you out of Orlando was the best option."

"You know, at first, I didn't want to go. I thought I was giving in to him by coming here. Like I was giving in to the fear he's created... It felt cowardly, I guess." She stirred her straw in circles and watched the melted ice in her drink swirl around as she spoke. A part of her didn't want to see what Chase thought of her revelation. Would it change his opinion of her? Almost every day carried risks for him, and she couldn't imagine him running from any of them.

He reached out and gently tipped her chin up so he was looking her directly in the eye. "You're the furthest thing from being cowardly. In fact, I think you've been very brave through all of this."

She shook her head in protest. "Are you kidding me? Brave? I'm scared of so many things right now. I'm scared of this guy finding me here. I'm scared that I'll never be the same when all of this is finally over. I'm scared of how it'll affect my practice."

Chase placed his large hands over her clasped smaller ones. "I'd say those are pretty normal fears right now. It doesn't mean you aren't brave."

She stared back at him and gave a small nod. He was right on some level, but she certainly didn't feel brave. "Well, I'm also scared of heights. How about that one?"

"Really?" he asked, still cupping his hands over hers, his thumbs gently grazing hers.

She tried not to be distracted by his simple act of comfort. "Really. Can't stand to be up high. Definitely don't like looking down when I am. It's not like I won't ride elevators or go hiking, but I'd rather just not know exactly how far up I am and how the people down below me resemble ants they're so small."

Chase looked at her with a thoughtful expression. "Then I think I know how this night should end." He let go of her hands to grab his wallet.

Whatever he had in mind was obviously not taking place where they were. She chewed on her lower lip, watching him for any clues as to what he had planned. He wasn't giving anything away though.

"I have no idea what you are thinking, but I'm not sure I like where this is heading," she said.

Thirty minutes later, she was right. Her mouth went dry as she stared up at the flashing lights that spelled out SKYCOASTER in front of them. Chase told her that he'd seen it from the hotel, so it wasn't far from the bar. But it'd taken them half an hour to get there, because they'd driven many roundabouts and side streets to make sure they weren't followed.

"Seriously?" She stared at him, the empty feeling in the pit of her stomach growing larger by the second. Had he lost his ever-loving mind? "I disclose that I'm scared of heights, and you bring me here?" Her voice squeaked on the last word.

Chase hesitated for a moment but didn't back down. "Out of all the things you said you were scared of, I thought this would be the one we could do something about right now," he said, his face earnest. "But it's your choice. We can leave as easily as we came. Well, maybe even a little easier." He gave her a crooked grin. "And I'd still think you're very brave."

Jordan burst out laughing, partly from the irony of his characterization of her, but mostly from her nerves. She watched the couple before them fall from the sky and swing outward. "So, you think falling from—how many feet in the air is this thing?"

"Probably about a hundred feet," he said.

"Falling from one hundred feet will help me with my fear of heights?"

"What would it hurt to try?" he asked.

He had a point.

"You know what this type of intervention you're suggesting is called? It's called flooding. By exposing me to my admittedly unrealistic fear, it's supposed to help me see that nothing bad will happen from being up high so, ultimately, there's no point in being scared. Though, I guess in this case, I'd actually be falling...which could be a little traumatic..." She was purposely trying to mess with him now. She'd already decided that this was something she was going to do. Something that felt right for her now.

Chase studied her closely. "Look, Jordan, like I said before, this is completely your choice. If you want to try it, I'm game to do it with you. If not, then we can find something else that I'm sure will be just as much fun. I did see a miniature golf course a little farther down the road."

He gave her a wink.

Jordan peered up to the top of the tower then back at Chase.

"What do you say?" He was holding out a hand to her.

She grabbed his hand. "I say let's do it!"

Walking up to the ride hand in hand, she felt a little lightheaded. She resisted the urge to turn around and run back to the SUV. Unfortunately, there wasn't anyone ahead of them. They were quickly ushered into an area where they were fitted with the flight suits. Jordan looked down at the suit.

"It kind of reminds me of a pair of overalls." She could hear the rustling of the stiff material every time she moved. "Well, overalls that feel like they were constructed out of a parachute."

"And built for two," he said, waggling his eyebrows at her.

Jordan rolled her eyes at him.

Once the outerwear was secure, the attendants had them both lean forward. She and Chase were now dangling in the suit suspended from a cable tether.

"Okay," one of the attendants said in a jovial voice. "When you're at the top, it'll be 'three, two, one, fly' and your flight will begin!"

A little too enthusiastic for me, Jordan thought as the two attendants headed toward the controls. She felt a tug and they were slowly being lifted into the air. The farther they went up, the more nervous she got. Before long, they were so high that they could see the entire beach city. Thankfully, it was dark outside, so there weren't a lot of people the size of ants to look down upon. Instead, she focused on the city lights and skyline. It was a beautiful sight to behold.

The movement stopped when they'd reached the top.

"Chase" she said, hesitant.

His reply was calm and soothing. "You've got this."

Before she had much more time to think about the next step, the attendant's voice boomed over the PA. "Three, two, one, fly!"

The next thing she knew, they were plummeting through the air. Initially, she didn't detect any tension from the stretchy cable they were suspended from. It was as if they were freefalling the hundred feet down and she'd abandoned her stomach at the top. After a few frightening seconds, the falling sensation dissipated and she was towed forward. The phase of the ride where they'd swing from side to side through the night sky began.

"This is unbelievable!" she said, her heart still racing.

"I hope that's unbelievably good and not bad."

"Unbelievable in the best way."

The ground was getting closer as they gradually dropped back down. She loved feeling the wind blow her hair as they swung back and forth in their descent. Only then did she realize she was holding on to Chase's arm with a viselike grip.

"Sorry," she mumbled, beginning to let go a little.

He used his other hand to hold her hands in place. "It's fine," he said. "That was awesome. You were awesome."

Jordan felt exhilarated as they neared the ground. "Have you ever done anything like this before?"

Chase looked at her thoughtfully, a mixture of longing and admiration on his face. "Nothing quite like this."

The look on his face heated her from head to toe while the words sunk straight into her heart. She was certain she'd felt nothing quite like it either.

The euphoric feeling clung to her for the duration of the ride back to the condo. They pulled into the entrance and she turned to him, her eyes sparkling. "That was a perfect end to this wonderful night. Thank you, Chase, for everything."

"I wouldn't have missed it for the world."

§

As soon as he spoke the words, he realized he meant them. There was nowhere else he'd have rather been than with her on this night. More surprisingly, the realization didn't even shock him.

He guided her through the parking garage and into the condo. Careful to remain on guard, he conducted an exhaustive walk-through of the condo when they entered. There hadn't been anything, so far, to indicate that their guy had discovered their location. But he was leaving nothing to chance.

Once he confirmed that all was fine, Jordan slid out of her sandals and removed her phone from her purse. "Oh, no. The music must've drowned out my cell ringing," she said, reading the notifications on her phone. "I have a couple of missed calls from the office and one from Karen."

"It's probably too late to call now. What do you think?" Chase asked.

Jordan glanced down at her watch, her brows lifting as she saw both hands situated squarely at the top. "Yeah, I'm sure Karen and Mike are asleep by now. I'll try her back in the morning and check in with Nancy. Hopefully, it was nothing important. The last time she called, she only wanted to know what I thought of the place. Well, and to assure me things were going smoothly at the office." She chuckled.

"She knows you too well," he said in a lighthearted manner. The thought struck him that he'd gotten to know her fairly well too, as he immediately understood Jordan's amusement—that the true intent of Karen's call was to assuage Jordan's worry about their practice. And after their experience tonight, he felt even closer to her. "Well, I guess this is goodnight." He moved toward her and lowered his voice. "I'm glad you enjoyed tonight. It was good to see you having fun." He rested a hand on her arm.

"And it was awesome to see you flying through the air."

"More like falling through the air," she said with a grin. Then she looked up at him and her expression became more solemn. "It's something I'll definitely never forget..." She took a hesitant step forward.

He knew he shouldn't, particularly after his statements at the restaurant, but he couldn't help but to pull her close and tuck her up next to him. For a minute, he'd allow himself to get lost in her, absorbing every detail that enticed his senses. He brushed his lips against the top of her head and breathed in the sweet scent that had haunted him since their first kiss. Her silky hair tickled his nose, but he didn't budge. His pulse quickened as he marveled at how they fit together perfectly, each of her curves finding a home against his solid frame. Having her pressed against him was a mixture of torture and bliss. Every one of his nerve endings was on end and uninhibitedly receptive to all that was her. After his minute had more than passed, he knew he had to let her go...for now. Using every bit of willpower that'd taken him years to develop, he wrenched himself back from her.

Looking down, he saw her eyes open slowly, still clouded with desire, and her dark hair tousled from the embrace.

Letting out a deep breath, she nodded her head in understanding. "Goodnight, Chase," she said, her voice husky.

Damn, he didn't want this night to end. He reminded himself that he wanted to do things right with her. The reminder provided only a minuscule amount of relief, while the more primal part of him thought of the numerous ways to do things right with her.

"Night," he said, retreating to his room while he could.

CHAPTER TWELVE

Chase had been sure he'd have had trouble sleeping, but the next morning, he woke up feeling rested and still a little energized from the night before. He threw on a T-shirt and cargo shorts and headed out into the living room. Jordan was already awake and talking on the phone. From the bits of the conversation he heard, he could tell she was briefing Karen on her Skycoaster adventure.

"I really did!" she exclaimed. After a brief pause, she continued. "I know. I couldn't believe it myself. But Karen, it was the best feeling." She looked up to see him standing there. "Oh, Chase just walked in. I'm going to go and see what we're doing for breakfast."

Chase couldn't hear the other side of the conversation, but he saw Jordan's eyes widen.

"I know it does, but it's not like that," she said, turning her back toward him. Her hair was swept up in a messy bun with escaped tendrils drifting around her face. She began to laugh while tucking a loose strand behind her ear.

He wondered what was being said on the other side.

"I promise," she was now saying. "And I'll call the detective back first. Keep your fingers crossed that it's good news."

Chase tried not to be distracted by how beautiful she looked with wisps of coffee-colored hair framing her flushed makeup-free face. "Morning," he said as she set the phone down. "What was that about?"

Before he could clarify that he meant the part about the detective, Jordan turned a deeper shade of red. He suppressed a smile. The woman had no need for cosmetics. She created her own often enough.

"I'm sorry. I didn't mean to pry. I was wondering why you were supposed to call Detective Larson today?" he asked.

"Right," she replied. "Karen said he called the office yesterday, shortly before they closed, looking for me. He didn't say what it was, but Nancy took the call and told him she'd be sure to get the message to me. Of course, she's used to me returning her calls almost as soon as she's finished leaving the voicemail." She turned her eyes skyward. "Last night was definitely an anomaly."

"Maybe they've got a lead on this guy's ID. The last time I spoke with Larson, he said they were subpoenaing the airtime minutes of Rigdon and were going to have him identify the number of the guy who hired him. From there, they would attempt to follow the numbers trail."

"But I thought the guy who hired Rigdon used a throwaway phone?"

"Yeah, he did, but there are a few ways they can still trace it back to a general location. Why don't you call him back now and see what's going on?" He hoped the detective had gotten a break in the case. The jerk didn't deserve to be running free while Jordan was confined to looking over her shoulder every day.

§

Jordan picked her phone back up and dialed Larson. He answered right away. She hit the speaker button so both she and Chase could hear him. "Detective, this is

Jordan Clayton. I received a message that you'd been trying to get in touch with me. Chase Armstrong is also on the line."

"Hello, Jordan, Chase. Yes, I was calling to let you know that we've arrested a suspect in your case. We were able to trace a location from the phone used to call Rigdon and set up the deal. Lucky for us, the suspect left it on, and we were able to isolate a possible residence within a one-block radius. We went ahead and compared the location to forensic cases you were assigned to. Don't worry, only the ones from public records. We found one match—a Mr. Charles Buckman. Interestingly, when we followed up with Keith Lancaster after your call, he'd reported that this same guy was very critical of your work. Keith told us Buckman's comments were the main reason he initially didn't want you assigned to evaluate his father."

Jordan immediately recognized the name as the father in a child-custody dispute she'd been hired to work. It had been a particularly heated case, with allegations of abuse and neglect made from both sides. Ultimately, the judge had used the information gained from the psychological evaluations to render a decision and placed the children in the custody of their mother.

"Yes, I remember the case," she stated.

"Well, turns out the wife had recently filed a restraining order against him following threats that he was going to get his revenge. During our interview, he confessed to hiring Rigdon. Bank records verified five thousand had been withdrawn from his account, just prior to the first pickup date Rigdon reported. Almost everything fits the timeframe perfectly."

Jordan listened without comment. She knew she should feel relieved, but strangely enough, hearing the details only made it more real to her. Putting a face and a name she knew with the man who'd been trying to kill her brought the whole thing home for her.

Bending her head down, she shut her eyes and

covered her face with her hands. It was a lot to process. She was vaguely aware of Chase now standing behind her, his hand resting on her shoulder.

"You still there?" the detective asked.

"Yes," she managed to get out. "It's just a lot to take in."

Chase circled his thumb around her shoulder, gently massaging her tightened muscle while he listened to the discussion. "You said everything almost fits the timeframe perfectly," he interjected. "Is there something that doesn't?"

"Well, he still isn't admitting to trying to run you guys off the road or sending the letter and showing up at the house. But there's little doubt we've got our guy. I think he figured out how much trouble he was in after admitting to the attempted hit and clammed up. Said he wasn't answering anything else without his attorney present."

"Yeah, I can imagine he would," Chase said. "So, he's in custody now?"

Jordan's breath caught at his question. She surely hoped so. Chase was still kneading her shoulder, and she leaned into him to intensify the pressure.

"Oh, yeah. He isn't going anywhere. Arraignment is tomorrow, and the judge will probably withhold bail, given the situation and potential threat to everyone. But I can call and let you know for sure," Larson said.

Jordan found herself feeling a little more grounded with Chase's help. "Thank you, Detective. I appreciate your work on the case. I can't tell you how much of a relief it is to know you've got him in custody."

"No problem. I'm real sorry you've had to go through this. I'll be in touch tomorrow."

"We'll be looking out for your call," she said before hanging up. She let out deep sigh.

Chase turned her around to face him, his eyes emanating concern. "Well, I'll say that definitely qualifies as good news, but I know it's a crappy situation. Are you okay?"

"Yes. No. It is good news. It's just… Is it weird that I still feel… I don't know. It's hard to put into words." She smiled wryly. "I guess I need one of those feeling charts like we use for the kids. The ones where they can touch the face that reflects their emotions."

"Are you still scared?" he asked.

"No, not scared, but vulnerable maybe? Like I've been taking things for granted that aren't really givens." She offered him a questioning gaze, not sure if she was making sense.

"I get it," he said softly. "It changes the way you look at things—but not entirely in a good way," Chase said, raking a hand through his wavy hair.

She nodded slowly. "I think so. I mean, I know what can happen from working with trauma victims, and I've reviewed more police reports than I care to remember, but it's so different to be in the situation myself. There's a part of me that wants to go back to how I saw things before this happened."

He reached out, placing both of his large hands on her forearms, his feet planted squarely in front of her. "It takes time, Jordan. Give yourself that. Things will get easier."

She nodded. He was looking at her with an intensity that made her feel like he was speaking from his experience. Given his life experiences, he probably was. She thought back to their earlier conversation. He'd said that he'd made a mistake when he'd been protecting someone. What had he meant? She wondered if he'd ever share the details with her.

Chase let his hands fall back to his sides, and she tried to concentrate on the present.

"So, what happens next?" she asked, pinning him with her stare. She'd directed the conversation into rough waters. Her emotions were raw, and any control she had was precarious. Dealing with whatever she and Chase shared now might be more than she could bear. But she couldn't seem to stop herself.

He rubbed the back of his neck. "Well, I'm not going anywhere until we hear from Detective Larson tomorrow," he said in a firm tone. "If the judge denies bail, this guy won't be getting out any time soon. With a felony conviction, he'll be in prison for years."

"And after tomorrow?" Jordan tried to pose the question casually, but her heart was in her throat as she waited for him to reply.

Her feelings weren't one-sided. She was certain of that. Though at the beginning she'd had her doubts, his attraction to her was readily apparent now that she knew him better. It was his entire reason for holding back that she wasn't sure of. If this guy was held behind bars tomorrow, Chase wouldn't be her bodyguard anymore. There'd be no more conflict of interests. His job wasn't well suited to a long-term relationship; nevertheless, she was willing to give it a try if he was. But a relationship with her had to be something he wanted as much as she did.

Chase looked past her for a moment and then met her questioning gaze. "Let's cross that bridge when we come to it. If this guy Buckman isn't a threat anymore, I'll probably head back to Orlando tomorrow. There are some things I've been putting off in the business that I need to get to."

Jordan crossed her arms in front of her. The hurt was likely reflected on her face, but she tried to mask it as much as she could.

Chase's eyes softened, and he grasped her waist, pulling her closer to him. His voice was earnest. "Look, Jordan. I have a feeling there may be no going back with you. So when we move forward, I don't think I'm going to want anything to stop it."

"What does that mean?" She looked at him with uncertainty. She was being direct, but she'd rather know than not.

"It means—" he raised his eyebrows, "—let's wait until we know for sure that this guy doesn't, by some chance, get out tomorrow. Because if he does—and I'm not trying to worry you, but it's my job to stay prepared—I'll be here, making sure you stay safe."

And then it clicked for her. He wasn't going to begin something before he was sure she wasn't still in danger from this guy. Whatever had happened in the past, the mistake he was referring to, must have been pretty awful for him. Part of her wanted to tell him to just let go. She trusted him and wasn't worried he'd repeat mistakes of the past. The other part of her felt grateful that he was so intent on keeping her out of harm's way, and she admired his refusal to do anything he thought might compromise that.

She let out a breath she hadn't realized she was holding. "And I thought I could be stubborn when I wanted to be," she said with resignation.

A slow smile spread across his face. "I prefer to call it determined...or maybe persistent. Unwavering?"

"You'd better stop now. I thought 'stubborn' was putting it nicely." She gave him the smile he was searching for. "You may not want to hear my alternative descriptors." She tried to ignore the fact that he still hadn't let go of her waist and was now using his thumb to trace small circles around her abdomen. Spirals of heat coiled from each ring.

The man was going to drive her nuts.

"Ouch," he said. "You don't think that was a little below the belt?"

Her eyes unconsciously drifted downward as if the answer to his question lay literally below his tapered waistline. She admired the view. His sculpted quad muscles expanded out from the edges of his shorts, leading down to equally toned calves. How he kept muscles like that and hadn't been to the gym once since he'd worked for her, she had no idea.

Catching herself in the middle of her impromptu excursion, she redirected her gaze back up in time to catch Chase's eyebrows shoot upward. The circling motion came to an abrupt halt. His look was equivalent to the one Coyote gave the Roadrunner when he actually caught him.

Her face had to be glowing crimson because even her ears were heating up. Still, she had to work at stifling her laughter at his nonplussed reaction to her unintended faux pas.

He swallowed. "Okay, I'm completely at a loss for words now."

Though a small part of her wanted to revel in the fact that she'd turned the tables on him, she knew better than to bait him. It'd be different if she was able to resist him, but with the strong level of attraction between them, she knew she'd be caught in her own net. Deciding the sensible thing to do was change the subject, she asked, "So then, with one more day in paradise, what should we do?"

Chase cleared his throat. "I think it's safe to say that I'm not sharing your line of thought just yet, so I'll let you choose," he said, his voice still strained.

"You know, you kind of had that coming." One corner of her mouth lifted slightly. "But if I get to pick, then there's no question—let's hit the beach." She twisted out of his grasp and left the maddening sensation of his fingers on her stomach behind. "Meet you back here in five."

§

Chase shook his head as she left. She was definitely something else. If someone had asked him if he'd consider removing himself from protection detail a month ago, he probably wouldn't have seriously considered the option. Though he'd put in more years in the field than he cared to count, he hadn't been sure he was ready to give up the sense of purpose that came with every new detail. But his perspective had changed since meeting Jordan.

With her, there was an excitement that rivaled anything he'd ever felt on the job. It was more than purely a physical attraction. He loved the way her mind worked, watching her experience new things, the bravery she demonstrated in the face of danger, her values, and how she genuinely cared about others. Being with her brought back a part of himself he'd thought he'd lost when the governor had died. He wasn't certain how he could make it all work, but he was damn sure he wasn't walking away from her tomorrow.

The warm Florida sun was beating down on them less than an hour later. They'd staked claim to a couple of lounge chairs and put a cooler filled with drinks in the sand in between them. He'd intended to relax and enjoy the beach now that their guy was in custody, but the torment from earlier only continued as Jordan slathered sunscreen all over her body, which was now glistening in the reflection of the sun. He tried to avert his eyes and lead his thoughts elsewhere. Maintaining his resolve to wait until tomorrow to pursue a romantic relationship with her might be the toughest exercise he'd ever endeavored—and considering the things he'd done, that was saying a lot.

She rubbed the lotion up the tops of her toned thighs, and his pulse quickened. With each breath, he took in the coconut scent wafting over to him as the lotion warmed on her svelte form.

"Can I borrow that sunscreen?" Chase said in a cantankerous tone. *Seriously? Who needs that much sunscreen?*

Jordan slanted her eyes his way while scooting around on the beach chaise to either get comfortable or continue to torture him. Given her actions earlier, he couldn't be sure at this point, but the effect was the same nonetheless. "Sure. All you had to do was ask. No need to get impatient," she chided him.

She leaned over to hand him the sunscreen. Yes, she was either teasing him again or unaware of how incredibly sexy she looked in her modest two-piece swimsuit. Thankfully, her voice interrupted this internal debate before his thoughts became painfully obvious.

"Other than work, do you get away to places like this much?" she asked, now stretched out with her long legs extended. Her eyes were closed behind her oversized sunglasses. It looked like she was having no trouble at all relaxing.

He began applying his own sunscreen and distracted himself with her question. "Not really. Not anymore, at least. When I was young, my family usually ended up on some coastline or another for our annual vacations. Those were fun times. My sister and I seemed to get ourselves into these crazy situations." His lips twitched as he finished the sentence.

She turned her head toward him. "Okay, spill it. I can only imagine the stuff you must've done as a kid."

He shrugged. "We never meant to cause trouble, but put two kids with very active imaginations together and my poor parents trying to catch a few minutes of alone time— ugh, the things we put them through." The memories had him shaking his head. "I remember one time we were in the British Virgin Islands on this beautiful little island. There were these land hermit crabs everywhere, running around in these amazing shells that we'd only seen sold in stores before. Well, it didn't take us long to decide that we had to take some home with us to keep as pets. So before we left for the airport, we put them in our pockets along with some wet food. You know, in case they got hungry."

"Oh my—what were you thinking?" Jordan covered her mouth with her hand.

"That they'd make awesome pets," he said, eyes crinkling at the corners as he suppressed a grin. "We were still in elementary school, so not a lot of forethought into the many holes in our plan."

"What happened next?" Her voice was animated and she sat up straight in the lounge chair.

He let out a chuckle before continuing on. "We ended up being at the airport late at night. Emily, my sister, and I both fell fast asleep before the plane arrived. The next thing I knew, we woke up to another passenger screaming and flailing about on top of her chair. The little guys had crawled out while we slept, and one had made its way into her skirt."

Jordan was laughing uncontrollably now. She flipped her sunglasses onto her head so she could wipe the tears out of the corners of her eyes. Finally, she stopped herself for long enough to respond. "How did your parents find out it was you two?"

"That's the worst part. They didn't even ask. They just knew. We had to apologize and then gather them up so they could be returned back to their home on the island. Luckily, back then airport security wasn't like it is now, so we had no trouble getting a tour guide to bring them back."

"Your poor parents! I'm sure you were an adorable kid at that age, but I can't imagine the passenger was very forgiving."

"Not at all. She finally calmed down once the little critters were taken away, though she sat as far away from us on the plane as she could. Looking back, I don't blame her at all. I probably would've reacted the same way if I'd discovered those tiny claws moving up my leg too. But back then, we were just despondent to lose our new friends. Had named them and everything—Fred, Barnie, Wilma and the Hulk, for obvious reasons, as he had an awesome claw and some type of green algae growing on his shell."

"Obviously, he'd be the Hulk and not Wilma," she said, clearly still amused.

"Totally." He reached over and ruffled her hair. "Yeah, those are times I'll never forget."

"Where are they now? Your family, I mean. Not the hermit crabs," she said with a smirk. "Do you live close to them?"

"My mom lives in Brandenton. Not too far away—though I'm rarely home for long, so I don't get down there as often as I'd like to. My dad passed away several years ago. It was unexpected—a heart attack. Living without him has been a difficult adjustment for her. She's doing okay now, but I know she wishes she saw my sister and me more."

Jordan shot him a sympathetic look and lightly stroked his forearm. "I'm sorry to hear that about your dad. I can't imagine losing someone so close to you in such an abrupt way. I've worked with clients who are grieving, so I can empathize, but I don't even pretend like I can fathom that kind of pain."

Chase placed his hand on top of her and drew in a long breath. Her comment reminded him of exactly how much loss he'd confronted over the last several years. "I don't think it gets any easier to lose someone you care about. You'd think the body would somehow reach a cap on how much grief you can handle at once."

"What do you mean?" she asked, her eyebrow raised.

Chase made no move to let her hand go. "Oh, I don't know. It just seems like there's only so much grief one person should be able to process in a given amount of time. But instead, when people you care about die close together, it seems that rather than getting better at coping, you get exponentially worse at handling it. Or I guess I do…" His voice drifted off as he spoke and a heaviness settled in his chest as the memory assaulted him.

"Who else did you lose?"

He knew she'd ask. It was the question hanging in the air after his confession. Maybe on some level, he'd meant to go there, but he was still surprised at his admission. He hadn't ever opened up to anyone about Robert. Even Mike, who he considered one of his closest friends, knew very little of the details surrounding his death. And most of what his friend knew, he'd learned from media reports.

Letting go of her hand, he hesitated for a split second, and then dove in before he couldn't. "Do you remember about five years ago when the Lieutenant Governor got shot?"

She looked at him inquisitively. "Do you mean Robert Gallagher?" she asked, her brow furrowed.

"I was protecting him at the time." Chase looked down as he told her, digging his hand into the sand and pulling up a fistful. Even to this day, it was hard for him to admit that. He felt like such an idiot. "I was still with the state patrol and the assignment was part of my job. Worse, it became my only job, and I still let it happen…" The familiar sensation of being detached as he spoke swept over him, and he watched the sand slip through the cracks of his fingers.

Jordan began to gently rub his arm again, but he didn't look at her, instead focusing on the ocean waves crashing in front of them. The sun went behind a group of fast-moving clouds and the water took on a dark bluish-black hue without the light from above. The murky transformation seemed to coincide with his revelation, as if even Mother Earth was aware of the reprehensible offense.

"Chase, you didn't let it happen. I don't know everything about what happened, but there was a lot of news coverage. It was a domestic dispute, and he was right in the middle of it. No one blamed you for his death." Despite the adamancy with which she spoke, her voice was calm and soothing.

"I blame me…and rightly so." He uttered the words with certainty. "Every day, I think about what I could have done differently. I was too close to him to be objective anymore. Even though I knew better, we got to be friends…more than that, he was like a brother to me." Chase shut his eyes, but it did nothing to block out the memory of that night or the fact that Robert was gone.

"How did it happen?" Her voice was so soft that it was almost a whisper, barely audible over the cries of the seagulls circling the water's edge.

"That's the thing. It was like any other night for him. He'd been single for about two years. His wife passed away in a car accident. She was five months pregnant with his son. He was never serious with anyone after that. On the outside, he seemed to like it that way, said being tied down wasn't his thing. I think he was too scared to love someone that way again…but he'd date several women regularly when he was traveling in to their area."

He paused briefly, hoping she'd get the picture regarding Robert's philandering ways without him saying it out loud. Comprehension registered on her face.

"That night, he was seeing a woman he'd met a few weeks before in Miami. She was a lawyer, very beautiful and, come to find out, very married. He didn't know it at the time. He enjoyed the nightlife, but married women weren't for him—for the obvious personal reasons, and he'd never let down the people who'd voted for him like that." He spoke forcefully. That had been something the media had gotten all wrong, and the attacks on Robert's character had made him feel even more guilt at the time. "They were having dinner at the hotel where we were all staying. The rest of the team and I were at another table close by. Around midnight, he motioned me over and told me we were done for the night. I tried to tell him it was no problem—to at least let us escort them to his room, where he wouldn't be in public. But the restaurant was virtually empty, and he didn't think he was in any danger. They were enjoying the pianist and a good bottle of Cabernet. After we left, her husband got there. He had a gun. Shot them both, and then himself. It was over in less than a minute." He laid his head in his hand.

"Chase, I'm so sorry that happened. I had no idea you were protecting him then. Mike never told me. But…" She stopped talking and moved in front of him on the edge of his chaise, looking him directly in the eye. "It still doesn't make you at fault."

His head flinched back slightly. She couldn't possibly believe what she was saying.

"How can you think that? It was my job to keep him safe—to keep him alive. He never even had a chance to get over her death…to move on…to run for governor. It was all taken from him," he said with bitterness.

"Don't you think he'd want to the same things for you? For you to be able to move on from his death…to live life without feeling guilty?" The wind had picked up and her hair was blowing back from her face, accentuating her eyes, which were filled with concern.

"You're right. I know he would," he admitted with reluctance. "I think I just feel like I don't deserve to sometimes…or that if I do, it might happen again. I know it's illogical, but every person I'm able to protect feels like one more person who stayed safe. That I'm actually doing some good or making up for what I didn't do before, because I was too caught up in listening to him as a friend."

Jordan seemed to be searching for the right words before she spoke. He could see her hesitation. "What would you have done differently?" she asked.

"You mean if I could go back to that night?" God, he couldn't tell her how many times he'd asked himself that same question and thought of ways to change the outcome.

She shook her head. "No, I mean if you hadn't become friends with him. What would you have done differently if he was solely another person you were protecting?"

"I would've told him either we stayed or he needed to go to his hotel room or somewhere more secure. I wouldn't have asked for his input or really cared about it."

"And do you think that would have worked? You knew him pretty well. How would he have reacted to an ultimatum?"

Chase saw her point. Mike had said the same thing in

as many words. But the truth resonated more clearly here with her. Maybe because she was the only one he'd let pry through the solid wall around his heart and he knew she wouldn't run from what she uncovered behind it.

"He would've been pissed. He didn't like to feel limited in what he could or couldn't do. It was why he sometimes chose to walk a mile through a main street in town surrounded by citizens, rather than to ride in the limo with the motorcade. It literally drove us all crazy as we scrambled to isolate potential threats on the route at the last minute, but at the same time, there was a certain respect that went with it. I admired that part of him on a personal level as much as I despised it as a professional."

She tucked a stray lock of hair behind her ear in an attempt to keep it from flying into her face as the wind changed. "So I think it's safe to say he wanted some privacy in the restaurant to enjoy his night, and he probably wouldn't have had it any other way, friendship or no friendship. To be honest, it sounds like he actually considered your request more than he might have normally, because at least he stayed in an area where he thought he was sheltered from the outside world."

He didn't say anything for a long time, realizing that he was more at peace with what had happened than he'd ever been. As his eyes met hers, he felt freer. Every step he'd taken since that day, every action, had been influenced by his feelings of guilt and regret. Now, his perspective was different. It had still happened; that would never leave him. But he no longer took sole responsibility for the loss.

"Thank you, Jordan. I'm not sure how or why I got into this, but it helped." The words were inadequate, but he didn't try to elaborate. He knew she'd get it.

She pulled him into a hug. "I'm glad," she murmured into his chest. "Client or not, I'm not sure we would ever be able to move forward if you hadn't let me into this part of your past."

Chase savored the feel of holding her in his arms. There was this connection between them that gained strength, not just when things were good, but during times like this, too—when he feared that the bond would diminish instead. And he had no doubts that what she'd said was true.

"Chase?"

"Hmmm?" he answered back, still not ready for words.

"I think we'd better head up now. It looks like the sky is about to open up on us."

Noticing the dark skies, he realized the storm must've been brewing for a while. The seagulls were lined up in a row along the waterfront, and cool winds blew sand across the small dunes in front of the condo's main deck. He reluctantly let her go.

She gave him a quick smile then rushed to gather up their things.

"You're right. It's moving in fast." The first few large drops of rain hit his shoulders.

He grabbed the cooler and her bag, but before they made it off the sand, the rain was coming down in sheets. Jordan scrambled up the stairs in front of him, clinging to an inflated lounge float that was aspiring to be a kite. The white cover-up she wore had become transparent, and her hair was plastered to her back. Even now—especially now—she took his breath away.

With his role as her bodyguard scheduled to end tomorrow, he could hardly wait to show her how much.

CHAPTER THIRTEEN

By the time they got to the elevator, there wasn't a dry spot on either one of them. Jordan looked at him through the beads of water stuck to her eyelashes and stated the obvious. "We're soaked!" She couldn't help smiling, even as the rain streamed down her face so heavily that she could taste it on her tongue.

Chase mashed the elevator button and then relieved her of the water float she'd managed to hold on to. "Gotta love Florida storms," he said. "We probably should've just stayed down there. They're gone in about the same amount of time it takes them to come in. By the time this elevator makes it to our floor, we'll probably be walking in to a sunny view from the balcony."

Jordan gazed over at him and couldn't help noticing that while she probably resembled a drowned rat, drenched looked pretty good on him. His hair was a mass of sexy, wet waves, and the shadow around his jawline emphasized his stormy green eyes. Her heart picked up speed as her eyes shifted downward. Droplets of water glistened off his sculpted chest, creating a trail of water that leisurely arched its way toward his chiseled abs.

The ding of the elevator ripped her from her

exploration of his body before she wound up in an impromptu reenactment of her earlier indiscretion. A good thing, too. There was no point in revisiting the same issue again. Hearing his account of what had happened with the governor today had shed light on why he'd put up the barriers he had. She wasn't sure of how much of their interactions had been impacted by his past, but she was certain they had been. After their talk, she understood why.

"Oh, well. Maybe the storm was a good thing. I may not have been able to leave that lounge chair otherwise. It's so relaxing here. I'm not sure I'm ready to go back to reality now that I've finally gotten away," she said, her tone wistful.

Chase nodded, sending an unruly, wet curl across his forehead. "I know what you mean. No wonder Mike and Karen escape to this place every time they get the chance. You and I both need to learn a thing or two from them."

"I think I already have. Well, from this whole thing in general," she mused. "I love what I do, but this has changed my perspective. I'm going to work much harder at keeping things balanced. If things hadn't gone the way they did…" She shuddered at the thought of how differently things could've turned out.

"I know." He placed a reassuring hand on her back. "And you're right. Sounds like a good new perspective to have."

Chase didn't remove his hand as they walked down the hall, and she marveled at how natural it felt. Somehow, something unexpected and extraordinary had come out of this horrible ordeal. No matter what happened tomorrow, she knew she'd always remember that.

She and Chase spent a relatively quiet night watching a movie, and then they turned in early. Yet once she was in bed, she didn't feel tired anymore She tossed and turned throughout the night. Despite trying to tell herself the worst was behind her, she worried that Charles Buckman would be released today. She mulled over possibilities in her head with new ones springing up, just as she finished refuting another. When she awoke to the sun streaming through the glass doors to the balcony, she felt like she'd scarcely fallen asleep.

She grabbed her robe and wandered out into the kitchen in search of caffeine. Lucky for her, Chase was awake and fresh coffee awaited. "Oh, thank you," she murmured in appreciation as he handed her a mug. The steam curled into the air and she gingerly sat down at the table.

"You're up earlier than normal," Chase commented.

"I'm not sure I'm officially awake yet," she said, her mind still foggy from the lack of sleep. "Slept terribly last night worrying about the news today." Even in her fatigued state, she observed Chase bristle in response to her remarks. "What is it?" she asked.

"Nothing," he said, lifting his own mug to his lips.

She raised her eyebrow. There was obviously something bothering him.

After a moment of silence, he set his mug back down and met her eyes. "I mean, nothing you did. It still makes me mad that this creep put you through all of this," he said, his tone forceful. "The sad part is I'm sure he's telling himself he's justified in getting revenge based on the biased report you gave, when his very actions support the conclusions you offered. Irony at its best."

Jordan's heart melted a little at his statement. He was being defensive of her. "I won't argue with you on that. But it comes with the territory," she said, her voice soft. "I've just never had it happen to this extreme, and hopefully, never will again, though it's common knowledge that custody cases can be risky for the professionals involved. If you would've asked me to speculate when this all first started, a custody case would have been one of my top guesses."

"Did you tell that to the detective?" Chase asked.

"Yes, but the problem remained that it wasn't a definite—merely a hunch based on statistics. They didn't want to rule anything out and take a chance on overlooking the real culprit, so they examined all of my cases that were public record. Fortunately, they didn't have to go any further than that." She took another sip from the mug in front of her. "So, what time do you think we'll know something?"

Chase glanced at the clock. "If the arraignment is scheduled for this morning, it won't take long for Larson to get back to us, particularly given that they're on Eastern time, so they're an hour ahead. But we still have a while, seeing as how we're both up early."

Jordan wondered what had gotten him up. He didn't seem overly concerned that Buckman would be let out on bail today. So she doubted he'd lost sleep over the arraignment set for today. Could he have been thinking about the potential change in their relationship? Her heart beat rapidly as she considered this. She was more than ready to have that discussion with him. Good or bad, she was tired of ignoring what was right in front of them. At least it would only be a couple of hours longer.

Chase put his hands on the table and pushed his chair back. "What do you say we go have breakfast somewhere? It'll pass the time. Not to mention—" he gave her a smirk, "—that I can hear your stomach complaining from here."

As if to substantiate his statement, her stomach chose that moment to let out a loud grumble. Her cheeks warmed and she flung a hand over her abdomen in a useless attempt to stifle the sound. "Okay, I think it's safe to say that my stomach seconds your idea. Let me get dressed and we'll get going."

They found a small coffee shop not far from the condo and joined the line of patrons. The aroma of freshly baked pastries and bacon filled the air, making her mouth water. Within a few minutes, they were escorted to an empty booth and handed menus before the hostess bustled back toward the entrance.

"Ooooh, listen to this!" Jordan exclaimed, reading the specials from a table card. "Coconut-crusted French toast topped with a caramel and chocolate drizzle and strawberries. Doesn't that sound amazing?"

Chase chuckled. "You are easy to please, aren't you?"

"Easy to please, huh?" she said, a grin spreading across her face. "I guess you've found one of my weaknesses. Give me good food, and I'm not going anywhere."

"That said, I may have to take you back to Orlando while you're sleeping then, since you seem to have fallen for all the cuisine we've had while we've been here." His mouth was in a straight line, but the curves of his lips rose slightly to betray his amusement. "Lucky for me, I know you sleep like a hibernating bear, so it shouldn't be a problem."

Ugh. He was never going to let her live that one down. "First you tell me I'm easy, and now I'm a bear. Which is it?" She bit her lower lip to hide her own amusement. She was sure if anyone overheard them, they'd sound ridiculous. But Chase made being silly fun and even more oddly, he made her funny, at least to him. While striving to work harder and more efficiently, she hadn't taken time to be so carefree. And now, it was akin to hearing an old song that made her want to dance—the awesome light-hearted feeling she got always made her wonder why she'd never replayed the song long before.

"Oh, you're not being fair now. I said easy *to please*, and well—" his eyes twinkled, "—the bear reference is actually pretty accurate."

"You're incorrigible," she said, though the rebuke had no impact as she was unable to stifle the grin forming on her lips. "And besides—" she leaned forward conspiratorially, "—it's in your own best interest to remember I'm an elephant."

A waitress approached, thwarting any witty comeback Chase might have offered, which was a good thing, because leaning in so close to him had made her impish remark backfire, with the heat turned back on her. The man had the sex appeal thing down. She couldn't get within inches of him without feeling like there was too much distance between them.

The waitress greeted them with her pen poised, ready to take their orders.

She struggled to remember what she was going to ask her about. Fortunately, her eyes fell on the picture on the menu in front of her. "How is the coconut-crusted French toast?"

"It's very good. One of my favorites. It is a larger portion though—are you two sharing?" she asked, pointing her pen at each of them as she spoke.

"She doesn't share her food," Chase deadpanned. "Storing it away so she can hibernate maybe?"

Jordan coughed on the sip of ice water she'd swallowed to cool down.

The waitress looked baffled.

"Scratch that," he went on, undeterred. "I've been forewarned—" the corners of his mouth twitched, "—that I should remember it's for the dry season." He relaxed back in his seat.

Jordan's mouth gaped open. In her periphery, she saw the waitress hide a snicker behind her order pad.

Chase titled his head and gave her an amused expression. "It's the season of low rainfall." He raised his eyebrows. "You know, when food is scarce and the matriarch elephant uses her superb memory to guide her herd to water."

Good Lord. Maybe this is why she never replayed the song. At least not publicly. She turned to the waitress, a flush across her cheeks. "I'm so sorry. He's just kidding." She shot Chase a look of reproach from across the table.

174

The waitress either found him humorous or needed to get to her next table, because she began to play along. "You keep that up—" she turned to Chase, "—and the dry season might arrive before you know it."

Chase met Jordan's stony stare with a restrained grin. "I think you might be right."

"So, before you get in any more trouble, what'll you be having this morning?" the waitress asked as she removed the laminated menus they'd placed to the side and put them back in her apron.

"I'll have a couple of eggs and a side of bacon with wheat toast."

"How do you want those eggs cooked?" she asked, staring down as she scribbled out the order.

"Over *easy* will be great," he said, emphasizing the word easy and flashing Jordan a heated grin.

Her face began warming up again and she kicked him lightly under the table.

The waitress paused over her pad to look back and forth between the two of them. "I had a feeling it wouldn't take you long to get into trouble again," she said with a knowing expression. Before she turned to leave, she leaned over and whispered to Jordan, "He's clearly trouble, but you two are cute together and the way he looks at you…" She fanned herself with her notepad. "He's not too hard on the eyes, either." She winked as she left the table.

Chase had the gall to look chagrined now. "Hey, what was that all about? Are you two conspiring now?"

"Wouldn't you like to know," she teased him. But inwardly she considered the waitress's remarks.

It wasn't the first time a woman had noticed his good looks. He frequently received appreciative glances when they were out. The attention didn't bother her. She was sure she'd look twice if she noticed him out somewhere.

What did cause her pause was that the waitress assumed they were already a couple. Many times, she felt like they were as well. She only hoped things worked out so they genuinely could be after today. Chase had been trying to avoid any romantic entanglements while he was working for her. But though they'd avoided becoming physically intimate, in her heart, she knew they'd connected on a level much deeper than that.

Thoughts of today reminded her of what she'd been meaning to discuss with him. "I've been thinking about staying here through the weekend before heading back…" She fiddled with the fork in front of her as she broached the subject. "Well, as long as everything goes okay at the arraignment today. I know you said you had to head back right away, so I thought I might rent a car for my return trip."

Chase stared at her with a blank expression. "You want to stay here?" he asked, raising an eyebrow.

"Only through Sunday. I really like it here, and I feel like I need some time after all of this is over to try to regroup. I'm not sure I'm ready to head back to where it happened right away," she said, her voice soft. "Plus, I know if I go back now, no matter how much I try to avoid it, I'll end up back at the office playing catch-up. So before I go there, I want to take a few days to process everything." She tried to gauge his reaction to her announcement, but he didn't give her any indication one way or the other. "Does that make sense?"

He stared past her for a moment, then returned his attention to her. "It makes sense. It'll be hard to leave here without you, but I understand the need to process everything before going back. At least, I do now. Hanging out with you twenty-four-seven may have rubbed off on me a bit." He grasped her hand, gently rubbing his thumb across her knuckles.

"I'm glad you get it." She gave him a small smile. "See, hanging out with me has its benefits." Tilting her head to the side, she added, "But if you start using words like 'increased insight' in the right context, I may have to offer you a job."

Chase shook his head. "I've still got a lot to learn about your world. I won't quit the day job just yet. At least, not in exchange for another one." He winked at her, but then he became serious again. "I'll book you a car. I already have accounts with different rental companies, so it won't be a problem. I can have it delivered to the condo..." He paused before continuing on. "Again, as long as everything goes as planned today. I won't leave here until that's a given."

"I appreciate that. And this," she said, motioning around the room.

"Food again, huh? Jordan, I promise I'll never let you starve."

"No." Jordan laughed. She'd probably laughed more on this trip with him than in the entire past year. "I mean this trip. Coming here with me. I know it's part of your job and you do it a lot, but I want you to know that what you do is awesome." She searched for the right words to express her gratitude. "You took on all of this risk to make sure I'm safe. I don't know how to say thank you for that."

Chase swallowed. "You just did. Nothing else is needed." He looked at her with an expression Jordan couldn't really read. "I'm just glad it was me."

When his eyes found hers, she felt like the only person in the restaurant.

"Me too," she whispered.

He squeezed her hand, and her stomach flipped in response. This time, she knew it wasn't nerves about the upcoming call.

After breakfast, they headed back to the condo. She looked through a magazine while Chase worked from his computer. The rolling in her stomach got worse as it got later in the morning. The detective would be calling soon. She took a few deep breaths and tried to focus on the moment. *Worrying won't change the outcome,* she thought.

A knock at the door caused her to jump.

Chase looked at her. "Were you expecting anyone?" he asked, already getting up from the table. He had his gun holstered on his side, his hand resting on the handle.

"No. No one except the office crew knows I'm even here," she answered quickly, her mouth dry.

"Okay. Why don't you go into the bedroom. I'll check the door."

She didn't waste any time following his directions.

This reminded her of the time they'd ordered Chinese takeout. Only she felt like a different person now. The gun he held no longer made her apprehensive, and she didn't hesitate to get out of the way so he could do his job. No matter how she tried to couch it, her sense of security would never be the same after this.

Chase checked the peephole as she left the room. "Who is it?" he yelled.

"Flower delivery," a voice responded from the other side of the door.

"Do you know who they're from?" Chase still didn't open the door.

"No, sir. Didn't take the order. There's a card attached."

"Okay. Can you leave them at the door? I'll be out to get them in a sec." Chase's request was a command rather than a question.

"Sure. No problem."

If the man thought the whole scenario odd, he didn't comment on it. Jordan racked her mind trying to figure out who might have sent flowers. Other than Karen, Mike, and Derek, the only person who knew she was here was Chase. And it was pretty obvious the flowers weren't from him. She heard the door open and close.

"Okay. Coast is clear!" Chase shouted out to her.

She made her way out of the bedroom and was greeted by Chase holding a vase filled with a bouquet of colorful roses. He set them on the table and handed her the card that'd been secured in the middle of them.

Jordan slowly took the card. Her heart raced. The flowers were beautiful, but until she knew who'd sent the arrangement, she was wary of the message that came with them. Opening the card with shaky hands, a feeling of relief washed over her as soon as she saw Karen's name in the signature line.

Dear Jordan,
Just wanted to let you know that we're thinking of you. The office hasn't been the same without you here. Mike and I are hoping that even though this wasn't a welcome vacation, you're able to find some moments to enjoy the coast. Now that you've discovered how cool our home away from home is, we expect you to come with us on our next visit!
Love you and miss you,
Karen, Mike, & Derek
P.S. Derek said to tell you things are pretty dull here without you, so you'd better get back to O-town as soon as possible.

As she finished reading, she let out a breath she hadn't realized she'd been holding. "They're from Karen, Mike, and Derek." She handed him the card to read. "Here you go. There's a message for you at the bottom."

Chase read it over and handed it back to her. "It sounds like you're missed in Orlando." He rubbed the back of his neck. "But I wish they'd let me know they were sending flowers. For a minute there, I was a little worried too."

Before she could reply, Jordan recognized the familiar tune of her cell phone ringing. In the midst of checking out the delivery, she'd forgotten about the upcoming call. She ran back to the couch and grabbed it from the coffee table.

"It's Detective Larson," she told Chase after checking the call screen. She accepted the call and put it on speaker. "Hello, Detective," she said, trying to project a calmness she didn't feel. "Chase and I are both here." She rubbed her sweaty palms down the front of her shorts and said a silent prayer that he hadn't been released.

"Well, I've got good news for you. The judge denied bail. Seemed he was a flight risk. Our guy isn't going anywhere. He'll be at the jail until the trial. On top of that, the prosecutor said the case for solicitation to commit first-degree murder is solid with the evidence that's been gathered."

Jordan's shoulders sagged, and she sighed in relief. "Thank you very much. I appreciate your work and the phone call. I can't tell you how much better I feel knowing he's not out there anymore."

"I know. I'm sorry it took us as long as it did, but unfortunately, these things take time." He sounded apologetic.

"I understand," she said. "It's a solid case though, and that's what's important now."

"Oh, yeah. This guy shouldn't be threatening anyone else any time soon. On top of the confession and bank records, we subpoenaed his credit card statements and found a recent purchase from Office Depot. Number ten store-brand envelopes—an exact match to the envelope the letter was mailed to you in. Purchase was made two days before the postmark, and the mail handling facility coincided with his address."

"So it's all coming together?" Chase clarified.

The detective grunted. "I'll say. It's good when it works out like this. Everyone can breathe easier."

"Second that." Chase bid him good day.

"Good day to you both as well."

Jordan turned to Chase after she'd hung up. "Well, that's the news we were hoping for." She smiled hesitantly at him.

"I'd say so," he agreed, watching her closely. "Somehow, I sense you aren't as comforted by Larson's call as you thought you would be."

"Oh, I am. Don't get me wrong. That is what I

needed to hear. It's just...there's a part of me that still feels guarded. I know it's because I didn't worry about things like this before and now...now, I might always worry about something like this happening again. I'm less naïve, I guess. Or maybe I truly realize how precious life is. This experience has changed me," she said, looking at him. "In more ways than one."

Chase moved toward her and gently drew her to him. She relished in the feel of his muscular arms wrapped around her. He made her feel safe and reckless all at the same time. Her breathing accelerated at his closeness, and all thoughts of the hearing and phone call were replaced by heated desire and longing. She wasn't about to take things further though. This was his call.

§

Pulling her close to him was like putting milkweed in front of a butterfly. The difference now was there was nothing holding him back. He unwillingly let her go and retreated a step.

"You need to fire me right now," he said hoarsely, his eyes burning into hers.

"What?" she asked, caught off guard. Her eyebrows furrowed. "Why would I do that?"

"Jordan, for once, could you do it without asking questions?" he pleaded, only half joking.

She chewed her bottom lip. "Okay, Chase. You're fired," she said in an uncertain tone. "Now, why did I just do that?"

He pulled her even closer this time. "So I can do this." His lips crashed into hers.

He explored the depths of her mouth with an urgency fed by a longing so fierce that it almost consumed him. He knew there was chemistry between them. There was no doubt about that. It was what had made being near her pure torture at times. Trying to do his job and resist what had quickly become the most incredible distraction he could ever envision had almost driven him crazy. But he could only thank his lucky stars that he hadn't given in to his hunger, because kissing her now lit an uncontainable fire within him.

An innate need to feel and taste her drove his passion. He moved his mouth down the delicate column of her neck, his lips caressing the sensitive area with each tiny descent. Her breath was raspy, and he could feel the erratic beating of her pulse beneath his lips.

He lifted his head to recapture her mouth with his, deepening the kiss, while his hands traced down her sides along her ribs, settling just above her hip bones. Her fingers were splayed across his back, pressing along the ridges of his corded muscles as she scraped his bottom lip with her teeth. He barely took time out to breathe. Who needed air?

Wanting to touch every part of her, he moved a hand up the front of her shirt, and she arched into him in response. He ran his fingers under the lacy edge of her bra, making a low moan of pleasure escape from her lips. That was all it took. Heat raged through him and he tore her shirt over her head. She immediately pressed her mouth back to his with the same urgency he felt.

Abruptly, she pulled back, her eyes clouded with desire. "Not fair," she said in throaty whisper. Without breaking eye contact, she grabbed both sides of his shirt, and it followed the same path as hers. Her fingers slid down his bare chest making his breath catch in his throat.

Crushing his lips back to hers, he lifted her up and settled her on his hips. She wrapped her legs securely around his waist. The heat radiating from her caused his entire body to throb. Using one hand to hold her close, he undid the clasp of her bra with the other. Her nipples grazed his chest, and he was completely lost in the firestorm between them. Without a second thought, he was carrying her into the bedroom with the sole purpose of making up for way too much lost time.

"Ugh. I was supposed to hit the road back today." Chase ran a hand through his hair and looked down at her tucked neatly into his shoulder with one of her long legs draped over his. "And now, I have no desire to ever leave this bed. Work be damned. If I would've known it would be like this with you, I may have had you fire me much sooner." He punctuated the statement by dropping a kiss onto her forehead.

She smiled back at him, looking pretty smug. "And what is 'like this' supposed to mean?"

He chuckled. "I'm hoping I don't have to explain that or I must've done something wrong."

"Seriously, Chase, I have no idea what you're talking about," she said, feigning perplexity. "This was—" she pointed back and forth between them, "—meh…average, run-of-the-mill—"

Before she could complete the sentence, Chase decided he'd heard enough. He pinned her beneath him and started tickling her mercilessly.

"Oh my gosh! You have to stop!" she managed to get out between breaths.

"Do you concede that words like 'average' and 'run-of-the-mill' are misnomers that have no place in this discussion?" he asked while continuing to tickle a particularly sensitive spot on her ribs.

"Okay!" The word rushed out of her mouth between giggles.

Chase paused while he waited for her concession.

Her eyes sparkled as she tried to squirm away. "Maybe 'average' was a bit of an understatement."

"A bit?" he asked, resuming the torture. Only with her squirming beneath him, her bare skin sliding along his, he was beginning to wonder who was actually being tormented.

"Incredible. That's a much better word," she said, laughing so hard that tears were pooling in the corners of

183

her eyes.

Chase stopped tickling her and raised himself on his forearms to look down at her. "Now that's a word I would have used." He was going to say more, but he was distracted by her lips just inches away from his. He leaned down and kissed her thoroughly before settling back into his previous position. If he didn't stop now, he may not leave the bed.

"Are you really going back today?" She looked up at him while her fingers traced little designs around his abdominal muscles.

"I don't want to go right now, Jordan," he said in a serious tone. His pulse quickened with every little circle she drew. "Believe me, I don't." He settled his hand on top of hers before her touch caused him to lose all ability to reason.

"But…" she prompted him.

"I have to rearrange some things at work and I have to be there to do it all. I'm scheduled to start another job as soon as I'm done here—the client was willing to wait for me to be available for a long-term trip overseas, and for the first time, I have no desire to do it." He shook his head. "I don't want to move on to another job, regardless of where it is or who it's for. I want to be with you and explore what we've started. Now that I know this idiot is behind bars, I plan to hold you, kiss you, and make love to you for as long as we want."

Her eyes widened at his admission. "I think I like your idea after all," she said. "As long as we want, huh?" She seemed to be turning the thought over in her mind. "Though you know I'll have to squeeze in work between all of that, once we both get back. Leaving unexpectedly was hard enough on the patients I see regularly, not to mention the backlog of evaluations I'll have waiting for me."

Chase tried to suppress his amusement at how quickly she'd begun to consider all of the relevant logistics. It reminded him of something he'd do. "Don't worry. I haven't forgotten that you're a workaholic," he teased. "It's part of who you are, so maybe I have some strange attraction to women who are like me in that way."

She gazed up at him. "I guess the 'opposites attract' adage doesn't apply to us in that way. And since it doesn't—" she let out a sigh, "—I understand why you need to go back. If someone is counting on you, I wouldn't want you to do anything else." She paused for a second. "I think what we've started here will be good, wherever we are."

"You know you're making this even harder, right?" he said, tucking an escaped lock of silky hair behind her ear.

He still couldn't get over how beautiful she was lying next to him. It was good that she understood his need to wrap things up at work, because a part of him thought it was ludicrous not to stay right there in bed with her.

"I'm glad." She brushed a kiss across his lips. "It'll be incentive for you to find someone to take your place instead of going off to… Where were you supposed to be going next?" she asked, tilting her head to one side.

He resisted pulling her right back to him for another kiss. He wasn't sure he'd ever get enough of this woman. "It would have been a detail with a lot of travel. I'd start in New York, but I'd be in Japan by next week. It's actually a client I've worked with for several years. That's why it's important for me to make sure he's okay with my replacement. I have complete faith in my guys, but they're not me. That'll take some getting used to for my long-term clients."

"You know, you don't have to stop this for me," she whispered. "I'm not going to say I ever envisioned a relationship with someone who's continuously risking his life to protect someone else's—in various parts of the world, for weeks or months at a time—but I'm willing to try it if you aren't ready to stop."

His heart expanded at her admission. "I know you would," he said, his eyes locked on hers. "But as much as I do care about you, I'm doing this for me. It's been something I've been considering a lot lately. Spending time with you this week…well, it kind of solidified where I was already heading. I might not have stopped this soon, but I would have stopped. I think part of what was driving me to keep it up was what happened with Robert, and you helped me to see that I had to quit blaming myself for his death." He pulled her in for a hug and then looked down at her with a grin. "You sure you aren't going to have Nancy send me a bill when we get back?"

Jordan smiled back at him. "Chase, that was all you. I just asked a few questions and listened."

"Uh-huh. Just a few questions? I think you're even cuter when you're being modest." He caressed her cheek with this index finger. "However it happened, I'm much better with it. I never realized I couldn't think about all of the good, because I was too focused on not repeating the bad."

"I believe that can happen to anyone at some point. I liken it to trying to drive in the rain with the windshield fogged up. Get rid of the fog, and driving becomes easier and a heck of a lot less stressful."

Chase considered the wisdom in what she'd said. Damn, she was beautiful, kind, and smart. How in the world had he ended up getting so lucky? "I like that. I like you." He bent toward her for another kiss. "And I really like being right where we are, but I'd better get moving. If I get on the road now, I can make a few phone calls to puts things in motion before it gets too late."

Jordan walked with him out to the parking garage, where his SUV was parked. He looked over at her and couldn't believe how this assignment was wrapping up. He was never one to dwell too much on the future. Maybe because his job required him to stay so alert in the present or because he'd never had too much time to think about it. But at this moment, he couldn't stop thinking about the future and exploring it with her. So much had changed in such a short time.

Jordan stopped when they reached his SUV.

He pointed to the Chrysler 300 parked across the way. "There's your rental. I texted you the code to unlock it. Keys are inside." He grabbed her and pulled her into his arms for one last time before he left. "I'll call you soon," he mumbled into her hair, breathing in the berry smell of her shampoo.

She rested her cheek against his hard chest. "Okay." She tilted her head back. "And thank you for taking care of the car."

"It was nothing," he said gruffly. He planned on taking care of her for a long while. "We'll talk soon." His hands were laced together against the small of her back.

"I'll make sure to turn my ringer up so I can hear it over the ocean," she said in an apparent attempt to lighten the moment.

"Okay, now you're just rubbing it in." He smiled and then leaned down to kiss her.

What he'd intended to be a quick kiss goodbye turned into a whole other matter when he placed his lips on hers. His tongue began an unhurried exploration of her mouth, reacquainting him with all that he'd be missing. Damn. She tasted sweeter than the French toast she'd shared with him that morning.

He might've been content with the easy pace, but a tantalizing whimper escaped her throat and sent his pulse racing. The kiss became more impatient, and he probed deeply within the recesses of her mouth. As his hand moved under her hemline to touch the satiny skin above her hips, the sound of a car closely approaching reminded him they weren't alone.

He broke away from her just as the car drove passed them. Taking a deep breath, he opened the door to the

SUV and leaned forward to wrap his arms around her one last time. "If I don't leave, I never will."

She nodded. "Drive safely." The words came out in a whisper, her voice still breathless from their kiss. She waved at him and then made her way back to the elevator.

He waited to make sure the doors had opened and she was inside before heading out. She wasn't a target anymore with Buckman in jail now, but he still worried about her. It was probably because he cared about her so much and knew all too well that there were more than enough idiots like Buckman to go around. Yet he couldn't shake the feeling it was beyond that. That maybe he was missing something. He tried to brush the thought aside. Though he'd worked through his guilt over Robert, the incident was obviously still making him a little paranoid when it came to people he was close to.

CHAPTER FOURTEEN

Jordan pried her eyelids open and looked around the room. Her disorientation gradually dissipated as the sliding doors came into view and the ocean sounds hit her ears. She barely remembered lying on the couch after Chase had left, deciding she'd rest for a few minutes before seeking out the white sand paradise she'd come to crave since her arrival.

Though the fan overhead was on, the room was hot from the sunlight drifting in. Her skin was clammy, and the blanket she'd kicked off while she was sleeping was hanging from her foot. She scanned the room, looking for a clock, and her gaze fell on her phone sitting on the coffee table.

Picking it up, she was stunned when she saw that she'd been asleep for several hours. "I must have been more tired than I thought," she mumbled as she stretched her arms high above her head.

Her poor sleep last night had caught up with her. She couldn't remember the last time she'd taken that long of an afternoon nap. Her heart rate increased as she recalled her anxiety from the night before. Taking a calming breath, she reminded herself that the nightmare was over.

Buckman wouldn't be threatening her anymore.

Wanting to savor the few daylight hours remaining, Jordan sprung off the couch and changed into her swimsuit as quickly as she could. It felt odd being here without Chase. In the short amount of time, she'd gotten used to him always being around. She'd known it would be an adjustment when this was over, but she hadn't realized how much she'd miss having him around to laugh or appreciate the sights with.

Her stomach fluttered as her mind drifted back to being tangled in his arms this morning, his talented hands leaving blazing trails of heat across her skin. The passion they shared was incredible. She grabbed her beach bag and threw in her sunscreen and an oversized towel. A smile flitted across her face as it dawned on her that he wasn't even in the same room or, given the hours she'd just slept away, even the same town, and he could still elicit a sensual response from her.

Without a backward glance, she was out the door and headed down the walkway to the warm waters. She'd decided earlier that she'd head to the state park not far from the condo. From the pictures in the travel catalog she'd been flipping through, it looked like she'd have the chance to see more of the rustic shoreline.

Heading east, she stopped to slip her sandals into her bag and decided to walk along the shoreline. The cool water swirled around her feet as the waves crashed beside her. Though the park hadn't looked too far away, she decided she'd better ask to make sure. A runner was approaching her from that direction.

"Hi. Could you tell me how far the state park is from here?" she asked.

She wasn't sure if she had his attention at first, as his glasses reflected her image back at her, and he had a baseball cap pulled down low on his head. He was probably close to her age and had a deep tan that suggested he lived here or had been here a while.

Smiling at her, he removed his glasses. "Yeah, St. Andrews?"

"That's it," she said, remembering the name from her reading. She wondered if he'd visited the park and would have some recommendations.

"It's not too far at all, maybe three-quarters of a mile straight ahead." He pointed back in the direction he'd come from. "You'll know you're there when you see the pier and the jetties."

"Jetties?" She furrowed her brow, not remembering anything by that name.

"Oh, sorry. Kind of a local reference point. Once you pass the pier, look for a barrier made up of large rocks stretching out into the ocean. Creates kind of an alcove from the Gulf. Good place for kids to swim because the waters are calmer there. If you want, I can walk down that way with you?"

She'd grown so used to keeping to herself and watching out for potential threats that it took her a minute to realize he was being friendly. Flirting maybe? She wasn't sure. "Oh, thank you, but that's not necessary. I should be able to find it now."

"Are you sure? It's no trouble. I live right over that way. Do you see the house with the deck coming out from the third level? That's me."

She looked where he was pointing. Sure enough, she saw a majestic house with a large balcony extending out from the highest floor. "I see it. Wow, what a view. I'm assuming you've been to the park, then?" She still wasn't sure where his motivation came from. Was he was being friendly, which was pretty typical of the locals they'd encountered, or was he was coming on to her?

"Many times. You'll enjoy it. There are a few trails around the bay. A lot of different bird species as well. Blue Heron, Great and Snowy Egrets, cranes, pelicans all hang out there quite a bit, and a few gators, too." He gave her a wink.

She arched an eyebrow. She wanted rustic, but hopefully he meant gators to watch, not encounter personally.

"Don't worry. They're just part of the ecosystem. You can watch them from the dock at Gator Lake. The only time there's been a problem is when people don't follow the No Feeding signs and throw in food. It can make the gators less fearful of people and, as you can imagine, more dangerous." He shook his head.

"I can see that. Then they're conditioned to associate people with food as well."

"Smart woman and beautiful, too." He smiled. "Sure you don't want any company?"

This time, there was no doubt he was flirting with her. He was an attractive guy, and she imagined he wouldn't have a problem finding someone to share the beach with, but all she could think about was bringing Chase with her to explore the park the next time they were able to get away. "Thanks for the offer and the trivia, but I'm good. Enjoy your run."

"My pleasure. Enjoy the park." He slid his glasses back on and tipped his baseball cap to her.

She gave a quick wave as he headed off and continued toward the park.

§

With U2 blaring in the background, Chase almost missed the ringtone on his phone sounding out. Mike's name popped up, and he couldn't help but feel a little guilty. He'd assured his friend that when it came to Jordan, he'd be hands off in any way other than to protect her from this perp. He hadn't intended to deceive his friend. It hadn't even entered his mind as a possibility when they'd made the arrangements. But it was different with Jordan, and being with her was something he had no regrets about.

"Might as well face the music," he muttered, hitting the answer button. "Hey, bro. How's it going?"

"Honestly, man, couldn't be better." His voice was full of elation. "I don't think any of us realized how worried we were until that jerk was caught. Derek's been the worst. He was driving us all mad wanting to know when she'd be back now that the whole thing is over."

A surge of jealousy burned through him in response to Mike's comment, catching him off guard. He reminded himself that Derek and Jordan were friends and he'd obviously be worried about her. It wasn't like him to be so irrational. But his feelings for Jordan were new to him. Maybe that was why he felt so possessive.

Mike didn't notice Chase's silence and continued on. "Luckily, Karen and I usually get the news first or we'd probably be just as bad. I probably shouldn't have given him such a hard time."

"What do you mean?" He wasn't sure he wanted to continue the discussion but found himself asking anyway.

"Nothing. Just harassing him that maybe we'd overlooked some feelings he might have for her."

Chase tried to keep his voice neutral. "I don't think so, dude. He and Jordan are friends. That's it." His tone was firm, despite his efforts, and he gripped the phone as he passed a slower car in front of him.

"We were only messing with him. We all realized early on that those two had about as much attraction as water and oil. What's more curious to me, my friend, is why you seem put off right now?"

Chase had said too much. Which was probably what Mike had intended all along. Now that the cat was out of the bag, he reckoned it was as good of a time as any to tell him the news. Hoping his friend would be happy for them, he jumped right in. "I'm assuming by your question that you figured all of it out."

"I've got a good guess, but damn it, Chase. You'd better tell me it's something I'm not guessing. Because ninja-warrior, tough-guy bodyguard or not, I will find a way to kick your ass if you added her to your list of *finished assignments."*

Chase bristled at his choice of words. He waited a breath to avoid telling him that Jordan was never going to be anyone's finished assignment. She was much too good for that. "Look. I know I told you this wouldn't happen. I never thought it would. But she's…she's amazing, man. Smart, kind, funny, and freakin' gorgeous on top of it all."

There was silence on the other end of the line, and then Mike began to chuckle. "Sounds like you got the picture. You told her yet?"

"Yeah." His voice caught a bit as he remembered exactly how he'd told her and everything that had followed. "Yeah, I did. It's awesome between us. I'm actually heading back to Orlando now so I can rearrange some work commitments. I want to stick around here for a while."

He paused for a second. "That's a big change."

Chase figured the silence meant he was probably trying to reconcile what he knew of him before with what he'd just told him now.

"Chase, I'm happy for you. And her, too. I never would've pictured you two together, but I can see now that you fit. You're two of the best people I know. Not that I wouldn't have kicked your ass if you'd hurt her."

An image of Mike scooping up a harmless spider and releasing it outside when they were in college came to mind. His threat of violence meant Mike thought a lot of Jordan.

"I would've expected nothing less," Chase said.

"So, now that we've got that settled, Karen and I are going out for drinks tonight. Taking a breather from all of this crap that's been going on. You in?"

Chase hesitated. He'd enjoy spending time with Mike and Karen, but he was beat and he had a meeting to scheduled for early the next morning, so he could reassure his long-time client that he'd be in very competent hands with his replacement, they just wouldn't be his.

"Come on, man. Derek already bailed on us. We need some fellowship."

"I want to. It'd be good to hang out again. How about a rain check though? I've got some stuff to catch up on tonight. You two have fun."

"Okay. I'm holding you to it. Dinner next week. You and Jordan both."

"Deal." Chase hung up.

As he drove the final miles home, Chase wondered why he'd reacted the way he had to Mike's baiting him about Derek. Sure, it could be that he was jealous of Jordan in general. But he's never really been the jealous type, and as far as Jordan was concerned, he trusted her completely.

No, if he tried to pin it down, it was his feelings toward Derek, not Jordan, that had caused the knee-jerk reaction. The man had never done anything specifically, but there was something niggling in the back of his mind that didn't seem right.

Chase thought back to what Derek had written on her card that came with the flowers this morning. *Things are pretty dull here without you.* Nothing inappropriate, so why was he bothered?

Then it came to him like a picture slowly coming into focus. He hit the call back button on his phone but was immediately sent to Mike's voicemail.

He veered his SUV off the interstate at the next exit and pulled into a rest area. Scrolling through his contact list, he found the general practice number.

Nancy answered on the first ring. "Clinical and Forensic Services. This is Nancy speaking."

"Nancy, it's Chase. Can you put Mike on the phone?" He kept his voice level, though his pulse quickened as he turned over the recent events in his mind.

"Oh, hey, Chase. He just went into a session. Is it urgent?"

Was it urgent? He wasn't sure yet. "What about

Karen?" He ran his fingers through his hair before landing them back on the steering wheel.

"Karen's working in her office. Do you want me to connect you?"

"Thanks, Nancy." Chase began inundating Karen with questions as soon as she picked up. "Karen, is Derek there today?"

"Chase?" she asked.

"Yeah, it's me. Sorry. I thought Nancy let you know I was on the line. I need to know if Derek is there at the office?"

"He's been here all morning. But he cleared his schedule for the afternoon. Said something came up…a family situation. He's okay? Nothing happened to him, did it?" she asked, sounding worried. "I thought he was driving a little recklessly when I saw him."

"When? what time?"

"Around lunch, I guess. I was trying a new way back to the office. I saw him heading south. And you all may get your kicks from teasing me, but I can tell you I don't drive like that. He really needs to tone it down." She paused. "Seriously, Chase, what's the deal? Is he okay?"

"He's fine." He kept his theory to himself for the moment. "Have you talked to him since then?"

"No. He seemed lost in his own world, weaving in and out of traffic. I tried to call him to tell him to be more careful, but he didn't answer. I left a message. He hasn't called back though. What's all of this about?"

How in the hell had he missed it? A feeling of dread washed over him as he ruminated the question. The thoughts were eerily familiar. Damn it. Not again. "Did any of you know Derek before he started working with you?"

"No, we put out an advertisement."

"Did anything ever happen between him and Jordan? Anything that would make him angry? Resentful?"

"No… Chase, you're worrying me. Why are you

fixated on Derek? The police got a confession from Buckman. He admitted to paying for the hit." She paused then let out a breath. "But he didn't admit to the rest. Oh, crap. You think it was more than one person?"

"Maybe." Even as he spoke the word, he knew he was right. Call it intuition or whatever; something had felt off when he'd left her. And he'd foolishly attributed his worry to paranoia.

Why would a suspect confess to a hit but then deny the less serious offenses? It could happen, but that should've been Chase's tipoff right there. Not wanting to waste any more time, he left the parking lot of the rest area. With no way of turning around, he reentered the Turnpike heading east. He'd been on this road hundreds of times before. The next exit with a westbound entry was miles ahead.

Karen seemed to be thinking aloud. "It doesn't make sense, Chase. Derek is the one who saved her that night."

"I know, Karen. Bear with me on this. I need to check some things out. Can you give me what you have on file, in terms of address, birthday, that kind of stuff?" He made a split-second decision and cut into the median, careful to keep a slightly left leaning trajectory, so he didn't get stuck in the deep mud in the center.

"I'll give you what we have, but it still doesn't add up. He's never done anything to indicate he had a role in what's been happening. If he did, he's one damned good actor to have fooled all three of us. Give me a minute to grab that file."

Now heading back in the direction he'd just come from, he drove as fast as he dared without getting stopped by the state troopers who patrolled the area. He had no time for a traffic stop.

He waited for Karen to get the information, drumming his fingers impatiently on the console next to him. His foot seemed to have a mind of its own when it came to the gas pedal, so he set the cruise control on the

SUV. After what seemed like way too long, she rattled off the details she had from Derek's employment paperwork.

"Got it. I'll call you back." He hit the end button before she could reply and dialed his office.

He briefed his secretary, Shelly, on the situation and the information he'd gotten. With what Karen had given him on Derek, the woman would be able to conduct a thorough background check and personal history review.

"Call me back as soon as you get anything. I need whatever you find as soon as possible." He blew out a long breath and tried not to think about how different the situation would be had he only made the connection before he'd left Jordan.

CHAPTER FIFTEEN

While watching the sun sink toward the water, Jordan stretched out her legs. A flat-topped rock in front of her made the perfect ottoman. She couldn't believe it was already approaching nightfall, having spent over an hour in this very spot. A beautiful spectrum of colors paraded across the evening sky, and she wished for the first time since being there that she hadn't forgotten her phone in the condo. Up until now, she'd been grateful for the uninterrupted silence and time to process the past few weeks, but she would have loved to have captured the vision in front of her on camera.

"Beautiful, isn't it?"

The deep voice behind her was familiar, but she couldn't place it. After turning around to face the speaker, she was surprised to see Derek standing on the rocks behind her.

"Thought you had the whole place to yourself, huh?" He jumped from the top of a nearby rock to a closer one while looking down at her.

A wide grin spread across her face. "What in the world are you doing here?"

"Well, that's kind of a long story. But it's suffice to

say, I heard you were staying in town for the weekend and thought maybe you could use some company." He sat down, taking a place next to her on the large rock she'd been using as her chair.

"Really?" She turned to face him as he took in their surroundings. Though it was good to see him, she didn't understand why he'd traveled all the way up here when she'd be back at the office on Monday.

He turned back to her with a sheepish expression. "I know. I probably should've called first. I'm sure the last thing you want is to be surprised." He looked at her meaningfully. "After everything that's been going on. But I was worried you'd tell me it was too much trouble. And believe it or not, after hearing Karen and Mike go on and on about the place the whole time you were gone, I thought it might be good for me to get away—take a break here as well. This whole thing was pretty stressful on everyone." He held a hand up. "Not that we had to go through was anything close to what you have, but it's been pretty tense on our end, too."

Her chest tightened as she listened to his explanation. Though none of the recent events had been under her control, the threats to her life had certainly impacted the entire practice. Until hearing Derek now, she'd spent little time contemplating how her partners felt about the whole thing. If it had been one of them, it would've affected her considerably. "I'm sorry you all had to go through this too," she said softly.

"Don't be. It's over now, and I'm glad it turned out the way it did," he said in a decisive tone. "It looks like we're out of sunlight. What had you planned on doing next?"

He was right. The water had taken on a metallic sheen, and the remnants of the colorful rays were dusting the clouds overhead.

"Well, I'd only meant to stay here for a little while and then go check out one of the lakes a local told me about. But——" she let out a chuckle, "—as you can see, I let time get away from me down here, so I'm not sure how much of the lake we'd be able to see now that it's dark."

"Oh, come on. Don't let a little darkness stop you." He grabbed her hand and hauled her up from the rock. "So, what's the name of this lake you'd planned to visit?"

She looked at him with a mischievous sparkle in her eyes. "Gator Lake."

He frowned. "And I'm assuming they call it Gator Lake for its inhabitants?"

"You've got it. But it's supposed to be safe to visit. As long as you don't feed them." She gave him a once-over. He was dressed in a pair of plaid shorts and a T-shirt. She looked around for anything else he might be carrying, but he was empty-handed. "And from the looks of it, that won't be a problem, because you don't have anything they'd find appetizing."

"You can say that again. And I'm sure I wouldn't taste so good to them. You, on the other hand, might be more appetizing." He raised his eyebrows suggestively.

"Gross, Derek." She rolled her eyes. "Don't even joke like that. I meant you have no food with you. I guess sometimes tourists feed them, and it can become a problem if they get used to it."

"Interesting." He gave her a thoughtful look. "So, how did you find out all of this valuable information on the gators here?"

She began making her way across the rocks that led back to the shoreline. She'd seen a walkway from there that led further into the park. "Oh. I just asked around a little. People are pretty friendly here. You'll see. Speaking of that, where are you staying?" She kept her fingers crossed that Karen and Mike hadn't offered up the spare room in the condo. She didn't mind having Derek around for the weekend, but she'd hoped to have some time to herself before returning back to her former routine.

"I rented a condo at the same resort as Karen and

Mike's. Thought that would give you some room, but it wouldn't be hard to get together, either."

"Okay." She tried to keep the relief out of her voice. "I bet Karen and Mike were surprised to have us both up here after they've been trying for so long."

His brow furrowed for a second but then his features returned to normal. If she weren't so used to relying on behavioral observations, she might have missed it. She pondered what he'd been thinking that caused the reaction as they made their way up the boardwalk to the parking area.

"Yes. It was kind of last minute, so we didn't spend too much time talking about it. They were right though. The place is gorgeous. When I first got here, I tried their condo, but you weren't there. Thought I'd go for a walk and try you again later if I didn't bump into you. But lucky for me, there aren't many people out today, so it was easy to spot you down on the rocks."

"I wondered how you managed to track me down. I accidentally left my cell in the condo, so I'm sure I've missed a few calls." Her thoughts automatically went to Chase. He'd be home now and probably trying to get in touch with her. She didn't want him to be concerned. "Would you mind if I used yours? Chase was going to call me when he got back, and I'd hate for him to worry."

He stared at her for a moment, and then began to laugh. "Would you believe I left mine at the condo, too? I thought about bringing it, but I didn't want it to end up wet or in the sand somewhere. I'm sure it's fine though. Chase will probably call Mike and he'll let him know I'm here with you."

"That's true," she said, grateful that Chase wouldn't be as worried if he knew she was with Derek.

CHAPTER SIXTEEN

Chase debated whether or not he should call Jordan before he heard back from Shelly. Though he was fairly certain Derek was involved in the threats to her life, he was relying on his gut instinct and the similarities in the vocabulary used in two messages she'd received. Not a lot to hang his hat on, but in years of policing, he'd learn to trust his instinct. He pulled her number up and pressed send.

The phone began to ring in his ear. "Come on, Jordan. Pick up." He spoke as if sheer will alone could bring her voice on the line.

"Hello, you have reached the voicemail box of Dr. Clayton—"

"Damn it." He didn't hear the rest of her message as he tried to work out what to do next. The beep following her recording brought him back to the present. "Hey, Jordan, it's me, Chase. Look, I need you to call me as soon as you get this message. It's important."

He hung up, feeling more anxious than he had before trying to get a hold of her. Why wouldn't she be answering? He remembered how she'd joked with him about turning her ringer up so she could still hear him.

Had she forgotten? He started doing the calculations in his head.

Derek had left around lunch, and it would be about a five-and-a-half-hour drive from Orlando to Panama City Beach. But Karen had said that he'd been driving fast. So…the timing sucked. If Derek wasn't already there, he'd be close.

Chase grabbed the back of his neck, pressing his foot on the gas pedal. He still didn't want to be slowed down by a traffic stop, but that was a chance he'd have to take now. There was no way in hell he wasn't going to do anything he could to get to her as fast as possible.

Passing several cars, he hit the call back button, trying to reach her again.

"Hello, you have reached the voicemail box—"

This time, he hung up without leaving a message. She'd return his call as soon as she saw the missed call notices on her phone. But why wasn't she seeing them now? His mind raced as he checked his mirrors, scanning the traffic around him. And why hadn't his office called back with the information he'd requested?

As if reading his thoughts, his cell began ringing in his hand. He recognized the office ringtone right away. Wishing it'd been her but grateful for any leads at this point, he hurriedly answered the call. "What've you got?"

"Nothing you're gonna like," Shelly began, sounding grim. "Your instincts were right on. The background on Derek was clean. Not even a traffic ticket. But after a little digging, it turns out the same isn't true for his older brother. Guy was convicted of first-degree murder. Details were pretty heinous. The victim was tortured and held captive for several days before he ended her life. He was sentenced to death—jury only deliberated for an hour before reaching a unanimous decision. It was that bad."

Chase's jaw was clenched so tight that it ached. She was right; he didn't like what he was hearing. And it sure as hell didn't fit the account Derek had given them on his brother. But having a murderer for a brother didn't mean Derek automatically shared the family trait. "So maybe the two apples didn't fall far apart, but it doesn't connect all the dots."

"That's because there's more. The defense called several witnesses during the penalty phase, a little of everything, really—psychologist, psychiatrist, neurologist, and a professor of neuroscience. They did everything they could to a paint a picture of the guy as mentally impaired, in hopes of getting a life sentence instead of the death penalty. But the state only called one expert."

"Jordan." Chase almost choked on her name. His throat was so dry.

"Yeah, and her testimony must've been pretty persuasive."

"Did you find any mention of Derek in the press reports?"

"He was in his early twenties at the time. Brother was fifteen years older than he is. Defense tried to argue he'd been a caretaker for Derek with Mom having a long history of substance abuse, but it was given very little weight. The two hadn't lived at the same residence for most of their lives."

Chase exhaled. The more he heard, the worse it got. "No way this is a coincidence. He's been planning his revenge for a long time."

"Yeah, seems like it. But we've got him now. What's next?"

Good question, considering Derek was probably in the same town as Jordan as they spoke, and because he'd been clueless, he was still hours behind him. "Leave it to me for now. If I need anything else, I'll call."

Chase could feel the anger building as he hung up. Derek had posed as her friend all this time while, in reality, plotting to do God knows what.

He tried calling her again, though he knew the attempt would be fruitless. Wherever she was, she either didn't hear or couldn't answer her phone. Even with the information he had now, the pieces didn't all fall together. If Derek was intent on hurting her, why had he stopped Rigdon when he'd attempted to follow through on the hit? He was certain Derek had been racing out of town to find Jordan, but what was he planning on doing? Up until now, his threats had consisted of scare tactics that could've led to fatal consequences, but no outright attempts to directly harm her. He didn't have all the information he would've liked, but he had enough to know that he had to do something else to intervene before it was too late.

He asked his phone to connect him to the Bay County Sheriff's Office. After going through dispatch, he was able to talk to one of the supervisors on duty. The officer was more than helpful when Chase explained the situation, and a squad car was dispatched to the condo to check on her. He was glad for the intervention, but he wanted to be there to check on her himself, to make sure she was safe and the creep wasn't anywhere near her.

A short time later, he received a call back from the police department.

"Hello, sir. This is Jason from the Bay County Sheriff's Office. I wanted to follow up and let you know we did go to the address you provided, but there was no answer at the door. Didn't hear anything from inside the condo, and no lights were on in the front room. Nothing suspicious. It appeared that no one was there. Waited a few minutes to see if anyone would show, but no one did. I've been dispatched to another call now, but I'll be glad to swing by again later if you still have concerns."

"Thanks, man. It'd be much appreciated."

He wondered again where she was. It was getting dark soon. Would she still be on the beach this late? Was Derek there with her? For the thousandth time since he'd turned around, he wished his specialty BMW included an option to convert to air travel. Though he was making good time, Derek had a significant head start on him.

§

"Excuse me. How much farther is it to Gator Lake?" Jordan asked a couple of guys as they loaded their surfboards into the back of a pickup truck.

One with blond, shaggy hair answered her. "Follow the path down a ways and around the bend. It's not that far. Park's closing soon though, if you drove."

"Okay, thanks."

Luckily, that wouldn't be a problem for them. She looked around for Derek, who was several feet behind her, bent over his shoelace.

"Hey, it's already dark. We'd better move fast. I don't know if the lake is lit or not." She waved at the truck as the surfers left the parking lot.

Derek jogged to catch up with her. "Sorry. Must be getting used to the laidback pace of this town already."

They traveled down the path until several signs let them know they'd arrived at Gator Lake. A lookout point at the edge of a wooden dock loomed in front of them, and they trekked over to it. There was a bench built in to the perimeter, but she didn't take a seat. She could tell, even in the darkness, that the best vantage point would be standing. The moon was out in full now, and she strained to see any movement in the lake.

"It's so nice out here." She looked over at Derek. "I wish I'd gotten off that rock a little sooner so I could've seen the lake during the daylight."

"Well, it seemed like you were enjoying lounging on the rocks. Besides, if you would've left sooner, I may not have found you out here." His gaze never left the lake as he answered.

She smiled. "True. I still can't believe how we ran into each other out here, of—" A splash near the water's edge stopped her in midsentence. "Derek," she whispered, "do you think that was a gator?"

"I don't know. I've never been anywhere where

gators were likely to pop up." He walked up behind her. "How deep do you think the water is? It's hard to tell now."

An involuntary shiver ran down her spine. Though it had cooled down some since the sun had set, she wasn't cold. Maybe it was the potential proximity to gators she couldn't quite make out in the darkness. "I don't know. I didn't read anything about that." She crossed her arms in front of her and rubbed her arms.

"Wonder how many gators are in here?" he asked.

"Not sure on that one either. But I doubt we'll get any answers tonight. It's too hard to see them. And only being able to hear them is making me a little jittery."

"Yeah." He paused for a second. "After everything you've been through lately, you're probably more—"

Headlights lit them up from behind. Then a park ranger approached them. "Hey, folks. Park's closed for tonight. If you drove, gate'll be locked soon."

Jordan smiled at the ranger. "Thanks. We walked up from the beach. But it is getting pretty dark. I don't think we'll be seeing much now, so we'll probably head back that way."

"I'll be glad to give you guys a lift back to the beach side."

Jordan and Derek both spoke at the same time.

"That'd be great."

"We'll be all right."

She looked back at him. "It's still a bit of a walk back to the condo. It might be better if we catch a ride partway."

Derek hesitated. "Fine by me. Just wanted to make sure you got to see everything you wanted to."

"I think I've seen about all I can at this hour." She directed her attention back to the ranger. "We'll take you up on that ride."

"It's a nice night to walk. The temperature is perfect

now," Derek commented as they made their way back down the beach, leaving the grounds of the state park behind them.

"Yeah, it's great without the humidity." She could still feel the wind through her cover-up dress she'd worn over her swimsuit, but the chill from earlier at the dock had left her.

It was darker next to the ocean away from the lights of the beachside condos and businesses. She slipped her sandals back on. No sense stepping on a washed-up jellyfish or a piece of broken glass.

"Actually, it's great with the humidity too." She smiled. "I mean, the trade-off is worth getting sticky and hot. When we first came here, it wasn't much of a choice, with everything going on. But surprisingly, coming here ended up being much more than an escape from the situation. It helped me to regroup…relax again." She stopped herself before getting into details about her time with Chase. It was still so new that she hadn't even told Karen yet.

"So you weren't worried at all while you were here? That he would find you?"

She contemplated his question for a moment. It was hard to answer without revealing more than she was ready to. In truth, she'd been on edge. Though, looking back, it had more to do with the events that had led up to their trip here. She wasn't sure how much time it would take to recover from the attack and everything that had followed, but putting her anxieties from what had happened aside, she'd felt safe once they'd gotten here. "Not really. You guys were the only ones who knew we were here, and Chase was careful to make sure we weren't followed."

"Yeah, I guess it's lucky he stepped in when he did." His tone was tinged with sarcasm.

Though his words were appreciative, his nonverbal communication suggested anything but. For the second time that evening, she wondered what he was thinking. She reflected back to his comments on how much this had affected everyone. Maybe he was still processing like she was.

"True. I owe Mike one for sure."

Coming up to a narrow passage between two condos, Derek pointed out a public beach access sign. "On the way in, I saw a little bar not too far from here. Let's stop and have a drink before we get back."

With more illumination from the surrounding structures, she saw that the passage led to a road. "How far is it?"

"Not far at all. It looked like a dive from the outside, but the parking lot was full. Come on. We'll give it a try."

She surveyed the distance ahead. They weren't far from the condo now. A few minutes' walk at most. And she wasn't tired, thanks to the long nap she'd had earlier. She debated whether or not Chase would be worried. Derek had reminded her that he'd know they were together. Besides, with Buckman in jail, there was really no cause for concern.

"I can tell I've almost convinced you." Derek nudged her in the direction of the entryway with his shoulder.

She changed her course, heading toward the path he'd showed her. "Okay. Let's check it out. But I don't want to stay too long."

"We won't. A couple of drinks and we'll get you back, safe and sound."

CHAPTER SEVENTEEN

Chase pulled into the parking garage and scanned the area for the rental car he he'd reserved for Jordan. Sure enough, it was parked right where it'd been earlier. There was no indication she'd driven anywhere. He parked his SUV and walked toward the rental. After punching in the code and looking inside, he saw she hadn't even taken the keys out. Now, he was sure she hadn't driven anywhere.

His feet pounded on the pavement as he jogged over to the elevator. The sheriff's office had said that no one was there the last time they'd checked, but maybe she was back by now. She'd been planning to go down to the beach today. However, it had been dark for hours now.

He cautiously approached the condo but heard nothing to indicate that anyone was inside. The combination to the front door was fresh in his head, and he didn't bother to knock. The best thing that could happen right now was for her to be irritated because he'd abandoned social convention and barged in on her. Worst case, he'd have the advantage of surprise on his side if Derek was in there with her.

His breathing was controlled as he entered the condo and methodically searched the rooms. This he could do.

Being miles away, with no choice but to drive, had almost killed him. Each room was dark. There were no signs of any type of struggle.

In the master bedroom, the sheets were still a tangled mess. His thoughts flitted back to everything they'd shared that morning, but he didn't afford himself the chance to think long about it. When he had her safe with him again, he'd let go. Until then, he had to compartmentalize; it was the only thing he could do.

Returning back to the main living area, he noted the blanket folded carelessly on the end of the couch. Had she fallen asleep? Walking over to the couch, her cell phone sat resting on the table. The screen indicated that she had numerous missed calls, mostly from him. Well, that explained why she hadn't been answering his calls.

He scanned the room, trying to find any other clues. Nothing else was amiss. It looked as if she'd left the phone behind when she'd headed out.

Not wanting to waste any more time, he rushed out of the room and headed down to the beach. Wherever she was, she hadn't driven, so that meant she was somewhere on foot. He made his way down to the shoreline, but he wasn't sure whether to go right or left when he got to the ocean. The lights from other resorts dotted the coast in either direction. Finally, he turned in the direction that led to the quieter side of the beach that ended at a state park. In the midst of the darkness, it didn't seem like the logical choice, but if it had still been light when she'd left, then she was probably heading away from the more populated area. At least, he hoped so.

He walked for several minutes with no trace of her. Beginning to doubt his choice of direction, he strained to see farther when a light from a fire flickering up ahead captured his attention. With any luck, whoever had built it would still be around. Sure enough, as he got closer, he noted the flames were coming from a fire pit settled on the raised deck of one of the beachfront homes. A lone figure was seated next to it.

Chase approached the house. "Hey!" he yelled to be heard over the crashing of the waves.

The figure waved at him but made no move to get up.

"Can I ask you a question?" He was standing right in front of the support beams of the house now. Being closer, he could just make out the profile of a man overhead.

The man walked toward him, carrying a bottle in one hand. "What can I help you with?" The dude sounded friendly enough, considering Chase was a complete stranger who'd wandered up from the beach.

"I was wondering if you've seen a woman walking this way? I'm not sure what time, but it would've been in the late afternoon or evening. Long, dark hair." As Chase asked the question, he realized how ridiculous he sounded. Even though it wasn't peak tourist season in the fall, there was no telling how many women walked down this part of the beach on an average day.

He guy took a swig from his bottle and looked back down at him. "I've seen quite a few today. The girl you're talking about not from around here?"

"No, she's not." Chase let out a breath. He had so little to go on. He had no idea what she was wearing, if she was alone or with Derek, exactly when she'd left.

"Rockin' body, blue eyes but kind of purple too, and pretty smart?"

Chase almost fell over in the sand. "That sounds just like her."

"Yeah, well, you're in luck, then. She's the only one I talked to today. Wanted information on the state park farther up the beach."

"Is that where she was heading when you talked to her?" He straightened his shoulders. A burst of momentum shot through him now that he had something to go on.

"Yeah. I told her about the jetties that way and one of

the lakes—Gator Lake. If you keep going in the direction you were heading, it isn't very far. You'll know you're there when the beach curves around and you see a line of large rocks jutting out into the water. You shouldn't have any problems spotting them, but the park's officially been closed since sundown."

Chase's stomach turned as he digested that last bit of information. If Jordan was at that park alone with Derek, there wouldn't be a lot of help around. "Thanks, man. I appreciate it."

"No problem. Some friendly advice though?"

Chase nodded, knowing he was going to hear it either way.

"Try not to lose her again. Girl like that, you want to keep close." He raised his beer in a mock toast.

"Don't I know it." He chuckled, but there was little real humor in it. He didn't need the guy's words of wisdom to realize that when he found Jordan this time, he wasn't sure if he'd ever be able to let her walk out of the room without him.

He started jogging to pick up his speed. Right now, he needed to focus on the finding-her part first.

§

"Derek!" Jordan exclaimed as the waitress set another drink in front of her. "I thought you said the second round was it?"

"I know we'd said we'd leave, but I figured a couple more minutes wouldn't hurt. The band is going to take a break in fifteen. I heard them talking. We might as well stick around until then. Come on. You need this as much as I do."

Jordan relented. Though she'd been ready to call it a night for almost an hour, it was apparent Derek was enjoying himself. She had nowhere else to be, so it wouldn't hurt her to stay a little longer. The band did sound great, and listening to them was making the time fly by. "Okay. But this is the last round. I don't want to go back to work Monday feeling like I need a vacation from my vacation."

"I promise this is it." He held his drink up. "To the beach, good music, new friends, and just endings."

Jordan took a small sip of her cocktail. She had no intentions of finishing this one. "New friends? I never think of it that way. I guess because you kind of fit in with us so easily from the beginning."

"Yeah, sometimes I feel like I've known you for a lot longer than the time we've worked together. It's something how everything seemed to fall into place when I started with the practice."

Jordan smiled. "It's pretty cool how that happened. And you wouldn't believe the number of applicants we got when we advertised for your position. Not that they were all good." She cringed, reflecting back on some of those interviews. "But when you showed up, we could all tell you'd really researched the practice and knew what we were about. It demonstrated a lot of initiative. You definitely stood out."

"Probably because there was no other place I wanted to be. It felt kind of like fate intervened then."

"Fate, huh? And here we thought we were lucky to have found you after a week of interviewing." She scooted her chair closer to the table to make room for a large group trying to walk by. "So, why fate? What made you want to start with us? You weren't even living in Orlando."

Derek squinted at her. "Are you interviewing me again? 'Cause if you are, you should've asked the questions before the drinks." He lifted his cup and drained it.

Jordan hadn't noticed the slight slur in his speech until then. She needed to get them out of there before he got much worse. "No, I'm definitely not doing any more interviews for a very long time," she answered blithely. "Curious, that's all. Remember, the three of us have known each other for years, but as you said, you're new."

He smiled at her. "I'm just joking with you." Then he playfully shook her forearm. "It was fate because I'd read about a case you worked back when I had some big decisions to make about where I was going in life. Reading that back then, well…it gave me some clarity."

She furrowed her brow. Though she'd had cases get media coverage, she couldn't think of any that stood out as particularly inspiring. Reading about her cases tended to make most people cringe. The details of the crimes revealed in them could sometimes be gruesome. "Do you remember which case it was?"

The band jumped into an older classic rock song, and his lips moved but no sound was audible.

"I can't hear you!" she shouted back at him, shaking her head and pointing to the stage.

He pushed his chair back from the table and motioned toward the door.

She'd have to remember to ask him about it again later. As she followed him out, her thoughts drifted back to Derek's disclosure about the death of his brother and the therapist he'd gotten to know then. Were the big decisions he'd mentioned part of that difficult time in his life?

Not far from the condo now, they walked further up on the beach, closer to the buildings. The sand was deeper and she felt the difference in her calves. Derek swayed on his feet, so she kept her strides short. She was thankful she'd stopped drinking before he had. Nursing a hangover wasn't how she intended to spend the rest of her weekend.

A surge of relief engulfed her when they entered the lower level of the condo.

"What floor are you on?" she asked Derek as they stepped into the elevator.

"I'll walk you up. I'm only a couple of floors above you."

"You don't have to do that. I'm fine now. Remember? No more bodyguards necessary." She laughed lightly.

Because of his glassy eyes, she thought maybe she should walk him up though. He must have drunk more than she'd realized in the hours they were at the bar.

"Well, humor me, then? It seems ungentlemanly of me to let you walk to your room alone."

"You're too much." She shook her head. "It's entirely up to you. I'm okay either way."

"Thank you." From the way he spoke, it was clear that he'd be getting off on her floor.

She led the way and turned to him after she'd entered the code and had the door propped open with her foot. "I had a good time tonight. It was nice catching up after being away. But now, I think you need to get some sleep."

"Yeah. You're right." He turned to go but stopped midstride. "Oh geez, I hate to ask, but do you have any coffee? I didn't get anything yet, and I have a feeling I'm going to need it in the morning."

Jordan pushed the door open. "Sure. Come on in, and I'll see what all we have here."

Derek followed her into the room. While she made her way to the kitchen area, he fingered the flowers that had been delivered earlier. "Did you like the flowers?" he asked casually.

"They're beautiful. Thank you." She rummaged through the cabinet, trying to find a container to separate some coffee grounds into. "Though, when the delivery came, it gave Chase and me both a start. We weren't expecting anyone and hadn't heard about the outcome of the adjudication yet."

"I didn't think of that. Must've been scary. Knowing this guy was after you and hell-bent on revenge." He spoke matter-of-factly, but there was an underlying bitterness in his tone. "Did you ever worry he might not get caught in time?"

Jordan paused for a beat. Something was off. While Chase had often gotten angry when she'd been threatened, his anger was never directed at her. The animosity in Derek's tone made it sound more like he was angry not at Buckman, but at her. She kept her voice neutral as she tried to discern where he was going with this. "I guess the thought was probably in the back of my mind somewhere, but I tried to stay logical about it. You and I both know these guys mess up sooner or later."

"Do you ever think you mess up, too?"

She spun away from the cabinet to face him. "What do you mean, Derek? What are you getting at?"

"What about when you're wrong?" he asked, his eyes devoid of any emotion.

"Then I guess I'm wrong. No one is right all the time." In that moment, Jordan understood that she didn't know this man as well as she'd presumed. She tried to recall what he'd said about getting to know the therapist who'd inspired him to pursue psychology…but he'd said something similar tonight about one of her cases being a motivator to him.

Which was it? Her intuition told her that it mattered, but she didn't know why.

"So, you'd risk throwing someone's life away without a second thought to the fact that you could be wrong?" Though it was a question, the scorn embedded in his words made it clear he wasn't looking for an answer. He already had it.

This was crazy. She needed to find a way to get out of the condo or get him out. But he was blocking her exit from the kitchen. If she could keep him distracted while she got past…

"Derek, I thought you meant in general. If you're talking about work, you know how it is. What we do is scientific. Any conclusions I give are based on that. It's the most objective approach we've got."

"Objective?" he seethed, narrowing his eyes at her. "Why don't you tell that to the people you've killed? Innocent people like my brother." He stepped closer to her.

Jordan let out a breath. There was no way she could walk past him now. Her pulse raced as he stood before her, but she tried to make sure her fear wasn't reflected on the outside. Who was his brother? Clearly, he was related to one of her cases. Murdered? Was he deeming her responsible for a death sentence? She hadn't had many death penalty cases, and even then, the appeals process took years…

It came to her in a flash. It was one of those cases that would always stay with her. The torture the victim had undergone. The video the man had taken so he could later relive the experience. The cold indifference he'd demonstrated as he'd drained the last breath from her body. In her mind, never had a penalty been more deserved. He'd have done it all again and again if sheer luck hadn't led law enforcement to his arrest.

She peered closer at Derek, trying to see any outer resemblance to the psychopath she'd evaluated back then—she didn't need a psych profile to know that the underlying personality traits they shared were all too similar. And he'd fooled them all. No one had looked for the fox in the henhouse. They'd all thought the perpetrator was someone from the outside while he'd orchestrated his plan from within, as one of them.

Derek eyed her with a calculating expression, more like she was a specimen he was studying rather than a person. "I can see you've finally figured it out. I must say, I wasn't expecting you to take this long. If I hadn't have led you to it, you would've never even made the connection. Same last name, even. Not as bright as you seem to get credit for," he scoffed.

She stalled for time as she plotted a way to escape. "Smith is a common name. And I didn't anticipate a new colleague would be related to a death penalty case from the past."

"No, I guess you wouldn't. That was part of the fun.

Watching you every day. You were like the rats we used in the university labs. I had complete control, and all you could do was run around in your little world and react to whatever I chose to do. It was perfect. I wanted to make sure you felt the same fear he had. Knowing that death was lurking right around you, but you had no escape. Having to wake up every day and live with that."

She could taste bile rising in her throat as she listened to him. "If that's true, why did you stop Rigdon then? He would have done it all for you."

"Are you kidding me?" His voice shook with anger. "I spent years planning this. Making sure you'd get what you deserved and it would be slow, agonizing. Just like my brother's. I wasn't about to let you go that easily." He stopped himself for a moment, and then his voice was eerily calm again. "Though the attack was an added bonus. I watched for as long as I could before I had to intervene." His eyes lit with a sick pleasure.

Despite his claim of revenge, he plainly enjoyed the thrill of watching others in distress. The ache in her stomach intensified as repulsion swept deeper within her gut. The man before her possessed no empathy. His plan for retaliation served as a means of justifying his twisted internal needs. But he wouldn't talk all night. She'd served her purpose for him now.

Though her eyes remained fixed on his, in her peripheral vision, she caught sight of a cutlery block set a few feet away. She didn't need to think twice. It would be her only chance at a weapon.

Jordan tried to keep her voice steady as the desperation of her situation rose. "What are you going to do? Karen and Mike know you're here with me, which means Chase knows you're here. You can't get rid of everyone."

He shook his head and arched an eyebrow at her.

"You never told them you were coming?" The words came out as a whisper as any hope of her friends putting two and two together in time to assist in her rescue dissipated.

"No, they have no clue. I don't have a room here, and I've made sure no one will remember us together. Besides, your fall will be an unfortunate tragedy brought on by a mix of alcohol and poor judgment. No one will be looking at it too closely. Though I will say the stop at Gator Lake was tempting. I almost considered revising my plan, but too many unknowns there, so I stuck with the original. What is it we say? The first response is usually the best one?"

Jordan cringed at his use of the word we. Derek had no place among psychologists. The oath they took to do no harm when becoming a doctor would mean nothing to him.

She had to act fast, before he did. In one swift move, she leaped forward and grabbed the first knife her hand encountered from the cutlery block. Adrenaline spiked her blood as she pulled it out and whipped around to face him. "Derek, get the hell out now," she said, the knife held out in front of her. Her mouth was so dry that it felt like it was full of cotton. She was surprised when her command came out strong and foreboding.

Instead of moving back, Derek came at her full force. She wasn't prepared for how fast he made contact and was only able to drag the serrated edge across his ribs. The superficial cut did little to deter him. He grabbed her arm, twisting the knife out of her grasp and causing her to cry out in agony as her arm was contorted in an unnatural angle. She tried to fight him with the remaining arm, but he was much stronger and was rapidly gaining the upper hand.

His fingers dug into her skin and he used the painful position of her arm to steer her ahead of him. "Try something like that again, and the little video you saw of my brother's antics will look like a day at the spa," he spat.

Her eyes watered from the burning pain shooting

through her shoulder and she blinked several times to hold back the moisture. Each step forward brought her closer to the balcony she was supposed to be falling—jumping from? What the hell had he said? "Your plan doesn't make sense." She winced as he clamped down even harder on her arm. "I've only had a couple of drinks."

"Yeah, you did screw that part up a bit, huh? I figured it'd be a lot easier to get you to loosen up some while you were here." He rolled his eyes as if her failure to get sufficiently drunk was a personality failing. "But you've had enough to do what I need you to now."

They were almost to the glass doors now, and Derek grabbed a pad of paper and pen from the end table.

"Here. This will be your chance to say good-bye. You can give Mike and Karen your best and, of course, don't forget your new *beau*." He placed the pen in her left hand, still wringing her right arm like a wet washcloth. Then he grabbed the pad of paper and positioned it against the wall in front of her.

"I won't write a suicide note," she protested.

He exhaled behind her. The warm air hit her neck and reminded her of the attack at her office. She fought the terror that came with it as her heart pounded so fiercely it felt like it was about to explode.

"Everyone knows I would never do that." Wetness escaped from the reservoir she'd been attempting to dam up and a lone tear trailed down her face.

He gritted his teeth. "Write it how you want, but make it clear you can't cope with the fears you have now."

She pressed the pen onto the paper awkwardly. Ambidexterity wasn't a skill set of hers, but Derek wouldn't react well to that revelation. Curling her fingers around the smooth plastic, she began to form her first letter. She needed to go slow. Needed to figure out another way to escape from this madman.

The ringtone of her phone startled her.

"It's probably Chase." God how she wished she was

with him now. *Will I ever be again?* Her breath caught with despair. No. She couldn't think like that. She wouldn't give up.

Derek didn't loosen his grasp. "I think you and I both know you won't be answering," he hissed.

"If I don't, he'll be worried."

"And you think that's relevant? Chase may be intimidating to some, but he's obviously no better than you are." His teeth were clenched as he spoke, and bits of saliva sprayed onto her cheek. "When he was hired, I thought it might make things more exciting. That would have been fine with me. You weren't nearly the challenge I'd anticipated, but he's been a minor nuisance at best."

His words chiseled away at her fear. Dropping the pen, she pushed back from the wall as hard as she could, hoping to throw him off balance.

Derek cranked her arm more.

She screamed as spots swam in her peripheral vision.

CHAPTER EIGHTEEN

Chase combed every inch of the beach in front of the cove, where the waves crashed up against the rocks in the moonlight. There wasn't a soul around. Even the concession stand was closed. He used the light from his cell flashlight to illuminate an information board he discovered around the pavilion. It showed the trails at the park, including the one to Gator Lake.

The route wasn't long and as he ran along the path, he prayed that Derek hadn't found her first. He couldn't lose her. Memories of seeing Robert's lifeless body after the shooting flashed through his head. Was this his fault, too? Had he let his feelings for her overshadow his responsibility? He forked a hand through his hair. God, how he'd tried to make sure they didn't. *What would you have done differently?* His resolve strengthened as he remembered her words to him on the beach that day. Not a thing. He wouldn't change any part of what he'd shared with Jordan. Their relationship wasn't an error in judgment. This time it was going to end differently. It had to.

The chorus of crickets was the only sound piercing the silence around him. The outline of a boardwalk up ahead came into view, but as he got closer, he could see that the lake was deserted. Like the beachside of the park, there was no activity nearby anywhere. He took in the smoky scent of nearby fires wafting through the damp air. The campgrounds probably weren't too far, but he couldn't think of any reason she'd have stopped there. Recognizing that the search there was fruitless, he retraced his steps.

After arriving back at the resort, he made his way back up to the condo. She'd check in here eventually. At this point, it was his best hope.

Approaching with caution, he was surprised to hear conversation coming from the condo as he got closer. He took post next to the kitchen window. The slats were closed so they couldn't see him from inside. The sound of Derek's voice made him bristle, and hearing Derek's instructions to Jordan had him battling the urge to blast into the condo. It was crucial to be fast, but he also had to be smart. He ducked under the window so his shadow wasn't evident inside and crept to the entrance. If only he had some type of distraction to ensure that he got to Jordan before Derek could do anything to harm her.

He dialed her cell number and let it ring. It rang from within the condo, but no one made any move to answer the device.

Damn. He was used to doing entries with his team. At least then, he'd have a flashbang so he could create a diversion. Nothing like a couple hundred decibels of noise and blinding light to pave the way for a smooth entrance. But he'd have to fly solo and make do tonight. He couldn't risk waiting for backup with Derek intent on following through with his threat.

While Derek complained about how easy it had been to carry out his plan, Chase slowly turned the doorknob. It wasn't locked. He held his weapon in one hand and eased the door open, praying that Derek was too caught up in his own monologue to hear the movement.

He let out a measured breath as he slipped into the entry hall. There was a wall separating the hall from the living area, and neither Derek nor Jordan could see him yet. He could keep that advantage for a few more steps before he'd round the corner and be in their line of vision. Leaving an arm's length in front of him so his weapon didn't give him away, he started making the slow semicircle around the corner.

He'd almost made it around when he heard a scuffle. Then Jordan screamed. Fury tore through his body, and his heart pounded so ferociously his ears rang. Upon entering the room, Derek was holding Jordan against the wall with her arm pinned behind her. He scanned his hands and spotted no weapons. Derek caught sight of him preparing to jump into the fight.

"One more step and I'll kill her," he said, his voice cold.

Chase didn't move. Even with the way Derek was holding Jordan in front of him, he'd have a clear headshot. "Let her go or, I can assure you, she won't be the one dead." His tone was matter-of-fact. His request, nonnegotiable.

Jordan stopped struggling, watching him from over her shoulder. Her eyes were wide with fright. The room was eerily quiet while he waited for Derek to decide his fate.

Rather than let her go, Derek shoved her hard in Chase's direction. She flew through the air, and Chase reached forward to grab her.

Derek escaped past them as Chase steadied her in front of him.

"Are you all right?" he asked.

"I'm okay." Her voice was unsteady. She bent her arm out in front of her and rotated her wrist. "It felt like he was about to break my arm, but I think it'll be okay."

Her defensive movement sent another course of fire through his veins. "I'm going after him. Call nine-one-one and lock the door behind me." Derek wasn't going to get away. He wouldn't let him. He darted in the direction of the stairs. The sound of echoing footsteps greeted him when he opened the heavy steel door. Despite the head start, Chase knew he was gaining ground as the steps got louder. He'd have him before they reached the bottom.

A door screeched open, and the sounds stopped. Damn it. Derek must've arrived at the same conclusion. Exiting on the next floor, he hoped he was on the same path Derek had taken.

A flash of color indicated a man had turned in the corridor in front of him. Remembering the two walkways both curved around to meet, Chase chose the opposite direction.

A few steps later, and he was face to face with Derek.

"Down on the ground!" Chase kept his weapon trained on the man in front of him.

Derek squinted his eyes at him and then looked furtively around.

"There's no where to run, and I don't miss," he said evenly.

"So you're going to shoot me, Chase? You can live with that?" He raised one brow.

Chase didn't need time to consider the question. "Absolutely."

Derek changed tactics. "You're way off here. This is a mistake."

"Save it, Derek. If you don't get on the ground now, I'll gladly put you there." The steel quality of his voice made it clear he was ready to follow through on the threat.

Derek glanced around at his surroundings one more time and then lowered himself to the ground.

Chase didn't trust him. "Hands behind your back." Derek complied, and Chase anchored his knee on his back to keep him from moving while he cuffed his hands behind him.

"You know, this isn't over," Derek said, his head turned to the side and pressed against the cool concrete floor.

"Oh, it's over," Chase said, nodding. "You won't be

doing much from behind bars. Consider yourself lucky you're still talking."

"No one will believe this. It's her word against mine. I've made sure to leave no tracks, and my record is clean," he said with a sneer. "As far as I'm concerned, you came barging in in a jealous rage."

Chase blew out a breath and contained the anger threatening to bubble out of him. He didn't bother to reply. He'd make damn sure Derek never got anywhere near Jordan again.

Police sirens reverberated into the night. The shrill, piercing sound escalated as his backup filtered in to the main level of the parking garage. He shouted out his location to the officers searching the halls.

Handing Derek over to the police brought him genuine closure. The niggling doubts he'd harbored since he'd left her to return home dissipated. This time there were no awkward pieces they were trying to shove into the puzzle so it would look complete. No, this time each jagged edge fit, and the image was clear—it was one none of them had seen or had wanted to. He lengthened his stride through the halls, wanting to see Jordan and make sure she was okay.

The living area was filled over capacity when he walked in. A first responder peppered Jordan with questions, but her eyes darted over to his. Though she didn't speak, he read the question in her gaze. He gave her an encouraging nod, and her posture relaxed.

After she declined medical attention, they were separated and questioned as to what had transpired. They both gave their accounts, with Chase confirming the details and supplying the conversation he'd heard while outside the window. The officers would relay their initial reports to Detective Larson for investigation.

Hours later, the interviews were complete, and the officers gradually filed out.

For the first time that night, Chase had a chance to pull her into his arms. The thick cords in his muscles began to slacken. "You had me so worried." He closed his eyes and held her tight against him. He wasn't sure he'd ever let go.

§

Jordan leaned into Chase, drawing from his strength.

He let out a ragged breath. "Damn, I couldn't believe how I'd missed it—that it was him."

"Don't feel bad. He had me fooled, too. I feel like I should've caught on to something, but I guess that's what makes people like him what they are." A shudder ran through her at how close Derek had been to her. Plotting his revenge and watching triumphantly as each act had driven her further and further into desperation.

"You mean subhuman?" he said dryly.

"That's probably a fitting term. Psychopaths like him don't have the same emotions we do, but they can do a hell of a job of mimicking them. It can make them hard to identify at first. And I guess we didn't have enough time before all of this to figure out who Derek was. Though what are the odds? It's nothing any of us would've been watching for." She paused for a second, wrapping her arms even tighter around him. "I'm just glad you got here when you did."

He let out another breath into her hair. "Me, too. When I realized what was happening, it felt like Robert all over again. That my feelings for you had put you in danger."

Jordan tipped her head back to look at him. "Don't go there. You got here in time. If we'd hired anyone else, I'm not sure I'd be standing here with you now." Her eyebrows furrowed. "How did you figure it out?"

Chase looked down at her. "Well, I was telling Mike about us."

Her eyes widened. "Mike knows now?"

"Yeah. He's cool with it." He grinned. "As long as I'm good to you. Otherwise, I've been fairly warned."

She chuckled. "He's always been like the older brother I never had." A comfort-filled warmth slipped over her. She felt immensely blessed at that moment. To have the friends she did, to have made it through everything okay, and to have Chase right here with her. But she was still confused as to how he'd known to come back. "So, how did your admission to Mike lead you back here?"

He shrugged. "It was a hunch at first. Derek used the same wording in his message on your flowers as the perp had in the letter we found at your house. And then Karen was talking about how he'd unexpectedly left the office in a hurry. Both could've been a coincidence, but it was enough for me to check him out. And that's when everything came together."

Jordan's eyebrows rose. "Wow, you have some wicked intuition. You may have to charge me for consults in the future," she responded lightly, but her appreciation was apparent in her tone.

He kissed her on the top of her head. "We'll see about that."

"So, what's your intuition telling you now?" she asked.

Chase stared directly into her eyes. "Oh, that's an easy one. No payment necessary. Well, maybe not a monetary one." He leaned down, pressing his lips firmly onto hers. "It's telling me to keep you close."

"How close?" she murmured, her voice throaty. She could feel tingles running from her lips down through her body. Damn, she didn't think she'd ever get enough of this guy. She hungrily eyed his lips, wanting a repeat.

"Really close." This time he kissed her with more force, parting her lips with his tongue and delving into her mouth until she was breathless. He pulled back for a moment, cupping her chin in his fist while his thumb ran across her lips. "Like not-an-inch-of-space-between-us close."

Her stomach pirouetted at his words. "What did I tell you?" She winked at him. "Wicked intuition."

"Admit it. You like it," he teased back.

"Not quite," she said. Then she paused. "I love it." This time, she initiated a kiss that had them both lost in a passion neither had known before one another.

EPILOGUE
SIX MONTHS LATER

"Jordan, you have a call on line one. It's a Mr. Keith Lancaster. Would you like to me to put him through? Or I can take a message?" Nancy asked.

"You can put him through. Thanks, Nancy." Jordan wondered why Keith was calling. "Hello, Mr. Lancaster. What can I do for you?"

"Hello, Dr. Clayton. Look, I know you're busy, so I won't take up a lot of your time. I'm really just calling to apologize," he said, sounding contrite.

Jordan considered his words. His petition for guardianship had been denied by the judge. Though it was clear to the evaluators that his father was suffering from some type of condition, her evaluation had shed light on his depressive symptoms, the most likely origin of his cognitive deficits. She hadn't heard anything more about the case since.

He went on before she could respond. "I wasn't ready to hear what you had to say...about my father's depression. I was wrong." He hesitated a moment. "I've always thought of depression as being a sign of weakness.

And my father is anything but weak."

His explanation resonated with her. She'd dealt with similar sentiments before, on numerous occasions. "I understand your concerns," she said. "There are some misconceptions surrounding mental health conditions, and you aren't the first to oppose a family member's diagnosis."

"Well, like I said, I was wrong. My father's been attending the group therapy sessions you recommended. And I can't tell you what a difference it's made. I feel like I have my father back now. The way he was before. I hated to think about how lucky we were that you picked up on it when I know I acted like a complete jerk in your office." He cleared his throat. "I shouldn't have listened to Buckman beforehand. And I'm sorry for what he put you through. I had no idea he was serious about the stuff he was saying. If I'd known, I'd have said something sooner." Regret tinged his pronouncement.

"It's okay." She attempted to reassure him. He wasn't responsible for what she'd endured. "You gave the detective what you knew. And in the end, it all worked out."

"Yeah, I guess so. But it's a mistake I won't make again." He blew out a breath. "Thanks for hearing me out today."

"I'm glad you called. And Keith, I'm happy to hear your dad's doing well." She was heartened to learn of the elderly's man progress. It was clear he'd benefit from the counseling recommendation, but hearing Keith relate how helpful the sessions had been was moving.

Hanging up the phone, her insides warmed at the sound of Chase's familiar voice coming down the hall. She listened as he wrapped up his conversation with Mike before entering her office. They were both chuckling over something. There was no telling with those two.

"Hey there," he said, bending down to give her a kiss. "You ready to get out of here for a while? I'm taking you to lunch. And before you ask, I already checked with Nancy. You're free for the next hour."

Jordan tipped her head back to take him in. "Me? Turn down lunch with a handsome date? That's not going to happen."

Chase's grin—the sexy one that made her stomach flip—widened. "And I hope that it's due to the overwhelming appeal of said handsome man and not because he comes with an offer for food." He winked.

Jordan laughed. Then she closed the window on her computer screen and stood up. "While the offer of lunch is enticing—" she looked at him, her eyes sparkling, "—the handsome man in front of me is irresistible." She put her arms around his waist and drew him to her.

She still couldn't believe how much her life had changed since he'd come into it. Just as he'd planned, Chase had stepped back from taking protection assignments and, instead, had gone on to assume an instructor's role in his business. His schedule was filled with training engagements on different aspects of security and self-defense that never took him away for long.

For her part, she now had much more balance in her days. Her passion for her practice hadn't changed, but she was much better at leaving her work at the office door. She'd learned the hard way that life was precious, and she wouldn't regret not having worked harder in the end. The relationships mattered most. So, in place of late evenings with records spread out over her desk, her nights were largely filled exploring the town with Chase or simply hanging around together, enjoying the tranquility that came with knowing that her stalker was incarcerated and no longer a threat to her.

Despite Derek's revelation that he'd left no evidence behind, the police department had been able to put together enough DNA evidence that, combined with the witness testimony, had made for a strong case and a straightforward conviction. She, Karen, and Mike had yet to fill the space he'd left in their practice staff, but after what had transpired, they were in no hurry to do so. She had a feeling their next hire would be someone they knew well. Nepotism did have its advantages.

Chase broke away from what had become a heated kiss. "Keep that up and we may have to do lunch at your house," he said huskily. "Besides, there's something I want to show you before we go." He tugged her toward the door.

Curious as to what he wanted, she allowed herself to be pulled down the hall. She glanced at him uncertainly when he stopped at the conference room.

He threw the door open, and they walked in. She was greeted with the chorus of a loud "Surprise!" from everyone inside. The room was adorned with several colorful streamers. In the center of the conference table was a huge bouquet of flowers.

She was momentarily speechless. Firstly, she had no idea what they were all supposed to be celebrating. Secondly, she was stunned to see her parents mixed in with her friends.

She turned to ask Chase what they were celebrating, but he was down on one knee in front of her...and then she knew. Tears sprung to her eyes.

"Jordan." He gazed up at her intently. "When I first met you, I was completely taken aback. You were beautiful, kind, passionate—and I'll tell you now, as crazy as it sounds, I felt an immediate connection when I touched you. It threw me off guard, because I'd never believed in chemistry like I had with you right from the start." He paused, took a deep breath, and then went on. "But as I got to know you...despite my resolve not to—" he looked at her sheepishly, "—I realized that those traits were only the surface ones, and though they were great alone, the qualities I admired didn't stop there. Your compassion, intellect, humor, and...patience with me—" he smiled, "—had me falling completely in love with you."

A round of chuckles circled the room at his comment, and Jordan didn't even try to stop the tears now streaking down her cheeks.

His eyes grew serious again. "When I couldn't find you that night at the beach, I was desperate. I couldn't imagine not having a chance to explore our future together—to build on what we'd started. A young man who helped me back then told me I should keep you close. What I didn't tell him was that I had no intention of doing anything else." He reached into his pocket and withdrew a black velvet jewelry box.

After opening the lid, he held out the most radiant diamond ring she'd ever seen. With his other hand, he gently grasped her trembling fingers.

"Jordan, I want you by my side for the rest of my life. Will you do me the honor of becoming my wife?"

At first, she just nodded. She was speechless. Finally finding her voice, she let out an unquestionable, "Yes!"

Her family and friends in the room went wild, whooping and hollering. Joy masked their faces. Her mom looked beyond ecstatic, and she had no doubt in her mind that the woman was already picturing grandchildren. She turned her attention back to the man in front of her.

Chase slid the ring onto her finger.

"Chase, it's beautiful," she whispered.

He stood up, now grasping both of her hands in his. "It's a brilliant cut. The jeweler told me the intense sparkle is the result of its many facets." His eyes softened as he spoke. "It reminded me of you."

ACKNOWLEDGMENTS

This book has been such a learning experience for me. I've written all of my life and have had smaller works published over the years, but preparing a full length novel for publication was an unfamiliar undertaking. The story of Jordan and Chase wouldn't have become what it is now without the support and critique of so many. It is with a heart filled with gratitude that I write this section now.

To my friends and family who read the earliest versions of this book, I want to thank you for taking time out of your schedules to provide me with commentary. Deanna and Melanie your suggestions and encouragement moved me to continue working to improve the story. To Deanna, I attribute the enhanced criminal elements, and to Melanie, I hope she is breathless enough for you now. I can't tell you both how much I appreciate your feedback.

I'd also like to thank Jennifer B. for offering to proofread the final version. You have a keen eye for detail and I'm so very grateful you provided your review and opinions. Now, it's your turn to sing.

For everyone that reviewed numerous mockups of the cover and helped me to find the perfect one, thank you. And for creating that perfect cover, I have to thank Robin Harper of Wicked by Design– you brought the characters to life!

To Kellie, Michelle, Wendy and everyone else that I bothered with "just one more question," thank you for always answering each request like it was the first. And even more, thank you for believing in my dream and helping me to achieve it.

To the awesome Mickey, where do I start? You were the one to initially lay eyes on a first novel by a new author. I'm sure that this is probably one of the most challenging jobs to fulfill in the editing world, but you did so with care and grace. You went above and beyond and with your assistance, I realized that what I'd thought was a completed manuscript was just the beginning. You truly rock.

To Rhonda, thank you for helping me take this novel to the next level. You didn't hesitate to tell me what needed to change, what needed to be rewritten and what needed to be cut, in a way that didn't alter my voice as an author. Your suggestions made Jordan and Chase's story even better.

And lastly, to my husband, I would still be "working" on my first novel if it wasn't for your support. Thank you for encouraging me. To my children, you are my inspiration to make dreams come true. And, to my mother, who nurtured creativity always. I love you all.

ABOUT THE AUTHOR

Nicole Luckourt professed in her fifth grade autobiography that she would be a writer when she grew up. Though life has taken her on many adventures and detours since that time, she has never abandoned her desire for creating stories and breathing life into the characters and plots in her head. With the publication of Expert Witness, her childhood dream has become a reality. She currently lives in the Midwest with her husband, two children, and several beloved pets. Her practice in the field of psychology inspires her writing and she is thrilled to be able to combine her two passions.

Nicole enjoys hearing from her readers. You can find her on her website: www.nicoleluckourt.com, and on Facebook, Twitter, and on Goodreads. Please join her mailing list for the latest updates on new releases.